Pra
Recen

"Entering the world of Anthony Giardina's deceptively placid third novel is like pushing off from shore onto a lake of childhood memory." —*Los Angeles Times Book Review*

"The characters . . . seem as real—or as unreal, maybe I ought to say—as members of one's own family. And Giardina's talent for capturing emotional nuance and writing about sex in a way that movie guides would classify as X-rated turns a story that might otherwise seem like thinly veiled autobiography into an unusually frank and compelling work of fiction about men and families in turmoil." —ALAN CHEUSE, *All Things Considered*

"Extremely perceptive . . . courageous . . . Giardina understands the paralyzing emotional and sexual limitations governing men in our society." —*The Advocate*

"A fine and complex and subtly subversive novel . . . I don't think Giardina makes a false step. Every emotion and detail and behavior in this book feels unalterably right." —LOUIS BAYARD, Nerve.com

"Hypnotic . . . rich . . . *Recent History* is a heartfelt work of art, not politics. It doesn't advocate, it aches." —*Daily Hampshire Gazette*

"Emotionally piercing, quietly beautiful . . . a gracefully written literary novel." —*Kirkus Reviews*

"Giardina's introspective, finely crafted first-person narrative . . . draws the reader into [his protagonist's] life with a candid, insightful narrative that probes important subtleties of identity and honesty." —*Publishers Weekly*

ANTHONY GIARDINA is the author of two previous novels, *Men with Debts* and *A Boy's Pretensions,* and a short-story collection, *The Country of Marriage.* He has written six produced plays, the most recent of which, *Black Forest,* premiered in 2000 at the Long Wharf Theatre in New Haven, Connecticut. His short fiction has appeared in *Harper's, GQ,* and *Esquire.* He lives with his family in Northampton, Massachusetts.

Also by
Anthony Giardina

The Country of Marriage

A Boy's Pretensions

Men with Debts

Recent History

Recent History

A Novel

Anthony Giardina

Random House Trade Paperbacks
New York

Copyright © 2001 by Anthony Giardina
Reader's guide copyright © 2002 by Random House, Inc.

This work was originally published in hardcover by Random House in 2001.

Library of Congress Cataloging-in-Publication Data
Giardina, Anthony.
Recent history : a novel / Anthony Giardina.
p. cm.
ISBN 0-375-75938-7 (acid-free paper)
1. Italian American families—Fiction.   2. Massachusetts—Fiction.   I. Title.
PS3557.I135 R43 2001
813'.54—dc21   00-062556

Printed in the United States of America on acid-free paper
Random House website address: www.atrandom.com

9 8 7 6 5 4 3 2
First Trade Paperback Edition
Book design by Mercedes Everett

three teachers

Carmello Chiarelli
1924–1985
Janice Slotnick
1914–1983
Jeffrey Kresser
1950–1997

I

Inca Boy

1

When I was eleven years old, in April 1961, my father arrived at school one day to take me into the woods. It was half-day, Wednesday. I usually walked home for lunch but that day he was waiting beside the Fairlane, in the suit he wore to work, the only man among the group of older, nervous mothers who insisted on coming and walking their children home from school.

On the drive—unannounced, with a mysterious destination—he tapped the wheel and hummed an odd little song that let me know he was nervous. I tried to follow the song, but couldn't. My father was a small, secretive man, quiet, well-dressed. He was known in the family into which he had married, a large and clamorous Italian family (as he was Italian, himself), as one who habitually stood back from the passionate center of action. You can see even now, in the home movies that survive from those years (he never took them, my Uncle John did), how he stands aside from the others on the beach, hardly noticeable sometimes, smaller and more compact and less expansive than the other, heavier, laughing men. What those movies don't tell you, though, is how he spoke, and the power he wielded because of the way he spoke. "Should we dig for clams?" someone on the beach would shout, trying to draw one last drop from the day. "No," he'd say, and point. "The tide's coming in." The others would stand back then, nod. How foolish they'd been.

That day, he'd brought sandwiches for us to eat, meatball; they were on the seat between us. By the time we were into the woods the submarine rolls had gone soggy, and the bag had a wet stain on the bottom. We had to park at the bottom of the hill where the road ended—the hill was adjacent to the old Girl Scout property, a large undeveloped tract in our town, which had been dominated once by a mill and watch factory, then, after these had closed, had managed to hold on to its population by becoming a bedroom community for the city of Boston. There were still large wooded patches left, one or two farms. My father led me up the hill, as if following some sort of map that existed nowhere but in his head.

We found a rock—a large, flat boulder—that seemed to be what he was looking for, then ate the sandwiches. He still hadn't spoken. He held a napkin six inches under his chin, a formal gesture, so as to catch any of the drops of sauce. Then, finally, he leaned toward me. He nodded once, and his lips made a small, familiar pursing motion.

"We're going to live here, Luca," he whispered.

He took another bite, then gestured, with his mouth full, across the ground in front of us. "This, this is our lot."

My father's voice had a slight rasp to it, as though he were in fact tougher than he appeared. It mixed with what was subtle and educated about him, and it was one of the things—there were many others—that gave the effect of there being at least two of him, two things not fighting it out so much as living inside of him in some interesting kind of harmony.

"That, over there, you see those sticks with the little orange flags? They mark out lots. Of course it's only trees now, but they're going to build a road up here. Everything you see . . ." Here he hesitated again. "They're going to blast away. The rocks and . . ." He gestured with his fist. "Make houses. You can't see it, but there's an orange stick way over there. That's where Uncle John's house is going to be. We're starting a neighborhood, you could say. The family. The Italians."

He laughed a little after he said that, as if this last part of it, the Italian part, so important to my Uncle John, could never be as serious to him.

Then there was a silence. I looked where he'd asked me to look, and took in all this strange information, strangely delivered; delivered, that is, as though while he was telling me one thing, he was also telling me something else. So I listened harder than I was used to. I listened for the second story.

We kept a photograph prominent in our house in those days, a photograph taken when my father was in college. He'd gone to Boston College, the first in his family to go beyond high school, on a hockey scholarship. The photograph was black and white: him and his teammates, a row seated, a row standing, hockey sticks crossed in front of the seated row, "Snooks" Kelly, famous in our house, stood beside them, heavy, jacketed, the coach. They were either jug-eared boys or else big-jawed boy-men who looked thirty when they were only twenty, and I suspect your eye would be drawn to my father even if you didn't know him. Seated in the front row, he is smaller and more delicate then the others, the one who appears most singular, and therefore blessed. There is a smile he is wearing that I used to sit and study. It was the smile of a man announcing: I am in this world, but not of it.

It was there now, curiously so, as he looked off into space, and ate his sandwich.

"Listen," he said. "This is for you. Here, living here, so you can have a better life."

I watched him consider his words carefully.

"Candace Road, that's a decent street, Luca, a nice neighborhood, but this is really something else . . ." Suddenly he trailed off. Something had begun to trouble him.

He had stopped—that was my father—as if too bold an announcement would trap him. He smoothed the wax paper in his lap. He took several seconds and then he looked at me. "You almost finished?"

I said that I was, though I still had half a sandwich in my lap.

That is the quality I remember of that day: my settling into a journey I believed was to be slow and luxurious, then being hurried by him, as if the direction in which he'd pointed us were being altered midstroke.

I have to say that in the days and weeks afterward, my father seemed more excited by what he was doing than he had that day in the woods. Sometimes, even months later, he would take out the architect's renderings and sit with us—that is, with my mother and me; I was their only child—at the kitchen table, pointing out this nicety and that. It wasn't uncommon that as he was speaking he would touch my hair. I would run down the street, afterward, on a kind of cloud. And return, an hour or so later, to find he had retreated to his office, my mother setting the table for the two of us.

She never complained. He was a law unto himself. There were things he required: silence, immense space. She kept his food warm, then, only at the end, when it was clear he would not be coming out, for hours perhaps, wrapped it carefully and put it in the refrigerator.

I thought, in those days, that I knew more about him than she did, and made a child's judgment as to her stupidity. I thought I knew something of my father's darkness, though that would not have been the word I'd have chosen then. I knew at least what he did at night. From my bedroom window, I could watch him in the backyard, sitting for hours some nights in the Adirondack chairs that had been set up near the rock garden, smoking Pall Malls with his head tilted at a slight angle, as though listening to a difficult voice coming at him. The words he heard disappeared from time to time, so he had to move his head forward, to catch something he might otherwise miss, which was out there in the dark.

Afterward, he would come inside, and if I was still awake, I heard their noise. My mother made a low besotted groan, and it took off from there, took off and ascended, and became like the sound of her dying. I associated those sounds with violence. I was young, and it scared me, but since in the mornings she was all right, even cheerful, after a while I stopped worrying.

Still, there were always two things about my father to consider. One was the nights when he elicited those sounds from her, and then, afterward, in the morning, by some alchemy I couldn't figure, made her happy. The other was what he did on Saturdays, when men came to our house. In addition to his work in the accounting department of Vanderbruek, the defense plant he'd been hired at out of college, and at which, over the course of fourteen years, he'd steadily risen, my father opened our house on Saturdays to men who wanted their taxes done, or men who had special financial problems, "tricky things," he called them. They were an odd assortment; the only thing that held these men together was the ridiculous way they all dressed, half in the world of weekend chores, in flannels and chinos, and half in the world of business.

Something in my father's bearing, I knew, made them want to appear respectable.

I would sometimes pass the window of my father's office, which faced our backyard, on the pretext of throwing a ball up into the air and catching it, and, in the light over my father's desk, always on, even on the brightest day, watch his alert, handsome face staring into the face of another man, some doughy, awkward stranger, with an intensity he only rarely directed at my mother and me. It was as though the man had just said something, and my father wanted to stop and ask him to explain. But I do not know how to tell you it wasn't a word or a piece of business my father wanted explained, but something else, a hazy thing that the man embodied, so that while he was listening, I knew my father wasn't really listening at all.

After the men were gone, there was another waiting to be endured. For the rest of the afternoon, my father sulked. Sometimes he took off in the car. I imagined he was chasing down one of the Saturday men to point out an error in judgment. Supper was always eaten in silence. Later, in the evening, he would go out and consult with himself in the backyard. His Saturdays followed that pattern, without fail. But just before dusk, in the spring and summer, the boys on Candace Road always gathered on the street to play Wiffle ball. It was a quiet street, full of small houses into which sound penetrated easily. By the time the game was in its second or third inning, the fathers had all come out of their houses to watch.

They were not, for the most part, successful men. They were tire salesmen, mechanics. Among them was a retired Army sergeant. No visible trajectory attached to their lives; the neighborhood houses lacked the silence and absences of ambition.

But at dusk on summer evenings, they came out and rested inside a moment of grace. Their sons on the quiet street. The soaring of the Wiffle ball, which, even sailing far, would break no windows. The smell of lilacs, apple blossoms in May. The fall of light in a suburban neighborhood early in the reign of John F. Kennedy. I do not want to romanticize, but there it was.

Frequently, my father was the last to come out. Even when he did, his mood was often such that he didn't greet the other fathers, merely stood there, stiff and in the white shirt he had worn to prepare men's taxes. But even he was capable of being seduced by this scene. At a certain point his shoulders settled, he'd light a cigarette, and the compulsion to leave—so strong, while reined in, so much of the time—leaked out of him.

Even guarding second base, I sensed this. In this game, in the perfection of boys at play, lay my power.

In October of that year, Uncle John's house was completed, and he held a party in celebration.

We'd often visited Uncle John and Aunt Emma in the two-family they lived in on River Street. Their sons were Bobby and George, who used to entice the younger cousins outside so they could piss off the roof onto them. But that night, when my parents descended the stairs and noticed that I was wearing my everyday clothes, a look crossed their features, as though there was something profound I didn't get.

We had seen John's new house in daylight, the most solid and finished of the several houses then in development, split-level houses surrounded by bulldozers and, in mid-fall, by heavy, dug-up mud. John's house had pillars and second-floor tiers and a facing of pink-tinted marble. A large effort had gone into making it grand, and my father, in the past, whenever he'd driven to the Hill to check things out, had come back and voiced a certain skepticism about what was going on up there. "Versailles," he had taken to calling John's house. He splayed his lips and made a sound, which was frequently followed by a call to the architect of our own house, to see if ours couldn't be simplified.

At night, though, the house underwent a kind of transformation. From far away, from half a mile down the hill, though the road was still unpaved and deeply rutted, we could begin to see the lights of John's house coming at us through the trees. My mother gasped when we were close. John had set up spotlights outside the house; what they lit appeared larger and more imposing even than it was. Surrounding it, in the dark, were high trees, so that the house poked out of the wilderness like it was making some supremely confident announcement of itself, and I remembered what my father had said about John's ambition, to make a neighborhood of Italians, and it began to make sense. I could not have said exactly what I apprehended when I looked up at the finished house, but I remember something quickening in me.

In the basement—carpeted, immense—there was immediately a competition for us. Who would we choose to sit with? The aunts' arms all went out, as if to grab us, and when they shouted greetings, it was as though with one voice. There were three of them, including Emma, John's wife. My mother's sisters all had black hair, long and rich and falling out of the bobby pins and clips with which they tried to pull it back. That hair was like a shout in the dark. Family lore had it that they were all unhappy women, but they never seemed that way. My father explained it to me: "They came from an island, Luca. An island in Italy. You have to understand this. They were little girls, and they lived in Paradise. And then their father took them here." (My mother, the youngest, was the only one born in this country.) "And since then, it's been nothing but complaints." Then he always added, low, conspiratorial, not for me to repeat: "Maybe it wasn't really Paradise, you understand? But let's keep that our secret."

I tried. But it was difficult sometimes, to believe in the vaunted unhappiness, or to see it as the central thing about them. They were vivid, even in their voiced dissatisfactions, and they stuck together in a way I admired.

Emma, in her forties, was pregnant then, tired out by the series of miscarriages that had come between Bobby and George and this late, last child. She sat with her sisters Carmela and Lucy on the couch. Carmela and Lucy had both been wild girls, and they had married the sorts of men wild girls married, sailors and musicians. They owned small houses, packed with children, and not until that night had there been any indication that one day these lives would prove to be inadequate. But here, in this house, came the first suggestion of the movement of history and, with it, a kind of panic.

As soon as we entered, they tried to pull my mother down with them, onto the couch, to assert that nothing really had changed, but my mother resisted their entreaties, moved past them, toward John. He rose from his BarcaLounger. He smelled of aftershave and wore a smoking jacket, with patches of suede at the cuffs. He had a large, smooth head, a businessman's head (he ran a fleet of trucks), with surprising blond hair—surprising, anyway, for an Italian—brush-cut, so that you could see the scalp through it. He planted a soft kiss on my mother's cheek, and then looked at my father, who remained at a distance, as if asking him to come closer, to stand with him in a kind of solidarity of success.

The two other uncles, Mike and Tony, were gathered around the pool table, where Bobby and George, the former roof pissers, posed for the rest of us, their hair pomaded and combed back off their short foreheads. They looked like the dark, wrongful heirs in Shakespeare, who carry small knives concealed. They held pool cues, and pretended they knew the game, but after a while John and my father came and took the cues away from them and began shooting.

My father was a very precise athlete, a man who wasted no motion. He knew how to hold the cue, and his shots did what he wanted them to. He looked unsurprised afterward, even a little bored. John was clumsier. Once, after a particularly bad shot where he scratched the table, he leaned down and rubbed at the nap, and said to my father, "Meola's bought a lot up here. Did you hear?"

"The dentist?" my father asked.

"Yes."

My father made a motion with his mouth that was like shrugging.

"And Doc Semenza," John said, preparing his next shot.

"So we're up here with the hoi polloi," my father said.

Someone, one of the uncles, had put on a record, Dean Martin, and when Dean Martin lapsed into Italian, Uncle Mike, who used to sing in a band that played at weddings (he worked for John now), began to sing along. At first John seemed amused by this, but as it went on, a kind of annoyance started to come into his face. Lucy, Mike's wife, picked up on this, as though John's shifting moods were setting the tone for everyone, and she shouted out, "You gonna get me something like this, Mike?" and then, glancing at John, as if for his approval, added, "In a pig's eye."

There were children in the room besides Bobby and George and me, five of them, some of them younger, and though they behaved in a respectful manner, every once in a while one of the smaller ones had to be reprimanded. This always came out louder, more angry than it needed to be. And every once in a while Carmela or Lucy would shout something insulting to one of their husbands, as though once that particular theme was introduced, it became a favorite.

Displaced from the pool table, my cousin George was leaning against a bank of windows, his hands behind him, staring at me. He had never much liked me, so his stare was unsettling, some hint of a challenge beneath it. That was the party: George staring at me, and bursts of noise followed by quieter pockets in which the only sound was that of my father and John moving around the pool table, the tops of their heads, my father's smooth black hair and John's bristly blond, lit by the glow of the lamp over the table. It was in one of these quieter moments that Lucy grabbed me, pulled me up close, and shouted, "So what are you gonna be when you grow up, huh, Luca? A fighter pilot?"

It had no meaning as a question, it was just Lucy's way of bursting through the uncomfortable silence of the party, but they all reacted as if their ears had been cocked. John, my father, the uncles all laughed, and then when the words "fighter pilot" were repeated, a second wave of laughter followed. George narrowed his eyes and looked me over again. He moved across the room toward me, turning once, to glare at the others. He hadn't laughed, the only one. When he faced me again, he said, "Come on. Come with me, fighter pilot."

We went upstairs. He flicked on the lights that illuminated the living room, a deep, long room full of soft furniture, pastels, and light wood, a room full of turns and nooks, with, at the end, a great stone fireplace. My father had described this room to us; he had come back from his first viewing of John's house and tried to make us laugh by describing the ornate furnishings, the sheer exuberance of John's yearning for a life beyond that which he knew. That was when the word "Versailles" first entered our vocabulary, and my father began referring to John as "Louis the Sixteenth." The memory of this derision stood between me and the room. I might have looked at it my father's way, and his way alone, if I hadn't been aware of the concentration with which George, standing next to me, was looking at it, a concentration that altered his breathing, made it reverent, and for a moment created a kind of intimacy between us.

He led me down the hall and opened the door to Bobby's room and allowed me to look in. "Bobby's room," he announced. Then he opened another door. Inside was a crib and pink walls. "If they don't have a girl, they'll go apeshit," George said.

George's room was identical to Bobby's. Both were brown and nearly bare, with only a bed and a dresser and a desk situated near the window. There were paintings on the walls, of boys catching footballs, boys playing golf. George sat at his desk and folded his hands. A neat pile of books lay on the corner of the desk: Geometry and Physical Science and *Animal Farm*. They had the overused look of books given to students in the lower depths of the high school, which was where George had always resided. The design of the room seemed a deliberate attempt to wipe clean the slate of George's previous life, to make of him a more ambitious boy, a scholar. George drew one hand up, to pat his pomaded hair, and a shadow of trouble crossed his features.

George's room was on the corner of the house, so he had two windows. He got up and went to the one that faced the side yard, the woods. His hands were in his pockets, and because of the light over his desk and the fact that there were no curtains yet, I could see the reflection of his face in the window, and the way he was looking at me.

He was short, shorter than Bobby, and less good-looking. Bobby was the handsome one, with a face like Fabian's and a tall body in which he moved like a swimmer.

"So, welcome to our new lives, Luca," he said.

He turned to me, and his face made a beckoning motion before he lowered his brow. He was thinking something over, whether or not to make some request. I said nothing, offered nothing. It was all too new, this sort of power shift between us.

"How old are you, Luca?"

I said eleven, soon twelve.

He sat down on the edge of the bed and touched his hair again. He looked at his school books, sullen and mistrusting, then reached under his bed. He pulled out a fat paperback and flipped through it. He chuckled. "This is good," he said. "This is very good."

He tossed it toward me. The throw didn't quite make it. I picked it up. It was a purple book with a picture of a Victorian gentleman on the cover, a man with a long mustache.

"You go back downstairs, and the next time Lucy tries to treat you like a baby, you read her some of that, okay? Read it out loud."

I knew that was not a good idea, but I nodded, because his face on the bed now wore a cruel little smile.

"You take it, and read it anyway. If you have any questions, you ask me."

That was all. He dismissed me. And the next thing was, I was sitting alone in John's living room.

I hadn't known that was what I wanted to do, but I was drawn back there, rather than to the party itself. I sat and absorbed it all. The room was dark. The only sound was the bubbles sent up by the filter of the fish tank. I'd come to sit here for a reason, but I didn't know exactly what that was. Our world was changing. I understood now why my parents had looked as they'd looked at home, preparing for this, charged and expectant. I sat there, and I tried to grasp it.

For the first time, I was able to see beyond my father's vision of this room, to what John was trying to do here. We were princes now, Bobby and George and me, but how did you go about being a prince? What did it mean for your daily life? I knew this: the book in my lap was something to be ashamed of. I knew vaguely but, still, enough what would be inside it: sex and more sex. George had given it to me because, for him, sex was easier than other things—easier for George than the books on his desk, or John's new insistence that he be a "college man," which we'd begun to hear for the first time.

A sound came from outside, but my reverie was deep enough that I did not get up to look until the sound had been going on a long time. At the base of John's driveway, my father was lighting a cigarette and with his free hand throwing rocks. That is, he stopped to light the cigarette and then he threw the rocks. He looked calm and unperturbed, just as if he had stepped out to have a smoke, and it was only in the motion of his arm as he threw that I knew something was wrong. He was throwing the rocks very hard, very far, and with great concentration. He was trying to hit our house, across the way.

After a while, he stopped. He disappeared, walked into the dark. I could see the lit ash end of his cigarette and then nothing of him, but I suspected he had gone over to our house and was inspecting it, testing the floorboards and the beams the way he did, humming, all the while, one of the songs with which he consoled himself. "Teach Me Tonight." "Don't Get Around Much Anymore." I watched, and I held the book George had given me, and at that moment, though I didn't know why, I wanted to fling the book across the room, to mimic my father's gesture with the rocks.

After another little while, John came out in search of him. I saw John stop at the end of his driveway. He looked to both sides, exaggeratedly, like a man in a cartoon, and like the man in the cartoon, I suspected he would choose the wrong direction. I almost shouted, from the window, to set him straight. But he chose right. When he brought my father back, ten or so minutes later, it may have been me, reading into the scene, but John had his arm around my father's shoulders, and I saw in those shoulders an immense resistance, as though John were leading him back toward a place he had decided, in the last ten minutes, he really didn't want to go.

Like everything else, that image disappeared, covered over by another, and another. I was in the seventh grade, and I made my good marks. Luca Carcera, beloved of the teachers. In the winter there were lakes, frozen over for skating, and I had friends. Sometimes we stayed late, skating; the sky took on, around the departed sun, a shade of deep yellow that exists in the world only when you are twelve, and disappears after. My father arrived to pick us up and stood outside the car, bundled up. "Nobody drowned, huh?" he shouted. "Nobody fell in?"

Sometimes he brought his hockey stick and came down to the ice to show us how it was done. He'd played left wing at BC and he had wonderful speed and when he turned on the ice he managed a terrific little jumping movement. I would never be as good as he was, none of us would. "Your father," they said, the boys who were my friends, breathless and in awe.

Afterward, he patted himself and found the pack of Pall Malls in his coat pocket and smoked one. Smoke came out of his mouth, and the smoke our breath made in the cold seemed a pure imitation. The car smelled of cigarettes and, once or twice, of the presence of someone else, a body that had recently been there. It was a poor-smelling, weathery body, whosoever it had been, someone who did not dress well or have the personal habits of my father, and we covered it, my friends and I, packed in with our skates. It went away. I looked out the window and saw the crust of the snow and something that flashed across my mind went away. To entertain us, my father was singing.

In the evenings, we drove to Natick, to Framingham, to visit furniture showrooms, to move among the great empty sofas and easy chairs. Or else my parents huddled in the kitchen, planning the house. "Do you want this, Dorothy, or do you want that?" my father would ask, as they

studied furniture catalogs. He was only slightly impatient, even indul-
gent at times. Sometimes they would retreat into Italian, tender when
they did that, or else angry. In the adjacent dining room, I sat writing
a play about Cortés, "The Conquest of Mexico," my assignment for
school. In the scene where Cortés faces Montezuma, I had him shout,
"Do you want this, or do you want that?" Meanwhile, my parents, in
English, moved toward agreements: a sectional in off-white, a beige easy
chair, a round kitchen table with teak chairs.

In April, we moved into the new house. The day had a ceremonial
quality, measured and carefully paced, like a presentation scene in the
movies, the birth of Ramses. My father held my mother's elbow at the
threshold, as if they were about to step into a lake and he was attentive
to the chill she might feel. With his hands in his pockets, in his best
camel's hair coat, he inspected the rooms and nodded. The rooms were
large and full of light; on the walls, the textured grass cloth shone. Before
us lay a new life, shimmering and empty as the model kitchens and dining rooms in the furniture showrooms. Moving trucks had preceded us,
and the movers had made mistakes. A couple of chairs, placed in the
wrong room, had to be dragged across the carpet. The carpet itself was
thick enough so that my father, lying down in the living room, could
move his arms and leave the impress of an angel's wings. He pulled me
down and we tussled and only in a region far back in his eyes did I see
signs of effort.

Later, Uncle John came. He wore an expensive raincoat and his
hair was wet. He had a cigar in his mouth and one for my father. He
always took a shower in the middle of the day because he sweated so
much at work. His midday freshness was legendary. My mother was
unpacking dishes in the kitchen, my father had gone to lie down in their
room. For this, I had been given the day off from school.

"Everything good?" John called to my mother. My father came
out of the bedroom at the sound, his hair mussed and standing up at the
back of his head, still in the camel's hair coat.

"Going back to work?" John asked.

"Yes."

"So. Moved in." John's hands were in his pockets, he rocked back
on his feet.

He offered the extra cigar to my father, but my father just looked at it. It had a pink wrapper on it, so we knew it was left over from when Emma had the baby.

"Yes. Moved in," my father said. It sounded grim coming out of his mouth, and John stared at him a moment, annoyed.

"You?" my father asked. "Going back?"

"I'll have a cup of coffee first, with Dorothy."

We all gathered at the bay window to watch my father drive away. John's eyes stayed on him a long time.

When my mother took the roast out of the oven at six, he was still not home. We were used to seeing him at 5:30, and there was less of a drive from Vanderbruek to here. At 6:30 she put the roast back in the oven to warm. Outside the window, I saw some boys cut across the lots, disappear into the frames of houses. Meola, Semenza; I knew the names already, and who would live in each of the uncompleted houses, and when I saw these boys, I didn't think they were the ones who would live there. They were just boys looking, gawking, and I waited for them to come out.

At seven o'clock, the lights of my father's car came around the bend and into the driveway. He entered, excited, holding a bottle of wine. "My new house," he said, like a boy.

We ate in the kitchen; my father kept reaching up to play with the chandelier that hung over the table. "Look at that," he kept saying, and flicked the dangling crystals of the chandelier they had chosen, one frozen winter night at Jordan's. We had not had a better dinner in a long time, and I kept wishing that I had homework, that I had gone to school that day, so I could feel now the exquisite pang of having to leave a scene so sweet.

That night they made love. I lay in bed listening. It was a windy night and there were tree branches that tapped against the house. My father had come into my room and stood in the dark, thinking I was asleep. He had leaned against the wall with his hands in his pockets, and I didn't think I was wrong in assuming what he was feeling was pride. Then he had gone in and made love to my mother, but the sounds tonight filled me with terror. Though I ought to have been used to them, tonight they seemed extreme, as though he were doing something to her beyond the usual. When I heard my mother cry out in that ripped-open way of hers, I went into their bedroom and stood in the doorway. I tried to fool myself by pretending what I was doing wasn't conscious—that I was sleep-walking—and thus excusable. When my father noticed me there, he made a gasp. Then he said "goddammit." He rose and I expected to be hit, though he had rarely done that. I had seen him naked many times but not like this.

On the bed, my mother's head was turned against the pillow.

My father tried to overcome his anger by taking my hand. "Never never never," he said on the way to my bedroom. "Do you understand, Luca? Never interrupt like that."

He tucked me in, exaggeratedly, almost secretly gentle. "You're scared?"

I said nothing. His face came very close. "New house. Your mother scares you, making those sounds?"

It was safe to nod, and he smiled, lightly and delicately. "Luca, that's the sound of happiness you hear. That's all."

He went away then. I drew the covers tight, and heard their attempts to discipline themselves, to keep quiet. The trees that would need trimming made their scratching noise against the outer walls and I thought about what my father had said.

One night early in summer, he brought home from Vanderbruek a man named Bob Painter. Bob Painter was a good deal larger than my father, tall and gruff-looking, with a round red face. He worked on the grounds crew. My father made sure we understood Bob was one of the foremen.

Bob Painter's effect on my father was a little startling to watch. He made this neat, taciturn man, who was always telling other people to temper their effusions, himself effusive, wanting to show off. My mother and I were both very quiet at the beginning. We were watching a man we thought we knew behave as we had never seen him before. He showed Bob Painter around our house, and, pointing things out, laughed at things that didn't seem funny. He laughed in a high and irritating way, and there were times, doing that, when he seemed to be dismissing us, and our whole lives, for the benefit of a stranger.

We sat in the backyard, on the flagstone patio. My father cooked steaks on the grill. Bob Painter was uncomfortable being here, I could tell. To my mother's question, he said he had three little girls, they lived in Woburn. Seven, nine, and eleven. "Like clockwork, we had 'em," he said to my mother. "Every two years." He was like a man you would see in an Army movie, a black-and-white one, a minor figure, the sergeant who loses his temper, gets in a knife fight, dies. Only at the end would you feel sympathy for him. I kept waiting for him to disappear, become as unimportant to our lives as he would be to that movie. His big round face had cracks in it, fissures. His cheeks were immense, long and drooping and marked by the outlines of broken veins. His face looked like it had been frozen in reaction to some sort of trouble. He had brought a six-pack of Schlitz beer, and each time he opened one of the cans he looked like he was in pain. He offered one to Mother, and she surprised me by taking it.

Did she flirt with him? I don't think so. But as it grew dark, she began calling him Bob in a familiar way that irritated me terribly. "Another Schlitz, Bob?" she asked, though he was clearly in charge of that area, holding them between his legs. He had an orange fringe of hair that swept back off his crown.

"My brother-in-law," my father announced, turning the steaks, "had an idea, Bob. This hill is going to be full of guineas."

He had never said the word "guineas" before. Perhaps he said it at work. The light was falling, and you could see where the lawn was starting to come up, shoots of green still vulnerable to our footsteps. My father looked at the shrubs ringing the patio and seemed regretful, perhaps knowing he'd gone too far. On the days when he had planted the shrubs, it had been as though nothing was more urgent and important than to make things grow here.

Bob Painter was again on the verge of speaking. Then suddenly he appeared to be embarrassed, thinking better of his own impulse. He sat quietly in the chair. He turned to me at last. "You got a room there, Luca?"

I said I did.

"Can I see it?"

"Sure," my father answered for me.

Behind me, in the hallway, Bob Painter's step made a heavy tread. His breathing, too, was heavy. There was not much to show him in the room. I thought maybe he had asked to see it just to get away from the uncomfortable scene below, but I was embarrassed, because this called attention to me in a way I didn't want. Like George's room, across the street, mine was stripped down: bed, bureau, desk, heavy dark rug. Over my desk, however, was a print my teacher had given me, after the successful completion of "The Conquest of Mexico," of an Aztec warrior. The warrior had a strong jaw, and a flaming burst of feathers grew out of his head. In his arms, he held a prone woman, a woman who had been overpowered somehow. He was, for me, a hopelessly romantic figure, and in Bob Painter's presence, I found I wanted to turn him to the wall.

Bob Painter stared at the print, though, with great interest. "What is this, an Inca?" he asked, and breathed in his funny, sucking way.

I corrected him.

He went on staring at the picture, then at me. "I have three daughters," he said finally. "You'll like them."

But why should I ever know them? I conceived for him in that instant a disgust so strong that whole sections of the evening are blocked out for me. All I remember after is wanting him to go, wanting the course of our lives, with its secrets and its blurred-over areas, to resume. We ate steak. The light withdrew. I went in to watch television. I listened to the sound of them on the patio, my mother's voice, now drunk, the loudest. I imagined my father again using the word "guinea," and I wanted my mother to lift a gun and shoot Bob Painter. Or me, I could do it. I could take an ax and finish the job. But my mother made her loud noises and then her murmuring assenting ones, and the men's voices rode under hers. It was like they were going away from her secretly, under cover of night, throwing their voices like ventriloquists, so that she could not know how far away from her they already were.

It was a Wednesday in July when he finally didn't come home. At first, it seemed only another of his latenesses. My mother kept his supper warm, we watched television together. When, the next day, we still had not heard from him, I thought she should call his work. I understood, though, that even if I suggested it, my mother wouldn't act. For an hour in the morning I threw a rubber ball against the side of the house, and caught it.

By afternoon, the waiting had become too much to endure, so I took the trolley into Boston. I was old enough to do that then, usually with friends, today, for the first time, alone. I knew my mother wouldn't know or care. I explored the streets of Boston, looking for a movie, finally settled on *Hemingway's Adventures of a Young Man* at the Saxon. I remembered nothing of it afterward, save for one thing, one detail.

I took the trolley home and walked to the Hill, then slowed my pace, certain that when I got to the top his car would be in the driveway. When it wasn't, I shut off a light in my mind and went and got my ball and threw it against the house. I must have made too much noise; there was a tapping at the window. Uncle John was there. He motioned me inside.

I remembered then what it was about the movie I'd just seen, the single scene that had lingered. The boy, Nick Adams, comes upon a boxer, punch-drunk, wasted, in the woods. Paul Newman played the boxer, and with him was a Negro. When the boy comes upon them, they share some melted ham fat, and then the boxer becomes excited. Something in the boxer cannot be contained. So the Negro knocks him out. Taps him, and he's unconscious. That was wonderful, that small and vivid display of power and control.

I loved that scene.

2

By August of that year, the houses on the end of our street, and Uncle John's, began filling in. Something was evident right away. A new kind of person had come here.

Uncle John had said the names, "Meola, Semenza," as though he were describing a delicate, expensive purchase he'd just made. But when they moved in, they ignored us.

In late summer, they began giving parties for one another. The rows of Cadillacs and Buicks began coming up the Hill. There were four houses on the end of our street, facing one another, and two at the end of Uncle John's. At first, on the nights of those parties, Uncle John would stand out on his lawn, watering hose in hand. Perhaps they'd made a mistake, forgot he lived there. He stopped short of waving to the well-dressed people going to the party at Meola's. His big house took on the appearance of a gatehouse at the entrance to an estate.

The sons of Meola and Semenza were also different from us. They played on the high school football team and wore, in their front yards, letter jackets, purple and yellow. They were compact, black-haired boys, guards, centers. They drove their own cars, too, and some nights brought their girlfriends up to the Hill. From where I watched, from my room or from the front yard (the grass had grown enough to begin mowing), they seemed to drive with an extraordinary calm. Beside them, their girlfriends, girls who wore their hair in "flips," and who were cheerleaders for the football team, seemed to have all the energy. The girls moved, in the passenger seats of those cars, talking and gesturing with their hands, and when they parked in front of the boys' houses, they waited for the door to be opened, and then moved inside, sometimes half-running, always followed by the boys, who moved more slowly.

It had been, in all the ways that counted, an odd summer. No one had bothered to tell me why my father had left. His disappearance, however, had been sudden and absolute. Apparently, he had not needed to take his clothes with him, wherever he had gone, because they still hung in his closet, and because it was summer and I was home all the time, I knew he didn't come to retrieve anything, unless he came at night when I was asleep.

I still had my old friends, and sometimes, after supper, I would get on my bike and ride to Candace Road to play in the Wiffle ball games. But the old neighborhood held no great interest. Coming home, I would get off my bike at the bottom of the Hill, walk slowly up, and approach the houses, which had their lights on, like a spy.

In their backyard, Bobby and George might be sitting at their picnic table, talking, and though they laughed frequently, I began to feel their diminishment, how they were coming to understand that they were not like the sons of Meola and Semenza, and yet not thugs either, in the way they had once been, in the way it had once been all right for them to be. Instead, for a time they were hiding, just as I was.

Then I would walk down to the other end of the street to look at the newer houses, in which there seemed to be a heightened sense of life: more lights were on, the football team sometimes gathered, or else the sons of Meola and Semenza were there alone, flipping cards to one another under the extravagant chandeliers hanging over their dining room tables.

There were girls, too: Meola had a daughter my age, in my class at school, though we never spoke. Her friends came over and they sat in the backyard. I stood in the dark with my bike, and listened to the high murmur they made. They spoke in the same language my family spoke, but it was full of hesitations and conjunctions, mysterious nuances that made it seem a language all its own.

And here is the essential thing, the thing I was most drawn to: when a man, the owner of a house, would come out the front door, and stand in the lighted entrance, it was as though he were surveying something. Nothing need be going on physically for the world to seem alive and full of movement. The men on Candace Road who would come out to watch us play Wiffle ball were not unhappy men, but this sort of proprietary moment was not possible for them. A curtain had been lifted for me, I suppose, certain important divisions in the world were made clear. And though it probably wouldn't have affected me the same way at any other point in my life, it did then.

Finally I would go home. My mother would always be watching television in the room we called the family room. She watched with one lamp on, and, frequently, with one arm slung behind her head.

"Where did you go?" she wanted to know.

"To Candace Road."

My mother did not understand Wiffle ball or my growing penchant for silent observation, so that was all I said.

"Want to watch TV with me?"

I would have to say yes, then sit with her awhile, though nothing on the square box in front of us interested me half so much as what was going on outside. I was watching only to be polite, because she had asked me, because I suspected she needed company.

I allotted her half an hour, then I went to my room. In summer, the windows were open, the breezes came in. I took off all my clothes and lay on my bed in the dark. Sometimes a car drove by, or there were voices, a boy and a girl. They spoke low, and I listened in such a way that even simple words—words like "No" or "Come in"—stayed with me a long time afterward.

On Sundays we still had the ritual of the beach to anchor us in the old world. The family still gathered at Nahant. We parked illegally. We carried picnic baskets of food, big coolers. We set up four blankets in a row. No mention was ever made of my father, but I could see, in the behavior of my Aunts Carmela and Lucy, a notation made. Emma was always protective of my mother, but Carmela and Lucy looked at her in a way now that suggested they were not unhappy at the turn of events.

On the blanket, eating her food, I don't believe my mother noticed this, or if she did, she pretended not to. She smiled as if nothing had happened to her, it was all right, being left didn't make such a difference. I asked her to come into the water with me. I would have preferred to swim alone, but I couldn't bear to leave her with them.

In the water, sometimes, she became a girl again. She told me how, when she was growing up, she left her sisters to the chores, took her towel down to the local pool, and swam all morning. "I was a fish, Luca," she said. "My sisters had to do all the work." So I saw, maybe, how things had once been, and why her sisters had looked at her the way they'd looked at her on the night of John's party.

When she came out of the water, Carmela and Lucy were usually lying back beside their husbands, often with one thigh draped over the men's legs. It seemed, since my father's desertion, they had become more interested in their husbands; they ran their legs up the fleshy thighs of Tony and Mike in ways they never had before. So I tried to distract my mother. I told her to watch out for crabs, to look down, down into the water. I felt all my stiffness and formality, as though I had become a kind of guide for her. In my hyperawareness of the intense sensuality of the world, it became an imperative to mask that sensuality, to stand as a barrier between her and it.

There was another side to my mother that seemed to come out exclusively on the phone. I was home a lot, so I heard. I lay in my room and read. I threw a rubber ball against the back wall of the house. I was too young for a job. My one task was to mow the lawn.

"Well, he can't see him," I heard her say once. And then: "Because I told him I would tell. I would tell them at his work."

After a moment, she repeated it: "If he tried to see Luca, I would tell."

In my room, I heard the words bouncing off the walls, off the picture of the Aztec warrior, the novels of John Steinbeck I was reading that summer—*The Red Pony, The Pearl*—and the book George had given me, called *My Secret Life*. Steinbeck was for the day, but at night, I liked to lie in bed and read about the Victorian author of *My Secret Life* "rogering" women. I liked to hear the women shout things like, "You're a horse! Oh my God, my man's a horse!"

"And they'd fire him right away," my mother said afterward.

Uncle John had explained nothing the day he'd motioned me inside after I'd gone to see *Hemingway's Adventures of a Young Man.* He'd said only, "Your father's gone away," or something like that. On his face had been the whole weight of the secret, but he had put his finger to his lips, as if to keep them shut. He shook his head, then made a stilted promise to my mother: "I want to assure you, Dorothy, that I will do everything in my power to make sure that Luca has a normal life."

After listening to my mother's conversations on the phone, I expected her to look different, but she didn't. She took care of her flower gardens and made up her face and prepared elaborate meals, enough for three or four. At the table, eating with her, I felt all arms and sharp, bony elbows. I felt ugly and like my bones would pop out and I would knock her in the face if I moved too quickly. I felt, too, and in dangerous ways, like that was what I wanted to do.

As soon as I gave up going down to the Wiffle ball games, I took to spending time in their bedroom. At the other end of the house, my mother watched four or five television shows in a row, everything that was on, so it was safe. My father's suits hung in the closet, five of them. I could see I would be taller than him someday, if I didn't stop growing. I would hover over him, but would I ever see him? Beside the bed was a wedding portrait, his tight smile, and then, on the wall, the BC hockey photo. When he was still here, he would have awakened every morning to the sight of himself poised to bolt.

One night my mother caught me in their room. "What are you doing?" she asked.

She was in the doorway, and I was on the bed, my hands between my legs, resting there. She cocked her head and smiled as though there could be nothing wrong with any activity I chose now. Then she rephrased the question. When I didn't answer, I saw the change in her face, the beginning of her allowing something in.

She came in and sat beside me on the bed. She looked where I was looking, at the BC picture. Then she got up and took it down, with a decisiveness I had not seen from her up to this point. Carefully, she put it away in a drawer. In the drawer also was a rosary, and some underwear she didn't use anymore. Then she came and sat beside me. She put her hand in my hair, which was thick and springy and resisted her fingers.

"Come and watch TV," she said.

"I don't want to," I answered.

The next day she did something. I was not home when she did it. It was early September. There was still a thickness of woods behind the houses of Meola and Semenza, and I had gone there to spy on Meola's daughter. There was a copse of birches, inside it Meola had placed a bench, wrought iron, full of fancy designs. Karen Meola came out with nail polish and a book. She had a broad, flat face and she was short, but she was popular. She painted her nails and I watched the way she lifted her heavy thighs to get at her toes. At a certain point she looked up, as if she'd become alerted—by nothing, by silence—to my presence. If she had discovered me, I don't know what would have happened. In two days, we would be back in school, and I would see her every day. But here, now, it was charged with strangeness, my watching her, and this was what I liked about it.

When I got home, there was commotion. Uncle John's car was parked in front of the house, and since it was the middle of the day, this was unusual. It was time for lunch.

But John was pacing in our living room, and when he saw me at the foot of the stairs, I could tell he wished I hadn't come home.

My mother stood in the middle of the kitchen looking as if she had just dropped something and was contemplating an imaginary mess on the floor before her. Her hair looked a little wild, and her eyes.

John turned on her. "Now what?"

And then, harder: "And how do you keep the house, Dorothy? Did you consider that before pulling this little stunt? You say he needs to see his son, fine—but is the way to do that to call and rat on him, so you lose everything? They'll fire him now for sure. You think like a woman, Dorothy. You think only with the emotions."

She looked at me, something secret in her eyes, as if I had been her ally in what she had just done; I, at least, would understand.

"What happened?" I asked.

John simply looked at me again, wishing I would go away. "Nothing," he said.

Then he went to the big bay window and touched the sides of his pants, perhaps searching for a cigar.

"You're going to see your father."

That night he called.

"I'm coming to get you," he said. "Friday night." After which he paused, then said, in a half whisper, "It's okay now."

But was it? In the way he spoke, there was the inference that our world, his and mine, was going to be restored, and that it was the only world that counted. But close to me, in the family room, my mother made her presence known, in small ways, by moving her legs on the couch.

"What would you like to do, Luca?" my father asked, from whatever room or bar he might be calling from.

"I don't care," I said.

Again, my mother had moved, as if she were following the conversation through the movements of her legs and arms.

"Maybe I can just, show you how I'm living now," he said. "Maybe that would be enough for a start."

"Okay."

He giggled. I knew it was just his nervousness speaking, though at first it cut me in a tender place.

"Your mother and you been doing okay?"

"Yes."

"I couldn't call because of, well, because of complicated reasons."

"It's okay."

He held a long pause.

"Friday night," he repeated.

When our conversation was over, I watched television with my mother for a while, out of politeness and a sense of impending and necessary desertion. She was watching *Naked City*. She favored police shows, doctor shows, anything featuring large and burly males moving heavily through the world, knocking obstacles from their paths. When the commercial came on, I spoke. "He says he's coming to get me Friday."

"I called his work," she said abruptly. "I told on him. I told them what he was."

I could see only the back of her head, the slightly mad way her hair sprawled upward, and her arm lay as if in readiness to pat her hair down.

"That's why he's coming, Luca." She touched her hair then, and continued watching the show.

Of course I understood something, though maybe not in the way of words. I understood that my father had made a charge outward, into the world beyond this world, and that this charge had always been coming, he had been preparing for it a long time. Our coming here, our ascension, the finishedness of this neighborhood itself—had been, I knew, a catalyst.

But when he came, I thought right away that he looked silly. He had fallen away from a standard, and it was only at his appearance that I understood how, in his absence, I had allied myself with Meola and Semenza, and with my Uncle John, the men who stood beneath the high archways of their doors and surveyed the world.

He was wearing a hat, but not a suit. Instead, a soft cotton shirt, buttoned to the neck. He stood beside the Fairlane, waiting.

Uncle John had come for the occasion. My mother had packed me food in a bag.

"Don't be silly, Dorothy," John had said when she'd handed me the bag, and my mother answered, "There might not be food there." Because so little had been said, every word carried an enormous, terrifying weight. *There.* Where were we going?

Behind me, as my father stood waiting, in the foolish hat, John had his hands on my shoulders, and I could practically feel his belligerence. It was only because John's anger seemed so oversized that I was able to sympathize with my father even a little, to move an inch beyond my absorption in this new world of ours to wonder what lesser world my father had chosen, instead, to inhabit. John's hands tightened on my shoulders and he forced me out the door.

My father smiled. I thought how I must look to him, standing before the door with my shoulders high, as though John were still gripping them, and with the bag of food in my hands. It was like I had become, in the time of his absence, a kind of girl.

"Let me look at you," he said.

So I went down the steps. He made a great show of circling my body. He touched my arms. "Okay," he said, as if he'd just had a thought, something secret, something he wouldn't tell me. He glanced once at the house to find John still watching him in a leaning-forward, aggressive manner that made him seem all pointy, rodentlike head. Then he looked around the neighborhood and seemed glad to be back. "I see they moved in," he said. "Down the street."

"Yes."

"And tell me. Do they . . . associate with you? With John? Are there . . . block parties, and such?"

"No," I said.

He looked down the street. "No, I didn't think so. Come on."

We got in the car, and he kept looking at me as if waiting for the conversation to start, as if it were up to me. He turned the radio on but seemed not to find anything interesting there.

"What's in the bag?" he asked.

I still held it, stupidly, in my lap.

"Mom made me something to eat."

He looked, briefly, angry. "Put it in the back, Luca."

I did, and then it was as if he regretted getting angry. "So? School started? Eighth grade?"

"Yes."

His voice was soft, but he knew how to put insistence into it. "And?"

A great many things had in fact happened in the first three days of school. Mr. McCluskey, the gym teacher, had let down the ropes that hung from the ceiling of the gym and announced that by the end of the fall we were all going to have to climb them. A shudder had passed through the group of us. Then a boy named Andrew Weston had gotten a hard-on in the shower, and that had made us all forget the ropes. Everyone already knew things about Andrew Weston—the secret, vague things you could know about boys, the malformed boys who were part of every class. There were others: David Campbell, Alan Carney. Mr. McCluskey had come into the shower room and put his hands on Andrew's shoulders and led him out. While the rest of us dressed, Mr. McCluskey sat in the gym office with Andrew and stared out through the Plexiglas at us, his mouth hard and straight, cautioning us not to say anything. Andrew had not come to our next class. Someone said his mother had come to get him.

That was not all. Karen Meola was in all my classes. We didn't speak. I looked at her fingernails, and thought, in a silence that seemed to me enormously loud and significant: *I watched you paint them.* There was a power to standing outside, to knowing things about people they didn't know you knew, that I had just begun to apprehend.

"Nothing," I answered. "Eighth grade. Same as last year."

After that, we listened to the radio. My father settled back. "We're going to the plant, Luca. In case you're wondering. We're going to Vanderbruek."

It wasn't entirely a surprise, though my mother said he'd been fired. Vanderbruek was at least familiar ground. They made tiny machines—my father used the word "coordinates"—that were used in aircraft and, no one was ashamed to say it then, in bombs. This was peacetime, 1962. The Russians were the only threat, but if the Russians attacked, it was important to have bombs. That was the simple justification my father had given for his work, though it had hardly needed justification. He was an accountant, one of many. But he was in charge of a group. The plant was vast, the size of a small town. The parking lot was like the parking lot of an airport.

He stopped at the side of the main road, near one of the lesser parking lots. You could not get into it unless you showed your ID. There were uniformed guards. The guard leaned out of his booth and stared suspiciously at my father, but my father waved to him, and the guard let him stay.

"You're probably wondering what we're doing," he said after a moment. It was that eerily silent time at the end of the day in a factory, just before everyone quits work.

My father took out a cigarette and lit it. The way he did it seemed slow and pleasurable, and after he'd taken his first drag he looked down at his fingers holding the cigarette and scratched one of them. "See, I don't work here anymore."

He squinted through the smoke out the window. His lips had thinned and gathered into what you could almost be fooled into believing was a smile. "You want to know why?"

And suppose I didn't?

He leaned slightly toward me. "I'm going to tell you this, but I'm going to try to tell you in such a way that you believe I feel no rancor toward your mother. I'm not telling you this to turn you against her, okay?"

"Yes."

"Good. Because she told them something about me. She's angry at me, so she called this place and told them something she shouldn't have. Someday I'll tell you what that something is, but not now. So I had to quit. They couldn't exactly fire me, but they made it clear it would be better if I didn't stick around. So I quit."

For a while then, my father watched me not asking the next, obvious question. I sensed that he liked it that I wasn't asking, but who could tell? I felt his eyes pass over me a long time.

Soon the cars started coming out of the lots. It was quitting time. My father stopped looking at me and started looking at the drivers. His face was very serious, mildly recessed, anticipatory. He looked the way a man looks when he expects to be slapped but has already decided he will not slap back.

Some of the men and women in cars returned his stare. Not all of them. There were too many workers at Vanderbruek for him to know all of them. But some of the ones who did know him stared and did not greet him. They might even have looked a little frightened of him. I saw one woman who looked that way, and she stepped on the gas as she drove past him. Then a big heavy Oldsmobile pulled up next to us and my father's friend Vinnie Fratolino rolled down his window. "I got the air conditioner on, Lou," Vinnie Fratolino said. Still, there was sweat on his massive face. My father leaned across me, so that our bodies were touching. He appeared glad that someone had stopped to greet him.

"What did they do to you, Lou?" Vinnie Fratolino asked. Behind him, the line of cars had stopped in the heat.

My father shrugged. "I had to quit. No other choice." Now his hand was on my knee.

"Assholes," Vinnie Fratolino said, and shook his head from side to side. "Excuse me, I should watch my language," he said, noticing me. His head was large and doughy, like a man's head in a cartoon. He seemed to have parts missing—vital lines and pockets—as if he'd been drawn lazily, all cheeks, with a big affronted expression pasted on.

"It's all right," my father said.

My father's gratefulness seemed to make his skin warm. He looked alert and happy, but Vinnie Fratolino stared at him with mild alarm. "So what'd you come back for, clean out your desk?"

"No, I promised somebody a ride."

Vinnie Fratolino nodded, then looked at me, and back to my father. "You need anything, Lou?"

"I'm fine," my father answered. "Hey, you better go, you're holding up the works."

Vinnie Fratolino turned around and seemed to be noticing for the first time the cars behind him. He lifted his hand and rolled up the window.

"Nice guy," my father said.

Before long, Bob Painter came out of the building behind the guard's booth, walking with his lunch box. When he saw my father, he didn't hurry, as I expected him to, but slowed down, and even stopped at one point to watch the cars going past. It was clear he'd have preferred no one see him get into the car with my father.

Finally, though, he had to. He sat heavily in the backseat and the car felt immediately full of him, his weight and his scent and his peculiar breathing. He sucked in air heavily, slurped it.

"You remember Bob, Luca?" my father asked.

Bob Painter's brow was lowered. He seemed a little shamefaced, as though all power was on my side, and after we nodded to one another, he looked out the window.

"The Inca boy," he said, and smiled in a crooked manner.

"Who spoke to you?" he asked my father.

"Just Vinnie, that's all."

There was a silence after that; it meant something.

Bob Painter had said to me, on the night of the cookout, that he lived in Woburn with his three little girls. There is a moment, before you know anything for sure, when you dare to imagine things: that we were going there, to Bob's house, for dinner, after which we would drive to wherever my father lived now. Bob was his loyal friend, a buddy. The gathering of inferences was like a storm that would pass over us. My father's life would be white and clean, a state of unspoken confusion and quiet.

The truth was, instead, that my father and Bob Painter lived together in a rooming house in the working-class section of our own town, a place I could have walked to, easily, on any of those endless summer afternoons of his absence. They had one room, twin beds. This was where they were taking me, this was the *there* my mother had been referring to. My father showed me around, the hall that smelled of disinfectant, the bathroom down the hall. As soon as we were in the room, Bob Painter sat in a chair and opened a beer, drank one after another, quietly, contemplatively, the sedateness of his behavior a kind of nod to my being here. On top of the bureau sat a bottle of Old Grand-Dad, but he did not touch it that night. My father kept an eye on him, then snuck me into the hall. "Don't worry about Bob, Luca. We're going out to eat. Then a movie. All right?"

It was what we did. In the diner, Bob Painter began to slur his words, and he looked at me, once or twice, angrily. My father kept his eyes on me, as if to reassure me of something—that Bob Painter's behavior could not crack the fragile vessel we needed to create. It was like he was putting his hand on my brow and saying: *Don't consider this man.*

We got to the Embassy early. My father remained alert through *The Miracle Worker,* sitting with his hat in his lap. Beside me, Bob Painter slept, snoring loudly. My father had to reach across me to nudge him awake. We drove back to the room in the car with the lights playing across our faces in a silence that seemed filled with my father's satisfaction, as though just getting through this night were some kind of triumph.

In the room, as soon as he was in bed, while still in his clothes, Bob Painter began snoring.

My father snapped on a light. We were private, away from Bob. The light wouldn't disturb him.

My father still had his hat on. We faced each other in chairs.

"How's things at home?"

"Good."

He nodded, searching for another topic. "You still go to the beach on Sundays?"

"Yes."

"They say anything about me?"

"No."

"I bet they do. I bet you've heard things."

"Bobby's sleeping with a girl," I said.

It seemed strange to be saying it. It was the only thing I could think of. It also distracted us from the thing he'd just said.

He looked at me curiously, his eyes bright in the reflection of the lamp. "Is that right? How do you happen to know that?"

"George talks about it. On the beach."

"In front of everybody?"

"No. Just me. We go away from everybody. George and Bobby and me."

"They tell you that."

"Yes."

He rubbed his chin for a while.

"And does George sleep with a girl, too?"

"No."

"Aha."

He played with the chain of the lamp. "Don't they think you're a little young for that?"

I shrugged.

"Are you tired?"

"No."

My father took my hand. He flattened out my palm, and moved his own finger against it, making the vague shape of the letter "W."

"Do you know what I'm doing?"

He did it again. It was what Annie Sullivan had done in the movie, the painstaking secret language through which Helen Keller had finally received meaning.

"Remember?"

I nodded my head.

"Amazing."

He shook his head.

"Listen, start bringing your glove on weekends, okay? We'll play catch."

He stared at me a moment, then he got up and made a bed for me on the floor.

3

In Ancient History, Mrs. Matheson (herself ancient, gold-plated, a figure seen as if through museum glass) divided us into pairs. A special project had been assigned, individually tailored for each pairing. "Luca Carcera, Andrew Weston," she announced. "The Athenian character."

We went to Andrew's house, afternoons (his suggestion) to work on it. Andrew Weston lived with his mother on the upper floor of a two-family house on the other side of town, the poorer side, not far, in fact, from where my father lived with Bob Painter. It was a neighborhood of two- and three-family houses with postage-stamp yards, in the vicinity of the shuttered watch factory.

Andrew Weston's mother sat at a large table pushed up to the window that caught the best light, with a pack of cigarettes (always, one was lit), an ashtray, and a stack of books. The table was full of plants, scraggly, half dead, but sometimes she would turn away from her book in order to push one further into the light, or to clip away a frond. She had long tawny hair she wore pulled close to her scalp, then hanging down in the back, a skeletal face that seemed always in motion. The books she read were the popular books of the time: Harold Robbins, Leon Uris, *Written on the Wind.* She read them all with a kind of annoyance, as if she were conducting a silent, impatient dialogue with the author. At any moment she might burst out with "Oh, that's *wrong*," or "That's *unworthy* of you."

Andrew did not treat her well. He was a small boy whose boner in the shower had astonished everyone. Any other boy would probably have had to leave school after an incident like that, but Andrew Weston managed to incorporate it into his persona. He was marked out, but he did not seem to care. His short hair flew up in the front into a dramatic stand of curls. In grammar school (the Westons had lived, briefly, near us), he had been a favorite of the girls, considered "cute," called by the mothers "a young dreamboat," but then he had made his transition, in the immense privacy of late childhood, and come out on the other side of it a friend of the girls, where the rest of us had made our lasting separation.

Within the confines of the top floor of the two-family house, he lorded it over his mother, barely acknowledging her as we entered the rooms. She glanced up with low expectations, her sharp features shrouded in smoke, caught between the cheap theatrics of her novels (even at twelve, I knew what was cheap and what was literature; John Steinbeck was literature, *The Carpetbaggers* was not) and the presence of two remote, silent boys who would give her, she seemed to know, very little. "The scholars," she would always say upon our entrance. "And here I am, reading trash."

From my first appearance, she looked upon me in a gauging, deeply focused way that let me know Andrew did not often bring friends home, and certainly not friends who were the epitome of regularity, such as I was in those days. "Who's *this*?" she asked, and if I'd been older, I'd have read seductiveness in the "*this.*"

In his room, Andrew required no help at all in writing "The Athenian Character." The first day, he went to his desk, opened the Ancient History text, and began writing. I sat on his bed. His walls were bare except for a Winslow Homer print. On the floor was a small record player and a stack of 45s. When Andrew caught me gazing at them, he suggested maybe I wanted to listen to a couple. "Go ahead, it's okay," he said. "Take advantage of my good taste."

Then he looked at me there on the floor a second longer than he needed to, as if the sight of me in the midst of this perfectly ordinary pastime had leaked out a small but vital piece of information he was snatching up.

On his way out of the shower room, led by Mr. McCluskey, Andrew had held his head in the firm, tilted manner one held one's head to staunch a nosebleed. But he had not cried. In the office, waiting with Mr. McCluskey, he affected the look of a boy who had already entered into some new compact with life.

As for me—as with the others, the larger group—we had made our own compact. We were not to speak of this, but it was okay to look at each other and raise our eyebrows and giggle. When the giggling grew too loud, Mr. McCluskey sent us a punishing look through the Plexiglas. Andrew stared ahead of himself, scratching his nose, waiting for his mother.

On the floor of his room, I listened to records. "Michael, Row the Boat Ashore," by the Highwaymen. "Loco-Motion," by Little Eva. Andrew's taste was like anyone else's. His mother knocked on the door and asked if we were hungry. "How about a snack?" she asked. Andrew didn't even condescend to answer. She opened the door and gazed inside, at me on the floor, Andrew at his desk. "He's a one-man band," she said, and smiled in a way that inquired: she may be stuck with him, but what was it in me that found no more suitable outlet than a friendship with Andrew Weston?

It was a good question. Even after I'd begun to understand how precise a characterization of Andrew his mother's had been, I continued to follow him to his house two afternoons a week, to sit on the floor and listen to records while he scratched away at the table. In his room, I half-listened for his mother outside. The phone did not ring, no one came to the door. If there was a father, his presence had become as ghostly as my own father's was in the house he had built and abandoned. Andrew had taken a volume of Thucydides out of the town library. "Listen to this," he'd announce gleefully, coming upon certain details of the plague at Athens. " 'Externally the body was not very hot to the touch, nor pale in its appearance, but reddish, livid, and breaking out into small pustules and ulcers.' " He made a face, and then seemed thrilled when he came to Thucydides' descriptions of the afflicted Athenians' diarrhea. At such moments it was like he was vaunting the deepest of his secrets, the utter boy-ordinariness of being thirteen.

We turned in the report and got an A. On the afternoons we'd set aside to write the report—Tuesdays and Thursdays—Andrew contin-ued to ask me if I was coming to his house. He phrased it less in the man-ner of an invitation than like some burdensome obligation he had taken on. I went. It seemed easier than saying no, than making an excuse, than going home to my mother's smiling, beautifully maintained catatonia. She sat in rooms, she watered plants (I thought of her and Mrs. Weston as engaging in a kind of war of plants, with my mother the clear victor), she watched mid-afternoon television. Somewhere I wondered how long this could be sustained: our lives had become like still lifes, like fruit on a table, spoiling in the light.

From my other friends I'd begun a long separation. My father's leaving had done that. I couldn't tell them about my father; that act of his had cleared out an area of experience, made it "the past." There was a barrier now around all the things I used to do. Only Andrew asked no questions, offered me the floor, his record player, the new records he bought, the quiet of the room, and his mother outside, smoking and wondering, vaguely, if we were hungry.

My only other social obligation that fall had to do with my cousin George. I was twelve, would be thirteen in November. I was tall for my age; still, twelve is young. But I had also always been known as the smart one in the family. How merited this was I am not sure. But it was enough for Uncle John.

With the building of the house, the settling of the new neighbor-hood, there was a new obligation for John's sons. They were to be like the others, the Meola and Semenza boys who were headed for college. It was all-important suddenly that they meet the new standard.

Bobby and George were both unprepared for this. They had planned on futures as advanced thugs: physical labor, caked grime under their fingernails, gray uniforms with their names stitched above their breast pockets in red, all that would be enough. But John kept looking at them as if they were made of wet clay, as if he could not hurry quickly enough to realize the vision that had come to him, I always suspected, too late. On Thursday nights he insisted I come and tutor George in English. "Straighten him out," John said, as if I were capable of doing that. Into my palm, he folded ten dollars a week.

What these evenings consisted of was sitting in George's room while George perched at his desk, or lay on his bed, thrumming any hard surface he could find with his thumb, while humming one of the songs then popular (though not the songs Andrew bought at Record Mart, which tended to be softer, whiter, more mainstream). George favored songs with heavy guitar lines he could mimic by forcing his lips together and letting out an "mmm" sound. He was seventeen, a senior in high school. *The Great Gatsby* lay on his desk, an old copy that had served maybe ten years' worth of seniors in the General class. George was supposed to read it and write a paper. I was to help him, but I had a larger task as well.

The high school had offered an informational night for parents, and John had come back from it with a fixed idea in his mind—the "College Essay." The guidance counselors had convinced Uncle John that whatever unimpressive record George had toted up in the previous three years, all could be rescued, his future assured, if he could only write a "College Essay" good enough. That was the core of my assignment.

But in George's room, we barely spoke. We were waiting for Bobby to come home.

Bobby, sixteen, had been "laying" Joanne Lacosta since early summer, since one night she had surprised him, when he slipped his fingers into her panties, by not stopping him. Then Joanne Lacosta had gotten "wet," and excited, bucking a little in her lower parts, until she'd said, "Please don't stick it in me," and Bobby had known, through some weird teenage intuition, that this was a signal to, indeed, stick it in her. Which he had done. All this he relayed to George and me behind a rock at Nahant one Sunday, the day after it happened. I had not been meant to hear, but I was with them, and George was crazy for the details: once Bobby had offered the first one, George's hunger couldn't be contained. So Bobby had to describe what it felt like to go all the way in, and what happened to Joanne while he was doing that (no, she hadn't screamed; her body had instead, and astonishingly, seemed to be inviting him), and what he had done when he came (nothing, but only that first time; afterward, he was smart enough to buy rubbers). And since then, the affair had gone on, continued through the summer and into the fall. In August, Joanne Lacosta had begun accompanying us to the beach on Sundays; she and Bobby were shy around one another, though she sent him certain secret-sharing looks. She wore two-piece bathing suits—green and black—around the bottom of which I could sometimes see little hairs coming out, little hairs that seemed to contain the carnivorous secret essence of shy, pretty Joanne Lacosta.

Bobby's room became, to George and me, a kind of greenhouse of sex. We knew where Bobby kept his rubbers, and George had stolen one to keep in his wallet. We touched Bobby's aftershave bottles, poured a little on our hands, and George said, sniffing, "This is probably what drives her crazy, this is the irresistible stuff." We even stared sometimes at Bobby's bed, and if the bed happened to be unmade, stared at the impression Bobby's body had made in it, in sleep, because he was a kind of holy figure now to us, his body consecrated by what he did with Joanne, three or four times a week.

It was the one great thing. It was the one astonishing, impossible thing. Staring at Bobby's bed I caught a glimpse of how far I was from it, and my life seemed an agonizingly slow climb toward something I only dimly perceived.

"You get hard, Luca? You get little boners?" George would ask.

Yes.

It made him smile, like there was something delicious about it. Here was the College Essay.

The evening was capped when Bobby came home. We were all figures in a dance that year, each assigned a series of steps. Bobby came home and went to his room. George rose and pounded on Bobby's door. "Whaddayawant?" Bobby called. "Get your ass out here," George insisted. Bobby came out. His eyes were lowered, like he wanted nothing to do with us. Sexual activity had cleared his skin, improved his grooming. He had a dark shimmer about him now, like George Chakiris in *West Side Story.* His slicked-back hair smelled vaguely sweet. He sat on the edge of George's bed and offered himself for our study.

George knelt before Bobby's open legs. "Let's have them," George always said.

For a moment, Bobby looked resistant; every week this went on. He couldn't believe how stupid this was. But then he offered them up, the fingers of his right hand for George to sniff.

This was their agreement. If Bobby, the younger brother, was going to get laid first, his promise to his less lucky brother was that he would bring home, for George's pleasure, at least the scent of sex. George would close his eyes and breathe in that scent, that secret cache stolen from inside Joanne Lacosta, while Bobby, on the bed, laughed at him. "You are so *nuts*, George. Stop it. You are so *crazy.*"

Once, at the end of this ritual, they both looked at me. "Go ahead, let him," George said, and Bobby nearly did, but then shook his head. "He's too young. It'd only fuck him up." For a moment, my heart had been beating very fast.

On my way out, Uncle John was always waiting, at the foot of the stairs, the ten dollars in his hand, to walk me home.

We both knew he was buying only hope. Even then I could sense the agreement he had made with himself, in his own mind, to keep two things separate: his real assessment of George (and with George, maybe, of the whole fate of his family) and this other thing, this belief certain men have, that life must ultimately be benevolent. Life must ultimately *yield.* It was the essence of optimism I faced at the bottom of the stairs: might I tell him that some miracle had occurred? Some progress made on the College Essay? John had fixed his sights on Northeastern for George. He had gotten hold of the application, which would not be due until February. "State three things that have shaped the development of your mind," Northeastern asked. At the bottom of the steps, I saw how fixed John was on this specific, accomplishable goal, so small, so reachable. If he could have written it himself, he would have. Had even gone so far as to announce once, "For me, very easy. Number one: when I was seven years old, having no food to eat . . ."

At the bottom of the stairs, he would not quite ask me, but only stare, his head tilted, that characteristic male hope in his eyes that taught me that every man, however old, is still a boy, waiting for the story to be altered in a favorable way. Sometimes he would say one word. "Progress?" Or "Success?"

All I could give him was a weak smile, a shrug. In that moment I knew he hated me. But I couldn't lie. He handed me the ten. In my mind there was a slight pull at the end, as though he didn't really want me to have it, knew I hadn't earned it.

The final part of the ritual was John walking me home. It was unnecessary, I lived only across the street. If I was old enough to tutor a seventeen-year-old boy in the College Essay, I was old enough to assay the fifty yards separating John's house from ours. But he did not only walk me home. We toured the neighborhood, "the Hill," as everyone now referred to it. We charted the progress of new houses. We stared into the woods, at felled trees, bulldozers left standing in a kind of sleep. There were living things growing around us, lifting up toward the pala-tial. John's own house, being as large as these others, was not quite di-minished. He had been the first, the pioneer. Someday they would come to appreciate this, though they hadn't yet. Whatever went on in George's room, whatever the ultimate success or failure of that venture, there was sustenance to be had here.

We would speak sometimes, though never of important subjects.

"The rock is from Italy," he would say.

Mastrangelo, the lawyer, had imported marble from Italy. The tini-est of facts rippled through the neighborhood, bypassing my mother and me, outcasts in our house.

"Imagine," he said.

We would reach the end of the street, where it was entirely woods. John would remove a cigar then. Slowly he would unwrap it. I didn't be-lieve I was there for him anymore; having come this far, my task was completed, I might now disappear. Slowly he would unwrap the cigar and with one hand light it and with the other cup the lighted end as he puffed until it took. Then he would drop the crumpled cigar wrapper on the ground.

It struck me, this gesture, because it did not seem offhand, but a deliberate, if tiny, defacement. The crumpled cigar wrapper lay on the virgin ground. John knew it was there. He puffed and stared down at the rows of houses, the farthest ones lit, the nearest plywood skeletons drawn up from the ground as if by the force of moonlight.

I wanted to stoop and lift the cigar wrapper but I understood that if I did, John would hold my arm hard and tell me to leave it.

After John had stood smoking for several minutes, he seemed to re-member me again. "I'm keeping you up, aren't I?"

"It's okay."

"When's your bedtime?"

"My mother doesn't care."

He mulled that over. "Your mother doesn't care about a lot of things."

I acted as though I hadn't heard.

"And how's your father? How's the weekends? Tough?"

"No. They're all right."

"I'll never get anything out of you, will I?" He chuckled.

We started home.

It was only then, as we walked again into the light falling from the streetlamps and from out of the living rooms of the houses we passed, that I could forget John's casual dropping of the cigar wrapper, could stop thinking about what it might mean, could again become absorbed by the houses and the lights and the views of interiors, the modern furniture and the hanging chandeliers. We were far then from the rooming house, from the breathing of Bob Painter, the enigma of my father's staring at me, the nights when I fell asleep, of the three of us, last. John had convinced me of something in these walks: the necessity of effort, the capacity of the world to be shaped to a man's ends. This was my romance, and in spite of all the confusing things I knew about him, John was slowly becoming its hero. In the grip of such a romance, Bobby's bedroom faded, as did the movement of Bobby's body into George's room, the offering of the fingers.

Bobby and George were lost to sex. But not me. I would not be that way; no.

All that fall, my father kept making marks in my hand, some of them blotting out earlier marks. But the word I was to shout in understanding—the Helen Keller scream of recognition—never arrived.

One Friday night, just as the weather took a turn into serious cold, my father was late coming to get me. I sat on the front stoop, staring at the tall birch tree that dominated the front yard. Uncle John sat with me, smoking, saying nothing, until he stood and said, "My ass is getting cold, Luca. I expect your father will be along sometime." Then he stared at me as if I should prepare myself for something.

That night, when my father finally arrived, it was on foot. He stood at the base of the driveway, not coming closer. It was evident he was waiting for acknowledgment, for us to see him and respond.

"What the hell is this?" John said.

"We're taking the bus," my father answered. "Come on, Luca."

"Where's your car? You break down?"

"I had to sell it, John."

I stood up, ready to go, even to come between them if necessary.

John rolled his cigar back and forth between his lips in such a way that I knew, even when he asked, "What do you mean, you had to sell it?" that he understood precisely.

My father, knowing that he didn't have to answer, zipped up his jacket and glanced away from us. "Come on, Luca," he said. His tone and the look on his face made me think I'd better come quickly. John followed me down the driveway. He stood close to my father, without words. They each blew smoke into the air. John lapsed briefly into a posture of what seemed like supplication, but it was as though he were looking over his shoulder, making sure no one noticed. "It's that bad?" John asked.

My father crossed his arms, huddled within himself, somehow managing to appear unembarrassed.

"How can you have let it get to this? *You?*" John's voice verged on a whine, as if, in spite of everything, he still expected my father to unzip this suit of clothes and emerge as the man he used to be.

"Listen, I've got a stack of bills for you," John said, breathing to calm himself. "They're at home, in my office. But under the circumstances . . ."

"Why don't you give them to me?" my father said.

John hesitated a moment. "All right."

He moved across the street, toward his house. We followed at a distance. In the large front window of John's house, we could see Emma rocking the baby, looking out at us, trying to get a glimpse of my father. She didn't wave, nor, seeing him, did she turn away. She had begun managing my mother's life for her, taking her shopping, making sure she got to the hairdresser.

"You all right?" my father asked, while we were waiting, just to say something.

"Yes."

A voice rang out then, sudden and shocking as the appearance of a deer. It was a woman's voice, and though it was coming from the wrong direction—from the houses peeking out of the woods past John's—it sounded enough like my mother to be her. It was high and musical, Italian-sounding. She was calling someone—a child or a dog—and my father, hearing that voice, snapped to attention.

He laughed lightly when he realized it wasn't my mother. Still, a change had come over his face. Something of his old melancholy, his handsome confusion, returned to him, replacing the slack and satisfied look he'd worn since he'd left us. We were waiting for John to come out with the bills, and I knew that in this caught state of waiting, with the woman calling her dog, my father's stomach was clenched—I could practically feel it—as though he had to be on guard against something that could still pull him back to this life.

When John came out and approached us, he said, "Are you sure you can pay these, Lou?"

My father's voice was slightly higher than usual. "Yes." It was as if he had to work past an obstruction, and I thought I knew what the obstruction was.

He remained in this silent, chastened state as we walked down the hill, took the bus, rode across town. Only women took the bus: nurses on their way to work, a woman and her son down the aisle from us. It was unusual for a man like my father to board; the women all seemed aware of him, but did not stare. It was half a mile from the place where the bus stopped to the rooming house. A party of French Canadian workers was in the hall. They were smoking in their T-shirts, and holding long-necked bottles of beer. It was their usual Friday night practice, a gathering at the end of the workweek. They interrupted their noise to allow my father and me to pass. There was a pause, too, so they could consider this man and his son in all the ways they probably habitually did, with suspicion and wonder.

The room was dark.

"He's not here," my father said, nearly under his breath, but just loud enough so that I could not mistake his panic.

He turned on a light and moved around the room, searching for a note on the table, or on one of the nightstands, then went to the window to look outside. He came back to the door and opened it, but there was only the smoke of the workers' party, so he closed it. He kept his hand on the knob.

He sat in a chair and put his hand over his face.

After a minute or so, he looked up. "You hungry?"

"I'm okay."

My father seemed alone then, and collapsed, like some plan of his hadn't worked. And because I understood it wouldn't be so bad for me if this plan of his failed, I said nothing.

But it wasn't good, either, to see my father like this. He was having trouble looking at me, and time moved slowly.

Finally, Bob Painter did come home, though he came home drunk and much later than expected. He came home, announced by a car full of the grounds crew from Vanderbruek. They dropped him off in front of the house, and we heard them; my father went to the window to look outside and listen, and I saw his face, complicated and full of too many emotions to count.

When Bob Painter came through the door, he glanced at me as he habitually did now, disappointed to see me, or as if my presence implied something—that I was a witness to facts about him he'd rather have kept private. He held on to the doorjamb, as if to keep himself upright.

"Who drove you?" my father asked. He was calm now, or else wanted not to show Bob what it had been like for him to wait.

"Wellsie." Bob Painter groaned, and headed for the bed, to lie down.

"I thought we arranged you were going to take a ride from Ed Kennedy?"

"We did, but listen. They wanted to take me out."

"Wellsie did."

"Listen . . ." A low growl seemed all he could manage. "It's important, that they wanted to do this. Can you understand that?"

Bob Painter sat halfway up in bed. "Get the boy outta here so we can talk straight, willya, Lou?" Sometimes Bob Painter's face took on a grizzled, unhealthy look that was frightening.

"He's not going."

"All right, so they wanted to take me out and I went."

"With Wellsie."

"Yes."

"Drinking."

"Yes. Oh shit." His hand went to his head. Bob Painter, big and burly and always seeming on the verge of violence, had started to cry.

"Can you understand what this means to me, that they wanted to take me out?"

"Bob, stop."

Bob fell into sobs, his hand going up and down in front of his face like he was rubbing something invisible to us.

"Can't."

"Bob."

"Can't. I can't."

My father looked at me but didn't settle on my eyes. He put his hand on my shoulder and led me out the door, past the workers, who were quiet to let us by. We stood on the porch, and I could hear his breathing, mixed with the voices that had started up. It seemed the men were listening to the sobs of Bob Painter, which were audible even this far away.

After a while, my father said, "This has got to change." He ran his index finger several times across his lips, as though he were cleaning them.

I kept my silence.

"This is not fair to you," he said.

Bob Painter came to the window and shouted, "Lou!"

We heard the voices of the French Canadians, mocking. "Lou!" they called, and hooted. "Lou!"

From somewhere out of the circumstances of that night came a plan, the suggestion that from now on when I came I should bring a friend. And there was no friend to bring but one.

I would like to say that there was nothing devious in my inviting Andrew, though of course there was, it wasn't accidental at all. I convinced myself that my father had made a mistake. Why shouldn't the adult world be capable of gross self-deception? He had believed that a life spent in a room with Bob Painter could somehow sustain him. The house, my mother, me: it had all been too much, and he'd run away. But he'd been wrong, anyone could see that now. If the voice of a woman on the street was enough to call him back, if all he needed was a nudge everyone else was too cowardly to make, I thought there were ways that I might help things along.

At first it seemed to work, too. My father's initial sight of Andrew caused his mouth to close in on itself, his lips to thin with uncertainty. We had had to get off the bus to go to Andrew's house to fetch him that first Friday night. From there it was an easy enough walk to the rooming house. Andrew was waiting for us on the front steps of his house, holding a large shoe box on his lap. He did not want to have his mother take any part in this, I knew that about him, knew how he came at things sideways, crab-walked through life so as not to seem committed to anything, while all the while settled and certain about selected things in a way that made me envious. When I had invited him to spend the weekend with my father and me, he'd sifted the invitation through some recessed part of his brain, taken a long time answering. I had almost given up when I heard the words "I suppose" come out of him.

Now he came toward us, his loping, sidelong walk that was—I had learned from other boys to form the words, though they applied only to Andrew, never to my father—a faggot's walk. My father saw, and I watched my father seeing, which is why it is stupid and dishonest for me to say I didn't know what I was doing.

Nor did Andrew finally escape his mother. She came out after we had started off. Andrew turned around, as if expecting this from her, and I did, too. She had come out to get a look at my father. She called to him. "Thank you for doing this!"

And my father shouted: "No problem!"

She said, "I hope he's no trouble."

"I'm sure he won't be. We'll have him back tomorrow."

"Your father lives *where*?" she had asked me, when Andrew had first presented the invitation to her. The arrangement, the course of my weekends, had fascinated her. But now they stood waving to one another, like any suburban parents, as if beyond the waving and the calling out of questions, they each connected to lives so ordinary and conventional as not to bear pondering.

Bob and my father both immediately knew Andrew. Their eyes went directly to the long and girlish swoop of his hair, his odd walk, and also to the fact that his eyes did not meet theirs when he reached his hand out to shake. There was a subtle kind of recognition in all this. Chastened by the events of the night when he'd taken a ride home from Wellsie, Bob made sure now he took the regular ride, the one from Ed Kennedy, so he was waiting for us in the room when Andrew Weston arrived. Things seemed to be settling dangerously, between my father and Bob, into a more conventional domestic routine.

Bob still drank, of course. When we got to the room, there was a line of empty Schlitz cans on the table, and my father eyed them, silently counting.

"Well," Bob said, at his first sight of Andrew. Then he glanced at me as if there was something he did not understand, something he was mad at me for. And then something, oddly enough, that he pitied me for.

That night it was *Birdman of Alcatraz* at the Embassy. First, though, was the diner, the awkward series of questions that Andrew deflected with the same swift expertness with which he dressed after gym. None of us was ever to see Andrew's naked skin again after the incident with the hard-on (he had been excused from having to shower, allowed into the locker room to change ten minutes before the rest of us), and my father and Bob were not to see any of Andrew either: he seemed to dodge through the empty spaces of the meal like a man dodging rain. I was not helpful. I volunteered only that we had worked together on a school project, a project about Athens. For Bob, this was an opening. "Oh, Athens," he said. "My daughter Maureen would be able to give you an interesting discussion about that. She's a smart one, too."

I caught my father staring at me across the table more than once that night, with a kind of grimness riding just in back of his eyes, as if the notion of my becoming like Andrew Weston—or like *him*—was more than he could bear.

"Did you bring your glove?" he asked me, with quiet seriousness.

"What?"

"For a catch."

"No."

He stared at me a moment, not unkindly, but allusive in a way he could be. "I told you to bring it. Remember?"

I ate my meat loaf.

"Do you play? Andrew?"

"Hmm?"

"Ball?"

"Oh. No."

We must have driven him crazy.

I had seen sometimes, in brief moments, how vested my father had been in my perfection, how even something so small as my ability to play ball well had been enough once to rip all the leave-taking energy out of him. Somehow he'd expected, no matter what *he'd* done, that certain things in me would stay the same. So I knew, or sensed, that the way to get back at him was to fall from perfection, to fall as far as I could.

At the end of the meal, when my father was in the men's room and Bob Painter had stepped outside, to stand on the curb with a toothpick in his mouth, Andrew and I had a moment, the two of us at loose ends within the diner. My father had handed me a bunch of change to leave on the table for a tip, and after I'd done that, I stared down the line of booths at Andrew. He was waiting at the door, looking at me as though he was trying to probe—it had become habitual by now—who I might be. It wasn't the sort of moment that I expected or wanted very much. It made things between us briefly, uncomfortably real. I wanted to make a joke then, to remind him of the things we liked to laugh about in his room—*diarrhea, pustules*—but I knew that wouldn't work right here and now. Andrew had a way of shrugging with his eyes, and that was what he did then. But I had a moment of believing it was all wrong, that I had stepped into something I wasn't going to get away from unscathed. Andrew was storing things up in a way I could only guess at.

Nor did the evening turn jolly after that. During *Birdman of Alcatraz*, Bob Painter kept falling asleep, and snoring. My father would nudge him, and Bob, awakened, would watch the movie as though it pained him, somehow, to try to comprehend the life of Robert Stroud, the convicted killer, who remained, for the movie's nearly three hours, unredeemed, and unrelieved of the burden of loneliness. Even his birds were taken away from him, midway through, and all that was left was the sweaty faces of the other prisoners and the guards, and the white sunless air of the cells. Under the lights of Main Street, afterward, and on the bus returning to the rooming house, we seemed not to be able to shake the movie's unsettling truth, that it was possible, unlike Uncle John and perhaps even my father and Bob believed, that life didn't finally yield toward goodness and forgiveness and the triumph of the human spirit, but, instead, might very well end as it had for Burt Lancaster, in the transference of the human body from one solitude to another.

I caught a certain look that night between Bob and my father. They were sitting on opposite sides of the bus, my father and Andrew on one side, me next to Bob on the other. Both men seemed thoughtful, and both were, for a moment, idly staring into space. Then Bob looked up and gazed into my father's face with a look I was growing used to, a look of longing and helplessness, eloquent and deeply private at once. My father returned Bob's look. I cannot say exactly what his face did, but ice entered my heart as I looked at him. It was as if that look were telling me, in no way I can quite describe, that though he did not have the capacity for emotional nakedness that Bob Painter had, he still felt as deeply and harshly and intensely as Bob, that they were alike in some important way.

Moments like that made me doubt that I could win my father back, that he was as close to coming back as I had tried to convince myself. And then something else happened to make me feel keenly the press of time, the need for something—if it was to happen at all—to happen very soon.

A few weeks before Thanksgiving, after another of the futile Thursday night meetings with George, I found Uncle John waiting for me at the bottom of the steps leading to his front door, with what I immediately detected was a new, troubled look on his face.

He had his hat in his hand and he was tapping it against his knees. "All finished?" he asked.

"Yes."

"Success?"

Tonight he didn't even wait for me to answer.

It was cold out, and John wanted first to know if I was warm enough. This was all preparation for something. He led me past my house, as usual.

"You like it here, Luca?" he asked. But he seemed anxious; there was nothing casual in the question.

I said I did.

"You think we did right?"

It was an odd question; of course they'd done right. My father's desertion changed nothing. The neighborhood was perfect. I tried to say all this in silence because John still cowed me out of words, though I believed he understood how enthralled I was by the neighborhood.

"I'll tell you one thing, though, that we did wrong. We didn't get the right architect. We got Zambetti, who we knew, and he was not . . ." John had stopped, not at the end of the street, but before Meola's house. There, he lit his cigar and waved it through the air, forming a wide, half-disparaging, half-envious circle. "Not for houses like this, anyway. You notice how much foundation he left showing, in your father's house, in mine?"

I had. It was a sore spot. It diminished us, the amount of gray at the base.

"You see how in these others, the brick and stone, they go all the way down to the base? That's important. That's a neater look. But what did we know?"

I did not move on, but stared at Meola's perfect lawn, which the Meola boys had not been expected to mow. Bonica, the landscaper, brought his men once a week.

"These are all, all these men, of the professional class." He sounded the old theme, pointed down the street, his fingers landing, in my foreshortened view, on each of the houses in turn. "Dentist. Lawyer. Cincotta's a . . . what? A tax man. Like your father. College man. A professional man knows these things. Me, I'm learning from the ground up. I've got a strong back and a weak brain."

He chuckled. "You cold?"

"No. I'm okay."

He paused, a long and significant silence, so that I might have known something important would follow.

"But it was still good for you, to come here, to have this time." His words trailed off, as if he understood he need not make them heard; they were for himself.

My mother and I began, soon after, taking rides at night, with a big-toothed realtor named Mrs. Chase. My mother settled on a rental house on Hobbs Road, a small house set within a grid of nearly identical houses, and one in which our bedrooms would butt directly up against each other. Our own house went up for sale, and was sold quickly, at a large profit. Still I retained the last-ditch belief that all these events could be forced to give way.

My thirteenth birthday fell on a Friday, the day after Thanksgiving. Andrew was with us again. The movie that night was *The Man-*

churian Candidate. Watching it, it occurred to me that I was studying six subjects in school, and then a seventh at the movies. All the movies of 1962 were about the same thing, with minor variations. Laurence Harvey wore a beatific expression throughout much of *The Manchurian Candidate,* as if nowhere in his imagination was there such a thing as resistance to the life that had been thrust upon him, the life of an assassin, condemned to kill even the girl he loved. He might have been Burt Lancaster tending to his birds, for all the hope that existed in those black-and-white images. I watched these movies and I watched Bob Painter watching them. As his drinking began to lessen, he stayed awake more. He was more reactive in his movie watching than my father. He made noises that called attention to himself, and I sensed in these small grunts of affirmation and denial a certain recognition and a fight against the recognition, as if, in spite of himself, he kept waiting for the redemptive moment these movies so rarely provided. *Give him a happy ending,* he might have been saying, in the grumbling silence with which he watched. *For Chrissake, give him something.* The movies of 1962 resisted him, unremitting in the bleakness of their conclusions, with only the occasional handclasp of a man and a woman—Frank Sinatra and Janet Leigh at the conclusion of *The Manchurian Candidate*—to indicate a belief that some compromise might be made with life, a dollop of pleasure or warmth squeezed out of the surrounding frost.

There was a reason Bob Painter may have been paying attention to the movie that night in a different way: his daughters were coming tomorrow. Mrs. Painter had at last agreed to his demand, would leave them to his care for a day. It had been five months. What exactly had precipitated the change in Mrs. Painter was a mystery, but tonight he had forsworn drinking. Fidgety in the room, snappish in the diner, he settled down only for the movie. My father gave Andrew and me to know that Bob was nervous. "These girls of mine, they're everything," Bob said. But if they were everything, why was he living with my father, when he could have been with them? That paradox, unspoken, rode with me all night.

In the morning, he was anxious, too. He drank cup after cup of coffee, shaved, lathered on Aqua Velva, stared out the window, and asked perpetually as to the time.

They were due at 10:00. At 9:45, Bob went outside, stood on the sidewalk to wait. He smoked a cigarette, paced, and from the window my father and I watched him. Andrew, in his sleeping bag on the floor, slept in.

At five minutes after ten, the car pulled up. A green Chrysler. Bob Painter crushed his cigarette underfoot. He stood with his back to us, but his back was expressive of desire, and his hands hovered just to the sides of his hips. I stared at the back of his head, the way the red hair curled and matted against his red neck, damp with sweat, though it was November. When his wife pulled up, I noticed he couldn't quite look at her face, nor she at his, but something was suggestive of the mood of their past days: the big, boxy, overused car, the slapdash parking job Mrs. Painter did. They had lived in chaos.

The two younger girls rushed out of the car, and Bob clasped them. The youngest, wearing glasses, hugged her father's leg and stared up at him. The middle girl was not so expressive, but wanted to be. Maureen, the oldest, the genius, Bob's pride, had not yet emerged from the car.

He went to the door and leaned in. Maureen was resisting, we saw that even from our perch at the window. Bob opened the car door and gestured with his arm toward the sidewalk, where the two younger girls waited. Mrs. Painter was not a clear figure to us. She sat behind the steering wheel in dark glasses—heavy, we could see that, with thick black hair, and pale—but she had turned, and stared at her estranged husband, her cheeks sagging somewhat, accusatory in her determination not to be his advocate in the matter of Maureen.

Finally the reluctant Maureen did emerge. All the girls had red hair, but Maureen's was the reddest. She made a dramatic figure there on the street, with her long hair and her size—at twelve, she was nearly as tall as Bob—along with her extreme paleness and the air of resistance even a stranger might have been able to read. Bob did not touch her, but he said some words. She did not nod her head, but seemed to have made some kind of agreement—temporary, conditional—nonetheless. Bob dipped his head back inside the passenger window, reached a final agreement with his wife. She drove off. With the little girls close by his body, and Maureen dragging slightly behind, Bob approached the house.

We moved from the window and took on our postures of waiting.

"Here they are!" Bob announced, as soon as he was through the door. "Aren't they wonderful?"

My first notion was that, in presenting them to my father, Bob was showing off some previously undisclosed part of himself. The little girls were shy and stuck close by him. Bob placed his hands on the sides of their heads. "Girls, this is my friend Lou Carcera. Lou, these are my girls. This one here's Patricia. And the little one's Jane."

My father stepped forward, the polite and formerly competent man who had smashed their lives. He shook both their hands.

"Maureen, come on inside," Bob insisted.

Maureen hovered in the doorway, taller it seemed, paler and more mature than she had appeared from the window.

"And this is Maureen."

Andrew was still on the floor in his sleeping bag. This was where she chose to look.

"That there," Bob said, "is Luca's friend Andy, Maureen. You'll like him. He's smart as you, almost. This here is Lou, and Lou's son, Luca, who's just a year older than you, Maureen. He might be almost as smart, too. But we're not sure. He doesn't say too much."

It was the first indication I'd received that Bob expected—even wanted—something more than I'd given. Maureen remained in the doorway.

"I've been telling him all about you," Bob said.

She was too good for us; that was what I thought. Andrew and I could be in this room, it matched us in enough ways, but not her, she was above it. Bob stared at her, waiting for her to make the transition, and when it seemed she wouldn't, he smiled apologetically at my father. "What do you think of this one's hair?" he asked, placing his hand on Jane's springy curls.

"That's curly hair," my father said.

"We don't know where she got it," Bob said. "We suspect the milkman."

He smiled hard, as if pushing the joke toward my father. Andrew had begun to stir on the floor.

"Get up, Andy, we've got a day planned." Only Bob called Andrew "Andy." "It's Luca's birthday, by the way, Maureen," Bob said.

She lifted her eyes toward me then, for the first time.

"Yesterday," I announced, in apology.

That was all. Her eyes went from me to Andrew, who rose halfway and moved his hair away from his face. She took him in, then stared at me again briefly, as if now she knew something about me. Still, the mask of absence remained on her.

"You'll all be great friends," Bob Painter said.

The plan was to ride in two cabs to a large wooded park on the Belmont line. We stopped at a grocery to get cold cuts and rolls. My father sat with Andrew and me in one cab. Bob Painter and his daughters were in the other.

I sensed a stiffness in my father that day. There had been no birthday present, but that was understandable, I knew he was experiencing financial troubles, and I thought I knew something else as well. His distracted state felt familiar to me, the state he went into when he was close to action. It was the way he had been in the days before his departure from home—wearing a faraway look, clearly no longer with us. Now that same state might lead to the opposite action. At least, that was what I hoped. We rode, and he had his hand on my knee, massaging gently, as though maybe he wasn't even aware he was doing that, and I remember feeling happy, certain about what was about to happen. I didn't know the rules of houses, but I suspected even after you sold one you could get it back if you changed your mind. Andrew was on the other side of my body, like a thing that had attached to me, so that when my father looked at me now, I knew he had to see two things, and I knew, also, that this made it difficult for him, a goad to return to a place from which he could guide me away from the undesirable.

We met up on the curb and Bob led us into the woods. Somewhere there were picnic tables, he thought he knew where. "I remember a beautiful spot in here," Bob said, but he seemed uncertain, and kept checking on my father, as if he, too, had picked up on the detachment I had noticed in the cab.

"I guess this'll have to do," Bob said finally, giving up when we were in the middle of the woods, in a sunny clearing, with no picnic tables in sight. "We can spread ourselves out on the ground. Otherwise we'd have to go back. I guess I'm lost. You girls mind that?"

Of course the little ones didn't, and of course Maureen did. She stood at a distance from us and accepted nothing from her father.

"You have to eat, Maureen," Bob called.

"I'm not hungry," she said finally. Her voice was low, deeper than that of any twelve-year-old I knew.

Bob went on eating then, with his gaze turned inward, rising out of this every once in a while only to look at my father, and then at Maureen, like two polarities he could not, for the life of him, bring together.

We dispersed after lunch. Andrew and I were sent to push the little ones on a set of swings we'd passed on the way there. Maureen followed, walking ten or so feet behind us. While we pushed the little girls, Maureen sat on a bench, staring at the ground, playing with her hair.

"Miss Superior," Andrew had begun to call her, under his breath.

I stared at her a long time.

"Miss Superior won't speak to us."

In the afternoon it got warm, and it was hot for us, pushing the little girls.

"Don't you girls want to spend some time with your father?" Andrew asked.

They stared at us like we were curiosities.

"Give us a higher push," the smaller one, Jane, said.

Finally, though, even they got tired and went and sat with Maureen. When they were all huddled together, I could see maybe how things were in Woburn, in Bob Painter's absence, a little world closing in on itself, female and long-cheeked and with its own rules and intonations, complete enough so that I wondered how Bob Painter had ever fit in at all.

I said to Andrew, "Come on, let's go find them," and I hoped, between now and finding my father, some idea would just come to me, because I knew this day needed something more from me, that it wasn't enough just to sit and wait for my father to make up his mind.

We walked into the woods and—I do not know where the thought came from—I became suddenly afraid for Andrew. I thought I was about to do something to him that was, at heart, cruel, and I also knew I had it in me to behave cruelly. The thugs at school had laughed at him, but then had left him alone—let him just be the distinct and isolate Andrew Weston—and that, I thought now, had been a form of kindness. I hadn't left him alone; I had pretended to be his friend. Now here he was, telling me he was hungry, and patting his stomach, like he was a child, and I looked at him all pale and pasty and thought how if I wanted to pick up a rock and fling it, I could, it would go far. If I wanted to go back to my old friends, the boys I'd played Wiffle ball with, I could do that, too. And I knew at the same time that Andrew couldn't. Andrew was like Bob Painter, like the men in the movies we'd seen: he had a single fate waiting for him, where for me—right then, in those woods, I was certain of it—there was more than one thing waiting.

But still I had this cruelty in me, and this wish to have my father back. So when I saw him, saw the back of my father's white shirt—he appeared to be standing in the woods alone, with Bob nowhere in sight—I grabbed Andrew's wet, soft hand and clasped it. The first thing Andrew did was to draw it away, and to make a sound that was like "Yeech." But I grabbed it again and I held it tight and when I saw Andrew resisting I felt like I could hit him, pummel him just to keep him there, his soft head was a thing I could crush just to make sure he stayed and helped me convince my father of something.

And then Andrew stopped resisting. He looked at me with a different look, one that terrified me, a look that had in it a bottoming-out softness and invitation that repulsed me, yet that I knew I was somehow responsible for. He dropped my hand and came close to me. I knew that if he came any closer I could not escape what I had started. It was like looking directly into the heart of someone else's most secret, needful place. I saw Andrew as a man in a cell, and I knew I had the power to release him from that cell, yet this was the most frightening of human potentials, because then he would somehow stick to me. Still, I did not move, and Andrew took a step toward me, very close.

"I found it!" Bob Painter called suddenly, invisible to us, from through the trees. "Lou! The tables are over here!"

My father had not been aware of the near presence of Andrew and me, and at the approach of Bob—the two of them clearly felt they were alone—my father seemed to be making a decision. He stepped forward. He put his hand on Bob's arm in such a way that I knew—his grasp was firm, and it had real feeling behind it—the gesture had a meaning beyond the simplicity of one man affectionately grasping another's arm. I knew, too, from the look on Bob's face—a collapse into something younger and infinitely more hopeful—that my father had intended by this gesture to communicate something.

"You'll see," we could hear Bob say, and all the relief in his voice. "It'll be good. We'll figure this one out."

I had planned, at the end, for the scene to be a simple one. My father would see me take Andrew's hand. The act would stop there. My father, seeing what I was about to let myself become, would have halted in his tracks, lifted me up, the two of us would have returned to the old life, safe from all this.

Instead, he nodded his head in agreement with what Bob had said, perhaps not quite convinced, but willing himself to be.

Behind us then, I heard the girls. They had been there all along, following us, though neither of us had known it. I took a step away from Andrew, but when I caught Maureen's eyes, I saw it was too late. She was too far away to have witnessed the scene between our fathers, but I could see in the widening of her eyes that she had witnessed all that had passed between me and Andrew. I knew, too, that had there been any doubt in her at all, the guilty look in my own eyes must now be telling her all she needed to know.

4

In the summer of 1967, Uncle John bought a boat, an eighteen-foot White with an outboard motor and no cabin. On Sundays, we fished near Egg Rock, off Nahant. I was seventeen that summer. I'd graduated from high school and was headed for BC, my father's alma mater, not because it was especially where I wanted to go, but because they'd offered us the best deal.

In the boat on Sundays were myself and John, sometimes one or two of the younger cousins, my Uncles Mike and Tony, and another man, a man named Biago Rufo. Biago Rufo was in his thirties then. He owned a roller-skating rink and a miniature golf course and was considered one of the rising young men in our town, more remarkable for the fact that he had been here for only ten years and still spoke a halting, broken English. For a year now, he had been dating my mother.

He was small and coarse-grained and he had bunched-up, curly hair. If you wanted to know why Biago Rufo had done so well after only ten years in this country, you had only to watch the concentration with which he fished, especially compared with the others. Mike and Tony held their lines in the water and drank beer and sometimes fell asleep. They said things like "This is the life, huh?" and smiled vaguely and benevolently at me. John did not even bother to fish. Instead, he lifted the outboard motor on its hinge and studied the propeller, because he had gone in too close to shore once, early in his career as a boatman, and scraped against rocks on the bottom. The propeller made a humming sound now; he worried about it, but mostly he was only looking for an activity. Week after week, he failed to become engaged either by the act of fishing or by the company in the boat.

Meola and Semenza had by now let John in. He had a social life. He'd bought a tuxedo. He and Emma went to parties, banquets in Boston; they gave to the Heart Fund. That he was still obliged to be the titular head of this family, to transport us all to Nahant on Sundays, to supervise the idleness of Tony and Mike, was a mild annoyance. And by now, he was worried about other things, as well.

Biago Rufo interested him only a little. That is, Biago's money interested him. But Biago himself was gruff, blunt-spoken, socially unambitious; he had no place, and never would, at the Heart Fund dinners where John smiled and smoked cigars and joked with Meola. While the rest of us fished and puttered, Biago Rufo listened to the water.

"No flounder," he would say after a while.

"They're on the bottom," John would answer; it didn't matter.

"No flounder," Biago Rufo repeated, as though it did.

Then Biago looked askance at Tony and Mike, could not understand either their sloth or their sensuality; could not understand, above all, why they owned nothing.

One Sunday my mother came swimming out to where we were anchored. She had swum a great distance, but she didn't look tired.

"You drown, Dorothy," Biago Rufo said. He was not the sort to let himself get excited by anything. (He was like my father in that way.) Even my mother's potential drowning he would handle with dispatch. He would leap in and save her and somehow manage not to get his hair wet.

My mother was over forty then. Her hair was still long. She had stopped aging, or else found a pocket of time in which she floated—still quite beautiful—as she was doing on that Sunday, staring up at Biago Rufo, and at me.

"You boys catching anything?"

"No flounder," Biago Rufo said. Then he gestured, short and neat, for her to go back to shore.

"I'm all right," she answered. "I can swim forever. Didn't you know that?"

She swam a couple of times around the boat, as if to demonstrate.

Then she stopped again. The water was an algae green and the sun was strong and her skin was very dark. We must have looked silly to her, holding our rods. Most of the time, we threw the fish back.

Biago Rufo had stopped looking at her by then, but she continued staring up at him, smiling in that just-baptized manner of hers, as if water could wash away anything, or worse, as if there were nothing really to be washed away.

I was seventeen, and I had not stopped to consider whether my mother loved Biago Rufo. But as she gazed upon him, I remember, distinctly, feeling that day that she did—felt, at least, something close to love, equally troubling and dangerous. And it seemed, at that moment, unacceptable.

I was dating, at that time, a girl named Carolyn Lafollette. In high school, we'd sung together in the chorus. It had been discovered in the ninth grade that I had a voice, a three-octave range. It was like an extra growth, a tumor; the family began treating me differently, like something might actually come of this. Then, like everything else, it settled, became unimportant. Carolyn Lafollette stood behind me in the chorus. I heard her clear, sweet, pedestrian voice when we sang "Kum Ba Yah" and "One Hand, One Heart." We enjoyed a chaste relationship, going no further than a hand feeling the hard outline of her bra while we parked at the drive-in. She flipped her elbow up to discourage me, but she needn't have. I had very little interest in her clean white body.

For work that summer, I had Vanderbruek. My father's old friend Vinnie Fratolino had gotten into the habit of calling my mother occasionally, to check on her. Sometimes he stopped by the house, let my mother serve him coffee, gazed at her with what I could tell was romantic interest. Nothing could come of it; he was married, and she had Biago. Nonetheless, he sat there, taking an hour of moony-eyed pleasure out of his day under the guise of helping us out. "What's the boy doing this summer?" he had asked one day. My mother did not consider such things. I had sent out my own applications for work—to the supermarkets, mostly—and when Vinnie Fratolino suggested he could pull strings at Vanderbruek, she had nearly ignored him. But I leapt at the chance. I was on the grounds crew, but Bob Painter was not there anymore.

It was an easeful summer. I listened to music. I mowed the great lawns of Vanderbruek, standing behind a mower that was like a chariot. I contemplated vaguely, unexcitedly, the white sepulchre of Carolyn Lafollette. On the bus, riding between the buildings of Vanderbruek, I listened to the old men, the bus driver and his cronies, finishing out the last years before retirement.

"How are you, Numb Nuts?"

"Not bad, Dry Balls."

They talked to each other, always, in the language of sex; sex was oily and ever-present as the smell of machines. Wellsie, the head of the grounds crew, took me around to various offices. He chatted intimately with gawky men in ties, engineers. There were whole hours of the day when there was nothing to do. It was the sixties defense economy, which kept us all with time on our hands and fat paychecks at the end of the week. Wellsie was on familiar terms with everyone. As soon as we left a man's office and the door was closed behind us, Wellsie would turn to me and whisper, "Nice guy. I fucked his wife."

The wives of hundreds of engineers had been fucked by Wellsie. I could believe it if I wanted. Also, that dozens of children had come from these couplings, children the credulous engineers believed were theirs. While they spoke, went on and on about a game of golf or a backyard barbecue they'd attended together, Wellsie would wait until the man had turned away, then, catching my eye, point to one of the faces in the framed family photograph on the engineer's desk, and wink. Wellsie resembled the actor Dick York, of *Bewitched*, though more raffish, and with wider shoulders. In the rooms where welding was done, where "coordinates" were glued and pounded into shape, where men wore no ties, there were always magazines hidden under counters, and Wellsie asked to see them.

In the magazines, men stood under waterfalls with naked women. They lolled in showers, in the stalls of horses. The women all had pendulous breasts, but Wellsie's only comments were about the men's penises. "Mine's bigger than that," he always said, and cackled, and the other men would laugh.

The world that summer was about fucking other men's wives, conceiving secret children, having an enormous dick. I mowed the lawns of Vanderbruek, and didn't exactly think about this, but ingested it nonetheless. Sometimes I thought: Bob Painter had to listen to all this, had to sit and endure Wellsie's bravado. I imagined Bob Painter's meaty, red face nodding. Yes, Wellsie, yes. I imagined him keeping his secret, and then, after the secret was out, as it had to be finally, the men making little jokes, cruel ones, confused ones, and then the jokes had ended. Because they'd accepted him, finally. Wellsie told me that. "Hey, they're just like everybody else, you come right down to it. They just like to take it up the ass." Bob Painter had stayed at Vanderbruek two years after my father had left, mowing these lawns, tending to the shrubbery, learning, painfully, I gathered, not to drink.

My father had opened an office of his own in town, above the pet store, the winter after he left us. He was able to do this, I was told, because of the sale of the house. Gradually, his old clientele came back to him. He was always very good at what he did. He saved them money, so his business thrived. He and Bob moved to a better apartment, then, just as my father's business began to peak, to a town in New Hampshire, with a little church and a tiny downtown. My father claimed he was tired of running into people on the street who wouldn't speak to him.

He and Bob bought a small inn on a lake a year later. My father was proud of the fact that he had got it as a "steal," had paid "nothing down." He put in a small office on the ground floor, and between the income from his accounting and the influx of tourists during foliage season, they did all right. Bob Painter got to use his skills as handyman and groundskeeper.

As for my mother and me, we remained, longer than either of us would ever have expected, in the little rented house on Hobbs Road. In a certain way, a calm enveloped us. We could anticipate no more changes, no further descents. We were to simply go on watching my father conduct the great experiment of his life, in which we both knew we counted a certain, measured amount.

Once a month, I was invited to stay for a weekend at the inn. The lake was small—a pond, actually—with a swimming raft in the center, and ropes to keep children from going out too far. I took the bus up, and they met me in the little town. They were back to having a car now. Even Bob Painter, who had lost his license in Massachusetts for a series of drunken driving offenses in the difficult late years of his marriage, maintained a license here. "Live Free or Die," their license plate read—a small joke they made their own when it came to certain choices, my father's continued smoking, for instance. Bob Painter picked me up in the car—an old Chevy wagon. He put his arm around me, affectionate now, but careful, judging precisely how long he might touch me. He whistled as we drove through the town. He said, "You'll want to take a swim as soon as we get there."

The two of them sat on the grassy bank and watched me. I had inherited a certain endurance from my mother. I could swim the length of the lake and back—just under a mile—without tiring myself, and my father liked that. They sat in their long pants, their chinos, and watched. Their faces were very red. Something was good for them about my being here, and when they looked at one another, I sensed a mild sort of congratulations passing between them.

In the winter, when the lake froze, my father plowed it and invited me to skate. But I had not received, in my genes, that ability of his, the speed or the agility or hard-charging grace of his body on ice. At BC, he had overcome his deficiency in size by developing an uncanny ability to dig the puck out of tough corners. It was something he liked to talk about, but on the ice, I couldn't meet him. After a while, he gave up trying to teach me things. He said, "You're no hockey player, Luca, that's for sure." At night, he would skate ahead of me, disappear under the eaves of overhanging trees.

In summer, though, they never joined me in the water. Some finickiness, some resistance kept them onshore. I floated at the end of my swim, and stared at them, putting off for as long as possible the moment I cared least for, when I would come out of the water and the two of them would look at my body. This wasn't much, it lasted only a second. Bob Painter quickly turned away, and my father's look of interest evolved into something else, a broad smile. My deficiencies as a hockey player aside, he believed I was turning into exactly what he wanted me to turn into. For years now, he had been saying, "You don't see that kid anymore, do you? What was his name?" I always came up with it quickly. "Andrew Weston," I said. "Andrew Weston, Jesus," my father always said, and sucked in air mock-dramatically. "What was *that* all about?" Then he laughed, and touched me, relieved.

But Andrew Weston was still with me. He had been in the chorus with me, two baritones. "Kum Ba Yah, ma Lord." "Climb Ev'ry Mountain." Before going onstage, we sat next to one another, in our black pants and white shirts, saying little. Little had to be said. When I drove him home after rehearsal we sat in the car in front of his house. He never wanted to go back in. We talked then. I knew little about his father, a pharmacist in Newtonville, who left early in the morning and came home late at night. The one story Andrew told me about this man was that he'd appeared as an extra in the movie *Six Bridges to Cross*.

From eighth grade through junior year in high school, we had had separate gym classes. Then, senior year, we were together again. Not a drop of public school water had touched Andrew's body in those years. Our gym teacher that year was Mr. Kroll, the football coach, less kindly toward Andrew than Mr. McCluskey had been. At the beginning of every year, Andrew needed to go through the same process, the note from his mother, the meeting in the gym teacher's office. Mr. Kroll, new this year, studied the note, then stared at Andrew, and said, loud enough for everyone to hear, "What's this?" We all knew, of course, but still, the football players in the class laughed, because they wanted to get on good with the new coach. "He can't take a shower," someone yelled. "He gets a boner." Then Mr. Kroll turned back to Andrew and smiled his big ape's grin. Andrew stood and endured all this, waited for Mr. Kroll's show to be over so that he could go back to his locker and dress. I knew I should have been defending him, but didn't.

One of the reasons it was difficult to defend Andrew was the way he had learned, that year, to draw me into his agony. Our scene in the woods the day after my thirteenth birthday had done it, created an opening. Andrew took that opening and ran with it. My gym locker was across the room from his. Still, I couldn't help but look at him, watch him in his ridiculous white underwear that his mother had bought him, and he saw me looking, lifted his lashes, said, in effect: I caught you.

Then he would lead my eyes down a row of boys—naked asses, tufts of body hair—to where Billy Plotkin stood, barely drying himself. Andrew wanted me to look at Billy Plotkin, but I might have looked anyway. He was on the football team, and he had grown his blond hair long that year. Mr. Kroll was always saying things like, "Plotkin, cut it," or "Plotkin, you look like a girl," but anyone could see Mr. Kroll needed his star Billy Plotkin more than Billy Plotkin needed him.

When Andrew and I sat in Calculus and Billy Plotkin came into the room, late (he sat ahead of us, two rows toward the window), Andrew looked at me. He raised his eyebrows. *We both see the same thing. We both see beauty.* We did. Andrew got at me, finally, because it was the truth.

Billy Plotkin had a girlfriend named Evelyn Navarro. Of course, a cheerleader. A beaky dark face, beautiful as his. The rumor was that they'd been sleeping together all year. Evelyn Navarro had been caught with a rubber in her purse. That was the story; no one believed it, but it was the sort of exaggeration that pointed to the truth. In the hallways they regarded one another with the tenderness and tacit understanding of twins, as if, even before their eyes met, a conversation had already started. In the locker room, Billy Plotkin stayed naked a long time, longer than anyone else, resistant to the transition back to clothes.

In the car sometimes, in front of his house, Andrew would say, "What do you suppose, do you suppose they do it? I mean, all the way?"

I only grunted. I did not want to give any indication of the fanatical interest I had in this question. Then Andrew gazed at the upper story, where he knew his mother was waiting.

"Oh Billy, Billy," he mock-moaned, and bucked on the seat like a girl, and escaped into giggles, and looked at me, and to let him know I was far removed from this, I laughed, too.

But in the hallway after class, I would see Billy, with Evelyn Navarro, their heads tipped toward one another, faces intent. What were they saying?

—Tonight I'll fuck you.

—No.

—You don't like me to say it.

—Not like that.

—Then how? *How?*

—Just, maybe, to do it.

—Like it's holy?

—Like you don't use words.

It was the way Bobby had made me think about sex: silence and cunning and immense daring. Joanne Lacosta had had a baby, a girl.

Bobby had married her late in the pregnancy, relaxed throughout, as though marriage was something he'd get around to when he felt like it. He'd resisted Uncle John's entreaties to come to work in the family business and gotten himself a job in a garage. An old problem with Bobby's ears had saved him from the draft. George hadn't been so lucky. He'd gone first to Fort Benning, then to Southeast Asia. Uncle John studied the maps, studied *Time* magazine. "It's not a *land* war," he often said, apropos of nothing, as if he expected you would be following his inner monologue.

—So let me just say it.

—Why?

—I like saying it.

She looks down, pretends she has to think about this.

—Okay, go ahead.

He pauses, bites his lower lip in anticipation.

—Tonight. I'll fuck you.

She smiles, in spite of herself. Someone else comes down the hallway, someone they must acknowledge. The bright smiles. The secrets.

Luca Carcera was not someone they need ever consider. He sang in the chorus, but no one except mothers and old people attended the chorales. He was in gym class, but his skills were only adequate. He was quiet, quiet, known, if for anything, for being smart.

And for being the friend of Andrew Weston.

All day long at work that summer after high school, I listened to the bragging of men. At lunch one day, Eddie Delavoise told the rest of us how he had gone into "town" (meaning Boston), picked up a prostitute, and "fucked her twice." He said it as if he were separating the edges of fat from a slice of capricola and laying it on a plate before us. The girl's name (he laughed when he told us) was Thumper. "That's the bunny rabbit's name. In *Bambi*." In my mind, during the day, I constructed, incessantly, the fucking of Billy Plotkin and Evelyn Navarro. I imagined it from first to last. How he would pick her up at the end of the day (in my mind, he worked where I worked, he mowed the lawns of Vanderbruek), fresh from a shower, in clean clothes. As soon as Evelyn Navarro was in the car with him, she laid a hand on his thigh. They passed down the summer roads. Kids playing Wiffle ball stopped their games to let them pass. The mute fathers, their hands in their pockets, watched. In the car, Evelyn Navarro said, "Oh please, I can't wait, I can't make it through a stupid movie, please can we go somewhere now?"

I knew nothing. I was seventeen, making it all up.

So they would not go to the drive-in, where they might by chance have parked beside me and Carolyn Lafollette, who would have been studiously watching the movie, dreaming of our bland college careers to come.

Or if they did go to that drive-in, they disappeared below window level immediately. Immediately Evelyn Navarro was covered. Immediately, she could not speak, was overwhelmed. I would drive Carolyn Lafollette to her house after the movies. We made jokes. We got along. We even clung to one another in our way. In my mind, as I dropped Carolyn off, as I waved good-bye and smiled, I saw Evelyn Navarro, before her house, get back into Billy Plotkin's car and say, "Oh, one more time, please."

I would come home to find Biago Rufo in our kitchen. He was dressed, of course, in one of his open-necked shirts, flesh-colored (which, in his case, meant lighter than his flesh) and the pants that Uncle John referred to as "guinea pants." They were high-waisted, beltless. He was a man who had no style at all. He waited up for me. My mother, I understood, was already asleep.

Our ritual—I had one with everyone, a function of my nature, I suppose—was to drink a cup of tea together. The kitchen was small, close. In the shadows of the backyard was a rock garden—my mother had insisted on one—and, beyond the fence, the outline of a restaurant, on a rise, two streets away. By the time I appeared in the house, he had the kettle on. His head, in close proximity, seemed enormous. He smiled at me. His smile had a kind of sadness to it, a peasant wisdom he had not yet affixed to his new language. When he spoke, he seemed dumber than he was.

He asked me, always, if I'd had a good time.

I said yes.

Then, what movie had we seen?

I told him. Whatever the answer, he shrugged. He had no time for the movies. He knew only a few American stars: John Wayne, Steve

McQueen. And for some reason I never bothered to probe, Aldo Ray. He had worked until ten, when his businesses closed, then come here, and after we drank our tea, he would leave, get into his little Fiat and drive off. The green car was one of his offerings to me: "You like? You can use," he said. But my father had bought me a used Falcon as soon as I'd gotten my license, so that I could transport my mother around, and do the shopping. My intention that summer was to teach her to drive.

Over tea, Biago made awkward attempts to behave toward me like a father. He made no secret of how he saw me: I was an abandoned boy. For Louis Carcera, he had only contempt. Rule Number One: you do not leave your family. But I don't believe Biago Rufo ever thought of himself in heroic terms. He looked at my mother and liked what he saw. They had met at one of the dinner-dances my mother and her sisters attended, hosted by a society of immigrants from the island where the sisters had been born. Now, while I was out on my charade-dates with Carolyn Lafollette, he came and put my mother to sleep. I thought of it as no more than that. But then, the hard part was I had to sit there and stare into the eyes of someone who knew how to do that.

After he left, I'd go to my mother's room. The house was small, our rooms nosed up against one another. Her door was never shut. Her form lay under a sheet. It was summer. She breathed easily.

Sometimes she woke up. Seeing me, she smiled. "Did Biago go?" she asked.

"Yes."

She moved. She allowed me to see the manner in which physical pleasure manifests itself in the body of a sleeping woman. For Dorothy Carcera, things were turning out okay.

"Good night, Luca."

Nights finished the same way, always. In bed, I ran through my private index file of the day's sexual images. Wellsie's conquests. The "fucked her twice" of Eddie Delavoise and then the image of the sliced-thin girl in the combat zone in Boston. The large breasts and the large penises in the magazines Wellsie had looked at. Biago Rufo's eyes: "She a nice girl, Luca?" and then the loud, efficient manner with which he sipped tea. The movement of my mother's legs under the sheet.

Always the last thing.

Evelyn Navarro, in her room alone, having been dropped off, cries out for Billy one more time. He appears at the window. He has climbed the tree and is naked, solemn and intent. The form I saw in the locker room enters the window of Evelyn Navarro. Enters her, with a strong, disruptive motion. The great cry I imagine as emanating from the throats of fucked women fills the room.

I used to go up to the old neighborhood at night, even that summer, when I was seventeen and too old to be doing such things. I'd go on my old bike, because the car would draw too much attention to me, and because being on the bike, an old Raleigh I'd outgrown, made me feel thirteen again. I'd ride with my ass high off the seat. I'd feel the wind.

The neighborhood was complete now. It had not needed Louis Carcera's family after all. A family of Armenians had bought our house, a big overweight mother and little boys, dark, with low, sloping foreheads. I knew only a half dozen of the families in the houses that had completed the circle; that is, knew who they were, remembered their moving in, the trucks, the couches and the bedroom sets. For the other, farther houses—the houses built in the second wave of migration—I felt a certain disdain.

One night the Meolas were having a party. Only a small section of my little copse was left, a division between the houses on one street and another, but it had been left, thick and dark. I had to leave the bike on the sidewalk, and slink through the backyard of a darkened house. It was unfortunate that I was wearing white, but I thought I could stay hidden.

Uncle John was at the party. I saw him right away, the loudest of the men. A summer party. The women in dresses that came halfway down their thighs. The men holding glasses of beer, highballs. The inevitable grill. Yet they were the fashion of the time. There was no higher aspiration than to stand in a suburban backyard with your wet hair slicked back, holding a drink. On the covers of albums, crooners still invited other men to live this life: to be unapologetically Italian, with golf clubs and an open shirt.

I hunched down. Uncle John told a joke. I listened to his party voice, not like any other voice I had ever heard from him. Anyone could see he was trying too hard. There was laughter—they were polite enough about it—but two feet behind him I could see the Meola boys, impeccable boys, college students now, one of them played football at Penn. They looked at each other. After John spoke, the lines of their mouths widened.

Then the party broke up. John and Emma were slow to go. Karen Meola was there with two of her friends. They went inside. I saw them laughing with one another in the kitchen. John kept on talking. I thought I detected a suppressed yawn on the face of Meola the dentist. His son, the Penn star, began throwing old hot dog buns into the woods, close to where I was.

Finally John and Dr. Meola sat on lawn chairs, alone. Emma had gone home. The Chinese lanterns glowed. The conversation—what I could hear of it—sounded inconsequential: the doctor's new T-bird, the man who ran the Ford dealership and his repute as a gambler, the things men talked about at night. I could tell, after a while, that Dr. Meola was sitting differently in his chair, less rigidly, more relaxed, allowing John this intimacy. Unforced laughter came from the two men. A story about a flat tire, a wife, a mechanic, the fortune these things could cost, the dupability of wives. Encouraged, John's voice rose higher and higher, until he had the dentist genuinely laughing, so that at one point, Dr. Meola reached out, touched the place on John's arm where the muscle was, and squeezed.

Another night, perhaps a week later, I came back. Karen Meola and her friends were there. They sat on the little bench. I hid from sight. Karen Meola was going off to Barnard in the fall, her friends to less prestigious places. It was the summer before all that.

Tonight, though, they were talking about the boys in our class. Names were being listed, and attributes. After some of the names, they simply laughed. I expected to hear Billy Plotkin's name, then, when it was clear they were concentrating on another, lesser class of boy, my own. But these were not the names they were concerned with. Instead, for reasons of their own, they concentrated on other, ugly boys. Charlie Morrison, who was going to Dartmouth. William Poirier, off to the University of Michigan. Albert Cutler, scholarship to Colby. They were the three smartest boys; they were of no interest to me, and yet their physical attributes, the things they said, the brief, highly charged movements they had made toward these girls—"He said, 'I could show you something.' I said, 'Oh yeah, Charlie, sure' "—were like stones they turned over, as if they wondered, deeply, what might be hidden beneath.

Morrison. Poirier. Cutler. They were the pimply boys. I had sat beside them. They had raised their hands. In gym we had shot basketballs, not quite as good as some of the others, better at History, English, boys who wouldn't quite be anything until they met their futures. But they had secret lives. This amazed me. They had spoken to these girls in those tones. They had moved, already, into the great dark area.

There was a silence and then giggles. The girls passed around a cigarette, Karen Meola shook out her long black hair and looked into the copse where I was hiding.

After they had all gone inside, presumably to leave, she came out again. I was still there because the lights had come on in the house whose backyard I used as an escape route. I would have to wait now, until they went to bed. Karen sat on the bench.

"Why don't you come out, Luca?" she said after a while.

The words hung in the damp summer air. Perhaps she hadn't really said them, or was talking to someone else. I lay down flat.

"Luca?"

She had gotten up, and was walking toward me, so I stood.

She had on a gauzy white shirt, cut-off jeans. Her legs were thick, she had a wide, flat face, and her hair fell in curly waves down either side of it.

She stood six feet away from me.

"God," she said, "I can't believe you still *do* this."

"Do what?"

"Spy on me. This is what you used to do when you lived here. When we were like—what—five?"

"Twelve," I said, and scratched my arm. We were silent and I thought maybe, for a moment, she was as embarrassed as I was.

"Why don't you go home, Luca?"

"Can I go through your yard?"

She tilted her head slightly, curious at my words.

I started into her yard. Before I was there, her father came out onto the back landing, and she told me to wait.

"You back there, Karen?" her father asked.

He couldn't see us; the dark and the distance and the first trees made us invisible.

"Yes. Here."

"Doing what?"

"Nothing."

"Okay. Come in, in a while."

He went inside, shut the door.

Karen came forward, stood beside me. "Make me a promise. Don't do this anymore. All right?"

"All right."

"Not that I care so much. It's just a pathetic thing to do."

She sighed, squinted her eyes at me, sent me a look of what I had to guess was empathy. "Do you want to smoke a joint before you go?"

I looked at her. Her eyes were very serious but cloudy, as though she was already thinking about something beyond me, the thing she would think about after I was gone.

"I never have," I said.

She went and sat on the white bench and lit the little cigarette.

"That's not what you and Carolyn do?" She giggled, then inhaled, spread her body more openly on the bench.

"No."

"Come here. I'll turn you on. I can at least do that for you."

I went to the bench and she handed me the joint. This was all foreign territory. I puffed as I would have a cigarette, and she laughed.

"No, no. Not like that. Watch me." She drew the smoke in, in a slow, luxurious, somewhat exaggerated manner, and closed her eyes. "Oh, that's *so* good."

She patted the bench beside her and handed me the joint again. "You are such a pervert."

I tried to do as she'd instructed me. It was different. The smoke was hot in my lungs.

"Better?"

"Yes."

"I used to take an extra long time out here, doing my toes, because I knew you were watching."

"How'd you know?"

"Oh, *please*. Did you think you were invisible?"

It was something to think about. All these years.

"But that was young sex stuff. When you're twelve. Boys watching you. Very exciting."

She handed me the joint again. I was getting used to the looseness of being here with her, doing what we were doing.

"This is different."

She hiked up one leg and put her arm around it and rested her head there.

"Why do you do it?" The question seemed offhand, musing, not urgent at all.

Again, I took the hot smoke in. It was impossible to tell whether something was happening to me. I thought of Biago Rufo, who would be waiting later, at the table. The tea. And here, it suddenly occurred to me, in this backyard, was life itself, the thing that could protect me from Biago Rufo. But though I was close to it, to *her*, it still seemed like a thing I didn't know how to get to, as though my allegiance, or else my deepest attention, had already been claimed by the other, watching side of myself.

"Is it working for you?" she asked.

"What?"

"The grass."

"I don't know. How do you tell?"

"You feel funny." She started to laugh. "But I guess you already do." She lay her head again against her knee. "I could go to sleep."

She was silent for a long time. Her father came out again.

"Karen?" he called.

"Go away," she whispered.

"Karen?" he called.

"Dad?" she called out.

"Coming in?"

"In a minute."

"Somebody out there with you?"

"No." Then, louder, "I have things to think about!"

He seemed to take that in. He jingled the change in his pockets and watched another moment before stepping inside.

Karen Meola lay back on the bench and put her feet in my lap. She kicked off her sandals. "There they are, Luca."

She laughed. Then she took them away.

"I'm going in," she said. "I'm very tired. I need to sleep."

I stood up. She didn't move in the direction of the house. In fact, she came closer.

"What is it with you, exactly?"

"I don't know. What do you mean?"

"I don't know what I mean."

Then: "Just don't leave for a few minutes, okay? Let me distract him." She went inside the house.

I'm not sure what it was exactly that made me come back, made me know I was invited. I began breaking dates with Carolyn Lafollette in order to go and lie in the copse, and some nights she never even came out. It had something to do with her father, something to do with the way she had stood close to me before going in to him. I knew it wouldn't stand up to much thinking. It excited me.

On the good nights she smoked her joint and looked for me. I didn't come out of the copse until she turned her head.

"You shouldn't wear white T-shirts, if you don't want to be seen," she said, with a dryness now, as though irony were the filter she needed to place between herself and the invitation she had extended.

I didn't say anything.

She took a long drag and stared up at her house, and no longer offered me any. It didn't work for me. The hot smoke hovered in my lungs, but I felt nothing. I waited for her to become stoned enough to suggest things.

One night, just after her father had come out looking for her, she lay her head against my shoulder. I understood that the two acts were linked somehow—the man on the back landing, looking carefully to either side, not speaking, wistful and hard-visaged, then going in, and then her head landing on me. I wasn't to do anything in response; I knew that, too.

We were creeping toward September. Carolyn Lafollette was fading into the past already. Sometimes at the drive-in—those nights were rarer now—I sensed some tiny movement coming from her, the suggestion—never made aloud—that if I wanted to cup the small, soft thing under her bra, I could. Carolyn Lafollette was ready for experience. But I hardly saw her now. I lived in a state of readiness, waiting.

The night came when Karen Meola reached a hand up to my neck, drew me to her, kissed me with enormous, wet lips, a very long kiss, her tongue at the end of it, like a P.S. at the end of a letter containing some further, some impossibly heady endearment. It went on like that for a while. I was tremendously excited. At the same time I knew—understood, somehow—that I was not really there for her, I was someone whose existence did not go beyond this copse. If she had had to stop and consider that this same Luca Carcera was the one whose scents and breaking skin and doleful presence had been a burden, no doubt, of her high school life, she would have stopped kissing me.

One night, she went further. She reached under my jean shorts. I knew I was not allowed to do the same. She reached and explored and satisfied herself and went inside. Her father, that night, met her on the landing. They had a brief, intimate conversation. His hands were in his pockets and her head was low, but as she followed her father into the house she looked back to where I was and offered me a sly smile.

I got on my bike afterward. I rode, high off the seat, and felt again the wind and knew that this was a brief and extraordinary pocket of happiness in my life, but it would not bear scrutiny and the best I could do would be to forget it. I suspected that if Karen Meola and I were to meet on the street, in daylight, she would pretend not to know me.

With the break in the pattern of my dates with Carolyn Lafollette, the summer rhythm of my mother's love affair was similarly altered. She and Biago could not count on my coming home at twelve, or one, depending on the movie. Karen Meola always went into her house before eleven, as if she were expected at a certain hour. I came home to find my mother and Biago sitting on the couch, or watching TV, an activity that usually bored him.

They could not go to his house. He roomed with an old lady in Watertown, had the top half of the house. It was the sort of thing a man of his type did until he was married. For my mother to be seen there would not do: their affair, I came to see, depended on my steady romantic habits.

"Tomorrow," I said to my mother on the night Karen Meola had reached under my shorts, "tomorrow I want to give you another lesson. Driving."

Biago moved his lips, thoughtfully, before speaking. "Good idea."

They were watching *The Wild, Wild West*.

"When I go away in the fall, she should have a way of getting around."

My mother smiled at me. It was as if we were talking about someone else.

Biago made a sound of assent. "He's right, Dorothy."

"We'll have a lesson," I said. "Tomorrow's Saturday."

She was not doing well with these lessons so far. The appearance of almost anyone on the sidewalk, or another car coming in the opposite direction, spooked her. Twice she had gone up on the sidewalk. But I went on, patiently, trying to teach her.

"I want to leave the car with you when I go to school," I said to her.

"Why? Don't you need it?"

"I can take the bus when I come home. I don't want a car there."

My mother's hands shook when she drove. She didn't bother to ask why this was important to me, and I knew if I left the car with her she would never drive it. She had lived a life in which other people drove. Even my father's leaving hadn't changed that fact. Now Emma took her shopping, or else she walked down the hill and waited for the bus.

Once, I was driving home from Vanderbruek and I saw her standing at the bus stop and before I recognized her I felt myself taken hold of by the sight of her, a certain hopefulness my mother could not quite let go of, and the way she had dressed herself up in a suit, and with bright lipstick, for wherever she was going. I didn't stop. I drove past her. I waved, but she didn't see me. I had to contend with a certain invincibility in my parents. No matter what happened to them, they seemed to go on without the remotest self-pity.

"Won't it be better?" I asked the next day, when we were driving. "When you have a car, you won't have to wait around for other people."

"Oh, I don't mind," she said. "It makes me nervous. The children."

"You won't hit them."

"But what if one runs out?"

I put my hand on her hand, to steady her, and she pretended for a while to pay attention, to take seriously the act of driving a car, even to pretend that this would actually happen. But I also saw the part of my mother that held back from simple challenges such as this one, the part that pretended, and thus must have been complicit with my father in his long charade.

Biago was waiting on the front lawn when we got back.

"How she do?"

"Good. She did good."

He scowled. "How you do, Dorothy? How many people you hit?"

"None."

"No? I don't believe it."

He had made a joke, unusual for him, but no one laughed. My mother went into the house.

"Tonight," Biago asked, "you going out with Carolyn?"

I shook my head.

"Why not?"

"I don't know."

He looked down, moved his head from side to side. "You break the po' girl's heart."

And I was, I was breaking Carolyn Lafollette's heart.

We went on talking on the phone, with Carolyn filling the lengthening gaps in our conversation. I wanted to tell her what was happening between me and Karen Meola. It was that kind of relationship, hers and mine. This was an important fact about me she should know.

But underneath was something else: a certain surprising ardor. She mentioned movies she wanted to see. *In the Heat of the Night. Hombre.*

"Paul Newman is supposed to be very good," she said.

"It's an Indian movie, isn't it?"

"Yes. But serious."

That was Carolyn Lafollette: monitoring the culture, preparing for Marymount, masking a nascent desire.

I gave in one night, took her to *Hombre.* She wanted to kiss. Her mouth was very small, her tongue so active my own withdrew, went to sleep. I thought of the skill, the direct line between passion and effect in the mouth of Karen Meola. I thought, too, of Biago and my mother, and I wanted to get home early.

"This movie's boring," I said.

"We're not really watching it," Carolyn Lafollette said.

"Work's been really exhausting lately."

I faked a yawn.

"Poor boy," Carolyn Lafollette said.

I drove her home. I did not consider then how little the imagined fucking of Billy Plotkin and Evelyn Navarro occupied my mind these days. Biago's Fiat was parked in front of the house. He came out of my mother's bedroom, fully dressed, only slightly startled.

"Short movie," he said.

"Don't make tea."

"Why not?"

"I'm tired. I want to go to bed."

He said good night to my mother and left, and I got on my bike and rode to Karen Meola's. Perhaps I was not too late. She didn't come out that night, and I fell asleep in the copse. When I awoke, I was startled by the silence. For all its seclusion, this was still a neighborhood of noise. Someone was always speaking, solitary voices breaking into the thick dark: people calling dogs, or children, or the distant splash of a body in a pool. The outposts of sound spoke volumes here, to me anyway, about the public life of intimacy. But tonight it seemed to have gone back to its old wild essence, and for a moment it was like being here with my father again, that day when it had been all quiet and strange, and marked out by orange flags. Briefly, in my half-sleeping state, the houses seemed to disappear, and became, again, all imagination. What if that was true? What if I was still eleven, and I had dreamt all this, my father was still with us? I had that sensation for a moment, that the world was still safe, all the mistakes could be undone. I thought of Bob Painter and Biago Rufo in rooms somewhere, strange men I would never need to know. The primary mistake—whatever that was—had not been made, whereby they'd been given permission to disturb things, to breathe on us, to move with such entitlement into our lives.

But the sound of a car disturbed the silence. A door slammed and I saw the lights go on in the Meola house and a sound followed, loud enough to penetrate the walls. Karen and her father were framed in the kitchen window. He was in a bathrobe, hovering over her, though he was not so much taller. Dr. Meola appeared to be hurling things at Karen. It was as if his mouth had the facility—the thrusting capacity—of an arm. Karen bent under the onslaught. Her hair hung down so that it covered her face, and it went on like that, long enough so that it became difficult to watch.

I escaped through the neighbor's yard, got on my bike, and rode home.

In August, Uncle John decided to give a party.

He had held off until now, for reasons that might have seemed strange if anyone had bothered to probe them. He had been accepted in the neighborhood, by now, for years. It was not a recent doing. And the others all gave parties. The women traded recipes. We knew this because when we ate at Emma's she always served some fancy concoction—shrimp bisque, artichoke dip—and she would say, "Oh, Julie DeMarco gave me this recipe." This was not snobbishness on Emma's part; she would have been incapable, I think, of snobbishness. She still kept her hand in with my mother, squiring her about, having her over for lunch, but she'd been absorbed by this other world as well.

Still, John had held back until now from inviting them into his house. "It's nice to go out," he said, and changed the subject.

Emma was the one who told us they were having a party. John even looked slightly embarrassed.

"You'll come," Emma said. My mother and Biago and I were all sitting at the table. It was a Sunday night; we'd just got back from a day at the beach. Sunday was the one day Biago agreed to leave his businesses, though he always checked on them on the way home. John bit his lower lip and said, "Sure, they'll come." There was a silence, and John said, "Luca can be the bartender. We'll set you up in the back. You know how to make a grasshopper? A Bloody Mary?"

The rest of them laughed.

"They'll come at you with all of their fancy drinks." Briefly, his eyes appeared hooded.

Emma glanced at him, and changed the subject. "We'll invite some of the children, too," she said. "The older ones. The ones who are going away to college. Make it a kind of celebration."

"Oh, sure," John said.

John had his secretary type me out a list of drinks and their ingredients, and picked me up some afternoons after I got home from work. We drove, and he quizzed me.

"Daiquiri!" he shouted.

"Sloe gin fizz!" Uncle John cried out, in the car. It was immensely important. Also, I could tell, annoying for him, like a burden he had taken on. He folded his hands and looked out the window for long periods of time, then snapped himself back to attention. "Gin rickey!" He clicked his tongue, as though he were tasting it. But it also seemed, at such moments, that he didn't care, and I could see how deeply divided he was, how little he wanted to be giving this party at all.

I hadn't needed, as it turned out, to know quite so much about mixed drinks. The bottle of sloe gin went untouched. It was mid-August, and I stood behind a fully stacked folding table and fixed a lot of gin and tonics, a lot of Tom Collinses, and opened a great many beers.

The adults had all shown up at John's party, but the children had not come. It was some sort of unspoken slight. Only the Armenians had brought their boys. The Meolas made excuses for their sons, for Karen. So did the DeMarcos, the Semenzas. They held beers and laughed. Emma had strung Chinese lanterns, a perfect imitation of the others.

Bobby was there with Joanne Lacosta and their little girl, Claudine, who had to be taken inside when she began crying. "Adorable," the women tutted. The women told me, all of them, not to put too much gin in their glasses, then came back for more. Their eyes took on that sparkle of middle-aged female drunkenness, and their bodies moved under their dresses, as though they wanted, more than anything, for someone—not their husbands—to ask them to dance.

In the dark pockets of the party, I heard Uncle John's voice from time to time, the words "buffer zone," "Lang Son." There was no response after those words. He spoke them with a loud guttural affect. Those times that I was able to see him, I watched the way he stood and gauged the effect his words had on these men. He seemed to be enjoying the look of embarrassment that came over each of their faces.

As the men approached the table, progressively drunker, they began to take me in. But they didn't know me; most of them would not remember my father, having come too late to the neighborhood.

"Open me another Budweiser, young man," Dr. Semenza said, then stood before me, sipping it. "You a college man?"

"Yes."

"Where?"

"BC."

"Ah. Fine school. Jesuits."

They would drift away.

Dr. Meola was drinking gin and tonics. He was drunk after two or three of them. He looked directly through me.

"Is that Beefeater you're pouring?"

"Yes."

John had bought a bottle of cheap gin, which sat next to the Beefeater. Dr. Meola eyed it, made very sure which bottle I poured from.

He took his drink from me while managing never to have looked me in the eye.

Bobby came and stood next to me. Claudine had been put to bed. "Pour me something, Luca."

"You're not old enough," I said, attempting a joke, something to push past those traces of the old formality that lingered between us. Though I had been present at the old finger-sniffing ritual, Bobby, I knew, hadn't really taken in my presence in those days.

"Shit. Rum and Coke, how about?"

While Bobby drank, we both stared across the party and saw John standing alone. He had a big goofy grin on his face, and a drink in his hand. He was staring into space. Already the Armenians had left. Biago was sitting in a lawn chair with my mother, the two of them having failed to engage anyone in conversation. Bobby was fixed on his father. "Nobody's talking to him," Bobby said. "Shit, my father thinks these people like him."

"They do," I said. "I saw."

"What'd you see?"

Bobby looked into my face, but I couldn't tell him I hid in the copse, watched Meola squeeze his father's arm. John broke into one of the party's clusters with an aggressive motion. They opened to let him in. The women's jewelry shone, and they touched the exposed skin above their breasts when they spoke.

"See?" I said.

But John could only leave the buffer zone and Lang Son alone for a short time. He would grab one of the men and begin telling him a long story, and the cornered man would glance at where the women were, and wait for his chance to escape John. I watched John drift to the end of his yard. He stood at the edge of the woods, staring into them. Suddenly, he went to where my mother and Biago were sitting, began motioning to them to get up and join one of the groups. Heads turned to them, curious and polite, but they looked attached rather than absorbed. I saw my mother, in conversation with a woman from one of the newer houses down the street, point to our house. The woman looked quizzical at first, then nodded, polite, and the next time I looked had turned away.

John came to the liquor table. "What are they drinking?" he asked. "What's the big seller?"

"Lots of gin," I answered. "Dr. Meola likes Beefeater."

John grinned. He wasn't looking at me. "Slip him the cheap stuff, next time."

Bobby started to laugh.

"What's funny?" John asked.

"You."

When Dr. Meola next came to the table, I turned away from him, and, disguising my activity with my body, poured from the bottle of Arrow gin.

"What's that you're doing?" Dr. Meola asked.

"Making you a gin and tonic."

"No. With the bottle. What's that you're pouring?"

I showed it to him.

"Goddammit, not that."

He was speaking loudly. The others in the vicinity stopped talking. I nearly said, "John told me to," then didn't.

"I'll have the Beefeater, goddammit." His face had gotten red.

John approached us. "Do we have a problem here?" He had put on an affected voice, conciliatory and smooth.

"He's trying to give me a glass of gin I don't want."

John looked at me, visibly distanced himself, asked me to come close. When I was close, he grabbed hold of my wrist, squeezed until it hurt. "The doctor gets Beefeater, you understand?"

"Yes."

"Pour it for him, okay?"

I did. John took the offending bottle and threw it into the woods. It made a loud crash, and after several seconds of shocked silence, a few of the women began to laugh and made little comments that had "John" in them, like he had done something witty and risqué.

John cupped his hands around the newly poured drink and handed it to the doctor like a communion chalice.

The party ended soon after. Couples offered their good-byes and drifted off. John brooded at the edge of the woods. Bobby and I went around, with Biago, picking up the plastic cups people had dropped, the discarded napkins. Emma had her own child to see to, inside.

"It's a shame the kids didn't come," John said, and sat among us.

No one answered. He looked at us, briefly, like it was our fault.

"What'd you do that to Luca for?" Bobby asked.

"Do what?"

"Squeeze his wrist. Hurt him."

"I did that?"

Bobby took my wrist, examined it for bruises. "He was only doing what you told him to do," Bobby said.

John whistled into the woods.

"They don't like hearing about George, by the way, in case you haven't figured that out," Bobby said.

"Well, the hell with them then," John said.

He took a long, considering pause. "I couldn't let Joe Meola know I was trying to pawn off the cheap stuff."

It was not quite an apology. He took out a cigar. We were all silent, and he turned to Biago. "You were the hit of the party," John said.

Biago gazed solemnly at the ground in front of him.

"Had everybody peeing their pants."

"I'm no a social man."

John took a second to scowl at Biago's language before responding.

"No? So how do you succeed if you're not a social man? You want the world to leave you alone? Things go wrong in your business, you have to know people." John's voice had drifted into contempt even before he put the cigar in his mouth and wet it. "You stink of the old country," he said.

Biago looked at him, held back from something, went inside.

"Tell you why they don't bring their kids," John began. "What is there for the kids here? What is there to grease their ascension into the world? This is all these people care about."

He rolled the cigar between his fingers before lighting it. "The finest colleges, and such. Who to know, who can help. And I bring them a wop brother-in-law. Somebody who talks like he's still in Naples."

"He's not your brother-in-law," Bobby said.

John looked at me. "No, he's not. Not yet anyway."

He puffed twice on the cigar and leaned toward me. "Let me see your wrist." He held it. "Did I hurt you?"

"No."

"You want your mother to marry that guy?"

I didn't answer.

"You understand, I have to keep up appearances."

Bobby snorted. John got up and disappeared into the woods behind the house.

Biago and my mother came out onto the back landing. "We go now, Luca. You come?"

Under his breath, Bobby laughed. "Guy's such a fucking wop."

"No, I'll walk," I said. I felt like being generous. I almost said, "I'll be late."

They went away. Bobby was still laughing under his breath. "It's funny people still talk like that."

"He's all right," I said.

"You think so?"

I didn't answer.

"God, my father hates him. Do you know that?"

When John came out of the woods, and just stood at the edge of them, holding the shards of glass from the bottle he'd broken, I wanted to ask him about that, ask him why he hated Biago, but something was going on in John that made him look strange. I don't think his clothes were actually disheveled, but they looked that way. And his face looked washed and a little wild, like he'd been crying, though I didn't think he had.

"You should have gone to college," he shouted to Bobby. "The both of you!"

Bobby looked startled. He stood up. He moved toward his father. "Come on. It's okay."

"You think so?" John asked, with evident sincerity, an open expression on his face, like Bobby could still tell him something new. Then his expression fell.

"I don't think so," John said, and lifted the shards of broken glass in his hands, and gestured with his hands that Bobby shouldn't come closer. "I don't. I really don't. I don't think it's going to be okay."

5

My father encouraged me to take a week off at the end of summer, to come up and stay with him and Bob at the lake. On my last Friday at Vanderbruek, though, the men of the grounds crew wouldn't just let me slip away. They had planned something.

I was to follow Eddie Delavoise's Plymouth to the house of one of the others—Will Monaghan. Will Monaghan lived in a small house built in a new development carved out of one of the old wooded pastures of Acton. He had an aboveground pool in the back, and that was what the plan was: to sit around that pool and drink beers. We could swim if we wanted, Will Monaghan said, though none of us had brought suits.

Within the confines of the hangarlike room that was our headquarters, the men were all farts and sex, but here, sitting around Will Monaghan's pool, they seemed almost meditative, waiting for the beers to kick in. Will Monaghan's kids, a boy and a girl, swam. His wife—lacquered, perfect as Donna Reed—came out with a bowl of chips for us.

"We'll never see the likes of you again," Eddie Delavoise said to me at one point, like this was a speech he'd been waiting to give. It seemed full of feelings and attitudes that Eddie Delavoise had no stake in, so it just floated awhile in the air, until it was absorbed into the gassy upper reaches.

"Next summer," Wellsie said. "He'll come back."

"So much I could have taught this kid," Delavoise said. "But he was shy. A baby." He had tried more than once to get me to visit Thumper with him, but I had declined.

They were all silent after that, the sun went behind the trees, there was a wind that made even the water in the pool ripple. End of summer.

"St. Germain said we lost that contract," Will Monaghan said, from out of the silence. He was slightly younger than the others, with hair that dipped over his forehead and then carved out deep inroads on either side of his scalp.

"Cutbacks," Eddie Delavoise said, with his lips pulled back over his teeth. "Goddamn antiwar protesters make them nervous, 's what I think."

"It's not them. Comes from on high," Wellsie said, and cackled, like it was funny.

They thought about it for a long time.

"Still need the grass cut," someone said.

"Can let it grow longer if they wanted. Let the hedges grow wild," Wellsie answered.

"That's a bad thing when the Dutchmen come," Delavoise said. The "Dutchmen" owned Vanderbruek.

"Get an education, kid," Delavoise said, and slapped my arm. "Save you from this shit."

The contract Will Monaghan had spoken of had been a big deal at Vanderbruek, and the loss of it a threat to the munificence of the plant. Only late in the summer had it really gotten to me (my absence of mind, my self-absorption) how closely our work here was monitored by the progress of the war, George's forays into the jungles of Lang Son a kind of payment for nights like this one.

A dog barked and Eddie Delavoise threw an empty beer can into the pool.

"That's defacing my property," Will Monaghan said, then did the same thing.

They laughed.

By the time dark came, we were all drunk, and the pool was full of crushed cans. Mrs. Monaghan came out onto the back landing of the house—there was a small porch with a light on over it—and stood there, watching us.

Will Monaghan turned to look at her, then said, under his breath, "Jeez, the wife is wondering what we're doing out here."

"Fuck her," Eddie Delavoise said.

"Jesus, Eddie, don't talk like that."

"No. I'm serious. Just fuck her." He chuckled.

Wellsie looked at me meaningfully, as if he wanted me to know something, wanted to plant a seed in my imagination.

"You boys drunk enough?" Mrs. Monaghan called.

"Yes. I think so, dear," Will said, in a polite choirboy's voice that made the others laugh. He sat on a belch.

"You could offer me one!"

But she only meant it as a joke. Her distance from us was important, her failure to partake in the dirty male ritual of drinking and flinging crushed cans into a pool was part of what made us, at that moment, want to worship her. She stood there and shook her head from side to side at our "badness," and I realized then how much I wanted this moment, this being among men, that it was better, somehow, more desirable, than my going off to school.

"Is that young man too drunk to drive himself home?" she called out.

"Who? Luca here?"

Eddie Delavoise slapped me on the back. "He's okay."

"I think you might all be too drunk." She looked at us another moment. "You drive him home, Will, okay?"

Then she went inside, after extracting the promise.

There were awkward farewells. We stood around the cars. Each of us had one more beer. Eddie Delavoise took a piss beside his car and the rest of us stood and watched him, as if we had nothing better to do. Then each of them in turn came up to me and said something—"Good luck, kid," or "Be careful," or "Be careful with the girls, don't get yourself caught"—as if they each owed me a piece of advice scraped from the rough hide of their own experience. Finally Will Monaghan got into his car and told me it was okay, he would just follow me home. He nodded, maybe a bit too formally, in the hope that I wouldn't object. "To make sure you get there all right."

I wasn't so drunk I couldn't drive. When I got to Hobbs Road, I stepped out of the car and motioned that I was okay, but Will Monaghan parked and got out of his car as well, and I wondered if now I was supposed to invite him in and introduce him to my mother.

He leaned against his car and lit a cigarette. "Okay," he said. "We made it."

"Yeah. I guess I'll go in."

His eyes took on, very briefly, a distressed look, like he wanted me to stay with him for a certain time.

"You want a cigarette, Luca?"

"No. Thanks."

He smoked it slowly. "Yeah. Bad habit." He inhaled harshly, like he was softer than he pretended to be, and was trying to toughen himself. "You going up to see your dad?"

"Yes."

"And Painter? Painter'll be there?"

"Yes. He will."

He seemed to be thinking about Bob Painter awhile, and shook his head, like he still couldn't get over it. Then he laughed. "Say hello to him, would you?"

I said I would. But he still didn't leave. He stared up at the moon and looked very young. He tapped his fingers against the side of his car, and doing this, he seemed to be amusing himself. But there was another part of his face I could see was keeping track of something—of time, or of something else that was beyond him—and I couldn't help but think of the way Wellsie had looked at me by the pool, and of the way Eddie Delavoise had said "Fuck her," and it was like looking at the inside of a marriage, the terrible fear that must reside there. Then a kind of click went off in his mind, and he pushed himself away from the car. He looked once more up at the sky as if some ordeal was over for him.

We shook hands then, an awkward gesture in which he seemed to be thanking me for not asking a certain question. He got into his car, and I stood and watched him drive away.

There was no sign of Biago tonight. My mother wasn't home, either, so I assumed they'd gone out. I stepped out onto our back porch, just to sit and maybe allow some of the things that had been stirred up as a result of the night I'd just had to settle down. I had a strong desire to go and see Karen Meola. I saw my mother then out in the rock garden, sitting in the chaise lounge with her feet up and head tilted backward, like she might be surveying the stars or else something I believed my mother to be capable of: thinking of nothing at all.

"It's late to be out there, isn't it?" I called to her.

She turned. "You're home. You never called. Where were you?"

"Out with the guys." It sounded so phony, coming from me, I thought even she would see through it.

"Come here. I want to tell you something."

"What?"

"You have to come here."

I stepped down into the garden, wobbling a bit, as if I were drunker than I'd thought.

When I was close, she said, "Biago asked me to marry him."

I looked away. It was an instinctive gesture, but I must have known there'd be some value in playing it up, because that was what I did. In my reaction there was a much more dramatic sense of disgust than I actually felt.

"What?" she asked.

"Nothing. What'd you tell him?"

"I told him I'd have to talk to you."

"Why?"

She looked at me as if that were a dumb question, but she wasn't going to call me dumb. I thought my mother might be beckoning me to come out from behind a screen, saying it was okay now, we could talk. Something seemed at risk tonight. I could feel it in the tension of the air, and in the sweet, fragrant end of summer scents, a hint that my mother and I might be about to break through toward one another. It was mildly exciting, and also made me nervous and defensive.

"You and Dad aren't even divorced, are you?"

"No. We never did."

We were quiet for a few seconds, as if the absence of that divorce posed some insuperable difficulty. And then, almost as if to acknowledge that it didn't, and to assure me that things would not change so drastically, she reached out and touched me in the only place she could reach, the back of my leg. She tried to draw me toward her and I was about to allow it, but at the last moment I resisted. Finally she dropped her hand, and looked at me, disappointed, or maybe something more than disappointed.

"I might go for a ride."

I waited for her to say something.

"On my bike, that's all."

"You have to tell me, though."

"Tell you?"

Her face was as clear now, as pure and uncomplicated as it had looked that day in the water when I'd first realized she loved him. All she wanted was permission. There were no rules to my mother's life, no hidden order buttressed it. All was drift. Here a strong wave had caught her. That was all there was to it. The story of our lives had, for her, no deeper dimension than that. And that was precisely the defect, because I believed in an order, even one that rendered us the losers.

"I'm going to go for that ride, okay?"

"Where will you go?"

"Just around."

"Don't you like him?"

I thought a little while before I answered. "No."

Her face didn't change right away. "Because of the way he talks?"

"No. It's not that."

"Then what?"

I scratched my arm. "He's crude."

She took that in, turned away from me only to stare in front of her and smooth the lap of her shift. "Some people think that," she said. "I know."

It seemed then that it was probably a good thing for me to say nothing. There was no way I could tell her what I really thought, because she could not come close to understanding it. I could not stand it that she was there for the taking. When I thought that, I also thought there was something about her I could never defend against the forces of chaos. My reaction to that was to go to the edge of the yard and throw up. It wasn't a big yard, so she knew what I was doing.

When I came back to her, she said, "Have you been drinking?"

"Yes. But it wasn't that."

"What, then?"

"I don't know."

A part of her that had never before surfaced came forward then. For a moment, it looked like she was going to be angry with me. It was as if, in that moment, she were allowing Biago or their sex or whatever else it was they had to loom larger than me. She even seemed to be testing herself, to see if she could do that. Then I watched the anger break and loosen in her. She couldn't quite stay in that self-driven place, and I knew that was a good thing for me.

"Do you feel all right?"

"Yes."

"Go inside. Wash out your mouth."

I did. From the porch I watched her. I wasn't invited back outside. She had asked my opinion and she had gotten it. Now, for the first time, there was a spoken division between us that neither of us could approach.

It was more because I had told her I was going to do it than out of any real desire that I got on my bike and rode to the old neighborhood. I rode and I thought about going inside Karen Meola. It seemed inevitable that that would happen. It was one with the night I'd just gone through, the bobbing beer cans and the mild drunkenness and the sight of Will Monaghan's wife staring at us and shaking her head.

But I did not go to the copse that night. Something stopped me at the last moment, an old loyalty or a cautionary sense of how the world really was. I made three slow circuits of the road. On my fourth circuit, I found Uncle John in his driveway.

I stopped, and didn't say anything, waiting for him to notice me. I knew it was his nightly custom to come out to close the windows of the car and take it into the garage for the evening.

When he caught sight of me, he smiled vaguely and said, "Luca," but no more than that. I knew that this was holy for him, as every caretaking thing was holy, and he didn't relish being interrupted.

"He asked her," I said.

"What?"

"He asked her to marry him."

John nodded. "I figured."

He put one hand inside the car to trigger the remote and then the garage door opened. Even in the silence afterward he didn't say what I expected him to say. He didn't ask me to conspire. Instead, he shrugged. "Hey, if it's love, there's nothing anybody can do."

He even chuckled at the end of it, like it might be okay. He stared at me a few seconds. He said, "Good night, Luca," and got into his car and drove it into the garage.

"You'll understand better when you're married," Bob Painter said to me, on the lake. He was rowing and I was rowing, facing him. It was early evening, and the trees, this late in summer, hung down over the lake. Every once in a while a bubble appeared where a fish surfaced. There were four guests, and my father was inside, taking care of things.

"Moods, and such."

He was referring to Maureen. Maureen had come up this weekend, without her sisters. She was a year younger than I, about to head into her senior year in Woburn. Academic accolades followed Maureen wherever she went. She had never forgiven her father. She was still what she had been that day at the rooming house five years before, silent and red-haired and judgmental.

Bob Painter lifted his oar. I did the same and we drifted. His hair was starting to go gray, but there were still bright copper highlights when the sun hit it. He presented his thick, brooding face to the woods.

"She always seems to have the same one," I said.

"Huh?"

"Mood. One mood."

It was an amazement to me now that I could smile at Bob Painter, feel comfortable with him. In some perplexing way, he had become the easiest adult in my life.

"But that's how women are," he said. "They stick to a position. Hell and high water. They don't *yield*."

He said that last word in a way that had Boston in it. We both looked at the shore, where Maureen was sitting, in an Adirondack chair painted green, reading the book she had brought with her. Her hair was now very long and frizzy, heavy, like it must have weighed a lot. She held it back with one hand while she read.

Bob Painter was always certain that I would marry. It was a comfort, to exist even for a short time inside this image of me he seemed to sustain, the Inca boy whose life would be regular and sure and desirable.

"She'll forgive me someday. Like you've forgiven your father." He nodded his head, and we resumed rowing.

Maureen put down her book and waded waist-deep into the lake. It was that moment of the day when nothing moves, when a conversation miles away might have reached us. Maureen wore a two-piece bathing suit, yellow with blue speckles. Her diaphragm was thin, bony, her skin translucent, the veins readable. She held her hair up. Bob watched her, expecting something. She plunged in and swam awhile. He went on watching her, his face hungry for something, or else trying to read meaning into everything Maureen did. When she was done swimming, she went back onto shore and dried herself. My father came out and began talking to her. He wore an apron—he had started dinner—and he took it off. He was a figure of splendid ease there, smiling at her, gesturing and feinting with his body, though she seemed not to be replying to any of his questions. Seeing us on the lake, he lifted his arm and waved.

"Swim to him, kid," Bob Painter said.

I just looked at him.

"Go ahead. Give him a present. Jump out of the boat. Go ahead. I can steady it. Show him you love him."

"I'm dressed," I said. "I've got clothes on."

"So take 'em off. There's only four guests, and they've all gone out to eat, prob'ly. Or go in your underwear, if you're shy. He'd love it, I tell you."

"What about Maureen?"

He raised his eyebrows. "What about her?"

On the shore, it was as if my father were waiting, like something had been prearranged. Even Maureen looked up for a moment; the air itself had gone dense with suggestion.

I hesitated a moment, then dipped my oar in the water. I pushed us farther out. In a little while, my father went in to attend to the dinner.

That night, when it was late, we all sat on the porch, in the green rocking chairs. Maureen sat closest to the porch light, reading.

"June bugs," Bob Painter said, and reached out to crush one.

"In August?" My father clapped him on the back, laughing. "June bugs are enormous, Bob." His hand lingered where it had landed, and he rubbed Bob's back.

"Fireflies, then," Bob said.

"Fireflies have lights," my father said, and laughed again. "They light up the night."

"I live up here how many years, I still don't know shit about nature," Bob said, and lowered his head. "Pardon my French."

Maureen's chair groaned.

Bob was fixed on her. My father watched his lover stare at his daughter. This was an old scene, Bob waiting like a dog, Maureen rocking, reading, utterly remote.

"Speaking of French," Bob said. "Maureen won a prize. What was it you won, Maureen?"

"Just a book."

"What book was it?"

"Le Petit Prince." Her pronunciation was flawless, but she threw it away; it meant nothing to her.

"What's that you're reading now, Maureen?" Bob asked.

"When She Was Good."

Bob nodded. Maureen turned, finally, took him in. My father's hand had risen some, was rubbing the top of Bob's back, near his neck, and Bob pushed it away.

It was too late to keep Maureen from seeing. Her eyes did that thing of hers: that reserved but highly visible taking in of information, then judging and classifying it in what seemed a thoroughly female realm.

She stood up.

"Where you going?"

"I might go upstairs."

"Read in your room?"

"Yes."

She stood at the edge of the porch, the ends of her hair in the light.

"You and Luca could take the car if you want. Drive into town."

"I don't think Luca and I want very much to do that."

She walked down to the edge of the lake and sat there, out of earshot.

"She doesn't like to see affection," Bob said.

"Oh, let her grow up," my father answered, casually but with some anger. Then he leaned forward in his chair, suddenly excited, turning to me. "Listen. Before I forget. I want you to go and see Snooks Kelly, at BC. My old coach. You'll find him down in the Forum. It's called McHugh Forum. Big. Building looks like a hangar. Tell him I said hello."

"Okay."

My father went on looking at me.

"It's too bad," Bob Painter said, "that you and Maureen don't get along better. See, that was always my hope."

"Bob has had a hope," my father said, and rubbed his face. "Bob Hope, I'm going to start calling you." My father laughed at his own dumb joke.

"It's not so bad," Bob said, "to believe that everybody could get along. Be friends."

My father was looking at him curiously. Then he turned back to me. "You're going to like BC. You excited?"

"Sure."

"He doesn't sound it," Bob said, morose and staring at Maureen.

There was a long silence, with the creaking of the chairs.

"The guests all back?" Bob asked.

"Snug in their beds," my father said.

Bob stood. "I guess I'll go up. The great thing isn't going to happen tonight, that's for sure."

He went to the edge of the porch. He put his hands in his pockets and stared at where Maureen sat, rocking slightly on the border of grass before it fell into sand. We could see now that she was smoking.

"Hey, that's bad for ya, Maureen!" Bob called.

There was no response.

"Jesus, who got her started with that?"

Bob turned back to us. "So you liked it, liked the guys at Vanderbruek?"

He pronounced the last syllable "brook." He had asked me this before. I answered now what I'd answered then.

"Wellsie tell you all his stories? His exploits, and such?"

"Yes."

"Don't believe him."

He tossed it off, looking to the side, mock-disgusted. He glanced at my father. "You know how goddamn lucky you are? You got your boy here."

My father stared at Bob, nodded finally.

"Lucky," Bob repeated. He looked slack and defeated, tired beyond words.

"We did all right with you, didn't we?" he asked suddenly.

I halted my own chair's rocking.

"I mean, your father's always been here for you. Of course, we ripped you out of that fancy neighborhood, and that was no good."

My father seemed as astonished by this as I was.

"But we tried to ease things. Did you understand about us?"

Bob's acknowledgment of the difficulty of these questions was, after asking, to turn away, as if to excuse me from having to answer.

My father, meanwhile, wore the tight, cautious smile that had become a habit with him. "That's enough, Bob, I think," he said.

"I always wanted to know. How much Luca understood."

"Well, okay. But maybe Luca doesn't want to tell you that."

He acknowledged that. "Maybe I'm just upset."

"I think so."

He held on to one of the porch supports, and it was, briefly, like his old drunken self, the way he would sometimes wobble into the room on Friday nights, clinging to the doorjamb.

"Sometimes I think, happy as I am with your father, if I'd stayed with my wife I'd at least still have my kids." He bit his lip.

"And what would that have been like?" my father asked. "For you?"

After a moment, he added, "Think about it."

Behind Bob, Maureen got up, crushed her cigarette in the sand, and began her approach.

Bob said, "I guess so. I guess you're right."

She had reached the porch by the time he was speaking those words. When he heard her footsteps close upon him, Bob's face took on a look of startled fear, as though some demon form had risen directly out of his consciousness and manifested itself at his heels. He swung around, so that the two of them had to stare into each other's eyes for a second. Something flashed before me then, a hint of the past, and with it, a strong sense of what their relationship must once have been. Bob's begging pose finally made sense. They had loved one another once, been allied in a way that was unusual. It had been fully visible there for a second. Then Maureen lowered her eyes and passed into the house.

"Anyway," Bob said, when she was gone, like he was trying to recover, and pick up his train of thought. "Give her a couple of minutes, so she doesn't think I'm following her."

He passed the two minutes staring at the door, as if she might come out again. He had nothing more to say to us.

As soon as Bob had gone inside, my father whistled, astonished at Bob's performance. Then he chuckled, low and deep. "Very dramatic, Bob is."

He folded his arms and rocked awhile. I resumed rocking, too, and there was that rhythm. I believed this would be the end of it, the two of us rocking until the need to say anything was past, and it would be okay for one of us to feign tiredness and go upstairs.

"Hey, do you want a beer?" my father asked.

"No."

"Do you drink? I've never asked."

"Sometimes."

He nodded. His elbow was on the arm of the chair and he played with his chin. Certain signs of age had just begun to appear on his skin, a demarcation of the territories of his face that hadn't been there until recently. He turned to me and smiled and I knew that meant something, though I didn't know what.

"It's hard for me to believe sometimes I've got an eighteen-year-old son."

"Well, you do. Seventeen."

"I know that. But close enough."

He edged up till he was next to me and put his hand on my knee. "If only you played *hockey*."

He'd meant it as a joke. We went on rocking.

"Those things Bob was asking you, those important to you?"

He had begun pulling the hairs on my knee, gently, so it didn't hurt.

"I don't know. There were a lot of them."

"That's right."

The smile had solidified, gone rigid. "I'm not the type of man who goes to confession, Luca. Bob's more that type. He's getting religion in his old age."

It was all too discomfiting—the night and its declarations—for me to think straight. But I did realize I could ask him a question then. I wanted to ask him how they had met, a man who wore a tie and worked among the accountants and a man who mowed the lawns. And how, after whatever that meeting had been, had the first assignation been arranged?

"It's a beautiful place though, isn't it, up here?"

"Yes." I could ask now, but I didn't.

"Next summer, you know, you don't have to go home, you could come here, we'd put you to work."

I nodded, and made no commitment.

"Somebody asked Mom to marry him," I said.

He turned maybe forty-five degrees in my direction, but didn't look at me. "Is that right?"

He nodded over and over again. "That's something. Well, good for your mother."

He paused, thought a moment. "What's the guy like?"

"Oh, he's this Italian guy . . ."

"Not Biago?"

"You know him?"

"Oh." He stared off and chuckled. "Oh God, Dorothy. Talk about going for the obvious. The Rossano Brazzi type. Terrible choice."

"She loves him."

"Oh. *Dorothea.*"

He'd said it in such a way that I was brought back to something in the deep woods of their marriage: the way they'd had of speaking to one another, lapsing into Italian as into a secret erotic mood.

He recovered. He nodded over and over. "What right have I to say what should happen to your mother?"

The sound of a car, of what sounded like teenagers calling to one another, arrived from a distance.

"No right at all, wouldn't you say?"

He slapped me on the knee, to conclude things in a hearty manner. Then he did something he had never done before, or not in a long time, grabbed me by the back of the neck and drew me to him and kissed me there, on the neck. He said, "You're beautiful, do you know that, Luca? You're a beautiful boy."

He had tears in his eyes, and I knew they had nothing to do with my putative beauty. Then he got up. "You know how to shut off the lights, don't you? If you're going to stay up?"

"Yes. But I'll be up in a while."

"You know to leave the one on over the desk, right?"

He rubbed his neck and looked at the lake again and smiled at me and went inside.

I had my own book and I tried reading for a while but I couldn't concentrate. Instead, I shut off the porch light and stayed there.

After about ten minutes, Maureen came out in a robe. She stood beside me, but said nothing. She was staring out at the lake, and except that I was rocking, and the chair was making noise as it rocked, she might not have known I was there.

"You all right?" I asked.

"Yes."

She sat on the steps and played with her hair a long time. She walked once around the house. I wondered if she expected something from me, but in all the years we'd known each other, Maureen had hardly registered my existence. Tonight was like that. It was like she'd been asking me, in her nocturnal wanderings, to not quite be there. But I was tired of that.

"What are you doing?" I asked.

She gazed up at me then, but didn't answer. I think I must have been as exotic to her as my father and Bob were, and there were times when I remembered she'd witnessed my little scene in the woods with Andrew Weston, and had probably reached her conclusions about me as well. It was an awkward situation for the two of us to have been thrown into, and the only reason I went on talking was because I'd had what amounted to an inspired guess. "They're making noise?" I asked.

It took her a moment but she managed to nod. Our beds were on either side of their room up in the living quarters of the inn (Maureen had a room, and I took the couch) and some nights we could hear them—at least I could.

I smiled. She took her time and studied my smile, like there was something exotic about it, too, and I played out that part, as if nothing they did fazed me.

"It's not that bad," I said, surprised to hear myself utter those words. "It's just like a man and a woman."

"Shut up, please," she said.

Again, she went down to the water, I supposed to nurse her broken heart. Yet there seemed something self-dramatizing in Maureen, like she was making more of this than there was, and for a moment, looking at her, I began to see it with new perspective, as though what I'd said weren't entirely untrue. When I went upstairs, they were still at it, and I lay in bed listening, the way I had once listened to my father and mother. Outside, in a weird sort of accompaniment, I heard a loon screech, three times.

I made one final trip to the copse before I left for college, not even knowing whether Karen might already have gone away. I suspected that I'd left it for too late on purpose. The fact was, something had gone out of this for me. I had come close to something potentially freeing, but then on the night my mother had told me about Biago's proposal, it had grown distant again.

That night I lay there a long time. There were lights on in the house, so I knew someone was home. It finally came to seem stupid, the whole ritual, yet I wanted closure. I'd had a final conversation with Carolyn Lafollette in which we'd said good-bye and promised to write, even hinting at a visit. Andrew Weston was going to UMass. Princeton had rejected him, and Yale, though his grades and his board scores were high enough for him to get in. The guidance counselors had all expressed astonishment.

There was no reason to anticipate Karen Meola would come out tonight, but I remained there for an hour, so I could tell myself later I had at least given it a chance.

I was about to go when I heard footsteps, and stood up.

"Can I help you?" Dr. Meola asked. He was standing maybe five feet before me, in a white shirt with the collar open.

"I was looking for Karen."

"I see. You're a friend of hers?"

"Yes."

"Karen's gone to New York. Gone to college."

"I didn't know."

His face took on a brief look of triumph. But there was something about him always nervous.

"You're—come here—you're John's nephew, aren't you?"

"Yes."

"Come here. Let me look."

I came closer.

"I know the story."

He jingled the change in his pockets.

"I know everything, young man. But she's gone now. She's safe."
He paused. "You can escape through the neighbor's yard, as you usually
do. I won't say anything."

There seemed a certain justice in it—that was the way I thought of
it, anyway, as I got on my bike—but I also had the sense that this had
been one of those events I wouldn't be able to reach a clear judgment
about until I'd had time to think. The feeling that had risen up in me—
something dangerously close to shame—was too strong to allow, so I had
to push it away, like it hadn't really happened.

When I got home, there was a strange car parked in front of the
house. I looked in the front window, and saw Andrew Weston and his
mother sitting with my mother in our living room.

I stepped inside.

"Here he is," my mother said, wearing her best social smile. Mrs.
Weston smiled, too. Andrew, sitting in our armchair, wore an absent, unhappy look. He was, I could tell, already gone.

"Andrew leaves tomorrow," Mrs. Weston said. "Did you forget?"

"No."

I sat across from him.

"He insisted he come say good-bye."

Andrew had never gotten his license, a thing about which he pro-
fessed not to care. I hadn't actually known his mother drove, but the
little green Dart parked in front of our house suited her, with its mingled
air of disuse and sideways hopefulness.

My mother stood then and came over and started picking small bits
of twigs from me, the things that had stuck to me from lying in the
copse. "Where've you been?"

"Nowhere," I said.

"I don't know where he goes at night," she said.

"At seventeen, they're lost to us," Mrs. Weston said, and smiled
at my mother in an official way, as if she were searching for some sort
of common ground, a place where they could be simply "mothers,"
and nothing more. How long had they been sitting there before I

came home? I could tell they had run out of conversation, because Mrs. Weston kept looking at my mother and narrowing her eyes, as if she didn't understand her at all. And in truth, I couldn't think of two women less alike.

"Are you sure you don't want tea?" my mother asked.

"Quite sure. This is just so they can say good-bye."

Then they both looked at us like we were four, and any sort of playing we might do with one another could be done under their watchful eyes. Except that there was something new in my mother's, something, if I didn't know her better, I might have called *shrewd.*

"Do you boys want privacy?" Mrs. Weston asked. It was not the sort of thing my mother would ever think to bring up.

"I don't know," I said. "Do you want to come into my room?"

Andrew shrugged, like it didn't matter to him one way or the other.

In my room, we stood in the light by my desk. There was nothing to say, and my sadness felt general, as if any loss, even the loss of my mostly ridiculous friendship with Andrew Weston, were something to be mourned.

Andrew started to giggle.

"What?" I asked.

He started to pick twigs out of my hair. "Your hair is like a nest for these things. Where have you been?"

I suppose that what happened next was a direct result of Dr. Meola's having found me in the copse, of the humiliation I had pushed down so deep it must have been aching for a place to come out. Whatever the reason, I found myself starting to cry, very sudden and in a way I knew would be over soon. Andrew didn't know that was true, so he held me, ran his hand over my neck, and said, "It's okay, really," over and over, and hearing him say it that way, and using the word "really," made me cry more.

I let Andrew hold me. It was actually nice, tender and sweet in a way different than it was with girls, because with girls I was always aware—maybe too aware—of the next place it had to go. That was how it had been, anyway, with Karen. The kissing had been great at first, but then it had become a mere prelude to her touching me. With Andrew it had nowhere to go—at least, nowhere I wanted it to go—so I just went on crying with him rubbing my neck the way my father had rubbed Bob

Painter's and Andrew saying, in that half-annoying, half-endearing way, "It's okay, *really.*"

When it was time to break apart, I looked at him with gratitude and I saw in his eyes that he was here in this room—*alive* and *present* in this room in a way very different from me. It made me, at first, step back.

But Andrew stepped forward. He pulled my head toward him and kissed me on the lips. It was sudden, and, I think for that reason, I let it happen, as if some other level of this moment's reality was going to present itself to me, some safer and more logical level, if I just hung on. At the same time, I could see to the place where that was an excuse, that I knew very well what was happening, and the reason I allowed it to continue was because it was not bad to be kissed by Andrew Weston.

Finally, though, I couldn't allow that, so I pushed him away.

"We need to go back," I said, not looking at him, and I went out to the living room, not even checking behind me or thinking he might not be following. That made things embarrassing, because Andrew didn't come out for several minutes. I sat on the armchair where he'd sat, as if there were a simple excuse for his absence. The mothers, in the meantime, kept looking at me and blinking, as if the whole scene had been evident to them, like they'd been listening at the door. But the house was small, they'd hardly needed to have gone that far. Mrs. Weston had a cool way of surveying me, like what she'd always suspected was after all true, and what a shame, what an awful shame, such a good-looking boy. My mother had taken on the recessed, half-astonished look she hadn't worn since my father left.

When Andrew finally emerged, his mother stood up. "Did you say good-bye?"

"Yes," Andrew answered.

"Well, there's still packing to do. It's endless."

She was carrying a pocketbook, and she clutched it to her. "Good luck, Luca," she said, and smiled, and the two of them went out.

My mother didn't say anything at first. "You should pack, too," she said, finally.

"I've got a couple of days."

We couldn't look at each other, and a discussion was out of the question, but what she was thinking was heavy in the air for the next couple of days. When she finally spoke what was on her mind, it was at a moment I least expected it, when I'd guessed she'd filed away her impression, or let it evaporate. Over breakfast, on my last day at home, she gazed out the kitchen window and her face looked poised to say something small, something like "Look at the cardinal" or "It's going to be another hot one." Instead, what she said was "So you're going to be just like him." And, as if that statement held no greater weight than the pointing out of a bird, she took an accompanying bite of her toast.

My roommate at BC was a tall, square-jawed, good-looking boy named Eric Davenport, from Milton. Eric and I did not have a lot in common, but for reasons neither of us bothered to probe, we each failed to make many friends from among the other freshmen, and so found ourselves a great deal of the time in each other's company. There were mixers where we stood at the edge of the dance floor, each of us afraid to go and ask a girl to dance. Eric Davenport had played rugby at Milton but had no desire to go on playing at BC, because, he said, he found the life of an athlete limiting and wanted now to explore other aspects of himself.

I spent less time than I'd anticipated haunting the foyer of McHugh Forum, where an exact duplicate of my father's famous team photo had a prominent place. Once, I saw the man who must have been Snooks Kelly (I recognized him from the picture; he resembled the actor Edmond O'Brien). He bustled in and out of the foyer with another man. He appeared to be in a hurry. I did not ask him to stop and recall my father.

I had one important visitor that fall, but before his arrival I received a call from my mother one day, telling me that George had come home from Vietnam. A party was to be held in his honor; I was expected the following Sunday, at John's. Could I make it?

On Sunday I took the trolley, got off in Watertown Square, and walked to John's from there. All the lights in the house were on though it was only mid-afternoon.

Inside, the house was very hot and I looked for my mother. She was sitting with one of her sisters, and stood when she saw me. There was something charged in our meetings now. She seemed always to be glancing at me from an angle, defended from me in a way she had not been before.

My aunts all made the comments that aunts make: were they feed-ing me there? I'd lost weight, was the general agreement. Somewhere in the distance was a large cake (I discovered later it had the United States flag on it), platters of cold cuts, the uncles and the cousins. But I was focused on my mother.

"Where's Biago?" I asked. I hadn't necessarily meant for the others to hear it, but there was a settling in the room after I asked, people shift-ing position and drinking from coffee cups. My mother's expression didn't change at first, then it darkened in a way she had of doing, as though I shouldn't have said what I'd just said. "I don't know," she an-swered. "Busy, I think. At work."

John was a muted master of ceremonies. For long periods it seemed he wasn't there. Then I would find him in a corner of the room, chatting with an uncle, but unengaged, playing with the wristband of his watch, or gazing out the window, as if at the state of his yard. George, the guest of honor, had apparently not yet presented himself. He was taking a long nap in his room. Joanne Lacosta was the focus of energy. The aunts pressed her dress against the shape of her flat belly (she was pregnant again), insisting she was beginning to show. Bobby stood by, managing his characteristic mix of sullenness and pride.

I found John downstairs at his pool table late in the afternoon, en-gaged in a solitary game. His lit cigar lay in an ashtray at the edge of the table. He looked up from a shot he was preparing to make and then went back to it. "I thought you'd be busy at school," he said. He dropped the red ball into the hole.

"You see, I'm getting better at this," he said.

I sat in one of the big Spanish chairs he'd imported. "You must be glad to have him back," I said.

For an instant, he merely gazed at me, as if to let me know I would not be allowed into the private regions out of which he might answer such a question. "Pour yourself a drink. You're a college boy now."

I said I didn't want a drink.

"Where's Biago?" I asked.

John set up another elaborate shot and completed it successfully.

"It fizzled," he said.

He lifted his cigar and stared out the window.

"They were in love," I said, trying to make it sound as if their separation, if that was what it was, had been all his fault.

"Love fizzles sometimes." He glanced at me before going back to his game. "Have a drink."

George finally came downstairs. He wore his uniform, though he'd done a patchy job of shaving this morning.

"Hey, Luca." He did not seem interested in the fact that I was there. It was like we had left off a conversation the day before.

"Congratulations," I said. "You made it."

He looked at me a second before saying, "They sent me back because I was shitting too much."

"Don't use that language here," John said.

George made a mocking show of zipping up his lips. "Well, it's true, anyway."

"You got a hero's send-off," John said.

George watched his father and rubbed his nose back and forth.

"Fix yourself a bourbon. You've been serving your country."

George said, "No thanks."

There was an awkward silence, relieved by Bobby's coming down the stairs. John glanced at Bobby, and they seemed allied in something now, a watchfulness concerning George.

In a little while we began to hear, outside, the arrival of motorcycles, and George sat up, alerted. John gazed at him, skeptical, waiting for George to move.

"They showed up, your friends," John said.

George looked sallow, and uncertain, as if he were staying with us only out of some notion of politeness he was getting ready to jettison.

More of his friends showed up outside. Their noise was deafening, until the motors shut off. I couldn't see, but I saw John watching out the window.

"Go ahead," John said finally. "Greet your guests."

George got up and rushed up the stairs. "Tell them to make a little more noise, while you're at it," he said when he knew George could no longer hear him.

We were all quiet then.

"Game, Luca?" John asked, though I could tell he had no further interest in playing. He continued to gaze outside, so I stood and joined him. The large machines seemed to create a kind of screen between John's house and the neighborhood. The women took off their helmets and shook their hair out, their legs and asses pressed into tight jeans. They sat on John's stone wall and put their helmets there beside them.

"How long has George been home?" I asked.

"Month," John said, and removed his cigar, and shook his head.

"My mother never told me."

"No. She wouldn't, would she?"

"At least he made it," Bobby said, from behind us on the sofa.

"Yeah, he made it all right," John pronounced, without turning around.

One day a month later—near Thanksgiving—I came back to the dorm to find Andrew Weston asleep on my bed.

Eric Davenport was at his desk. He had his Philosophy book open and he was leaning back on the two rear legs of the chair. One of Eric's new affectations was to wear his hat indoors. He indicated Andrew on the bed and flattened his lips.

"What's he doing here?" I asked.

"Things didn't work out too good for him at UMass," Eric said. Then he stared at me a little longer than was natural for him before returning to his Philosophy book.

I sat on the bed and shook Andrew's leg. His hair had grown longer, and shaggy, in a way that actually made him look better. I couldn't help noticing that. When he opened his eyes, he appeared frightened. "Oh. You."

"Yeah. This is my room."

"I know that."

He pulled down his sweater and turned slightly to the side. "I need to stay here awhile."

I looked up at Eric, who was listening while pretending to read philosophy.

"What happened to you?" I asked.

Andrew sat up and put his face in his hands. "I stayed there as long as I could. I've got to transfer. That's *not* the place for me."

Andrew's teeth had started to chatter.

"Are you sick?"

"Everyone's from *Peabody.*"

His eyes had gone wet, like he might be about to cry.

"Why are your teeth chattering?"

"Because I'm *sick.*"

"Lie down. Listen, does your mother know about any of this?"

"She mustn't."

"Okay."

Eric got up then and took the blanket from his bed and covered Andrew. "Poor guy's sick." He tucked in the sides, gentle and concerned, a calming presence for both of us.

"Tell Luca what they did," Eric said.

"Oh, it's nothing."

"No, tell him."

Andrew closed his eyes.

"He's packing up to go home for a weekend," Eric said. "He gets home and his mother opens his suitcase and there's pictures of naked guys taped to the insides."

Andrew's eyes closed tighter.

"They'd snuck into his room. His roommate helped."

"Where do they get those pictures?" I asked.

Eric stood up, made sure Andrew was all right. "You can get them," Eric said. "If you want those pictures, it's easy enough to get them."

For a week, Andrew Weston slept in my room—for two nights, until he was better, on my bed, while I took the floor, then we switched— and came with me to classes. I was on the meal plan, so I let him share my food. He got better. He read novels incessantly and stayed up later than Eric and me, sitting at one of our desks with the lamp turned away from where we were sleeping, pointing it toward the window. It was as though he couldn't go to sleep until he finished whatever he was reading, but one night I awoke and found him staring at Eric, who slept with his mouth open and snored loudly.

Andrew played with his hair while he stared.

As always, he was guarded with me; though I had been his only friend in high school, and though there were by now things I knew for certain about him—though he had gone so far as to kiss me—these things remained, still, out of bounds, not quite discussable.

"What if I came here?" he asked one day. "Transferred. This place seems all right."

I shrugged. He had already done what damage he could: Eric's behavior toward me had altered some, grown more polite and solicitous, as if I, too, were recovering from an illness. Meanwhile, the looks of several others, when they saw Andrew with me, took on a level of comprehension that hadn't been there before.

"You could do that," I said.

"Or maybe not college at all. Maybe I'll just go to New York."

"And do what?"

"Work somewhere."

He sat on a bench and lifted his knee and rested his head against it. I gauged the signs of wellness and determination in him. I wanted him to go and I dreaded his going, because then Eric would ask me questions about him.

"The only thing is, everything is going to break my mother's heart."

He looked at me and smiled in a way that seemed to have nothing to do with what he'd just said; for a moment, he might have been reveling in the hopelessness of his own situation.

"You could go home and live with her," I said. "That probably wouldn't break her heart."

"No." He shook his head, as if to clear it of his mother. "What about you? Will you be all right here?"

"What do you mean?"

"Oh, you know."

"I don't."

There was always, with him, the sense that he knew things about me that I wouldn't find out for years. That was the kind of friendship it was, like hanging out with a disapproving sibyl.

He pulled his hair back. "You didn't mind when I kissed you."

I hated him for saying it because I suspected it was half true.

"I saw it in your eyes, for a second, you didn't mind."

"Why don't you go fuck yourself, Andrew."

He laughed. "If that was possible, believe me, I would."

Finally he was ready to go. He called his mother on the hall phone and cried loud enough so that everyone could hear him. It didn't matter. He had decided to allow his life to take up whatever space it needed. The night before Andrew left, Eric took us into Brookline and bought us steaks with the birthday money his parents had sent him.

"Just remember, nobody can hurt you," Eric said, and cut into his steak.

"Oh, it's so easy for you," Andrew said. "It's so easy for everyone."

"No. Just don't let them hurt you."

Sometimes they talked, in the dorm, while I was out at class. I came home and found them engaged, deep in conversation.

That night, we took our usual positions, Andrew at my desk, the lamp pointed toward the window so that its light wouldn't disturb us. When I woke in the middle of the night, the light was off and I heard a sound, muted, unfamiliar. Instinct told me I shouldn't look. But I listened. There was a lapping, slow and steady, with a kind of falling rhythm, and under it a low, more or less continuous moan. Then I did look, only for a second, and as if I were pretending not to. The covers of Eric's bed had been pulled back and I saw Andrew's head, the back of it, in the vicinity of Eric's lower belly. That was enough. I turned away, and I stayed that way, but until they were finished, and for a long time afterward, I was attuned to every sound they made, every murmur on Eric's part, and the accompanying murmur on Andrew's.

Andrew left. In his aftermath Eric and I were careful with one another. I counted the days to the end of the semester, and considered requesting a new roommate for next year. On Sunday nights, I spoke to my mother, but I hesitated getting at the truth of what had happened with Biago, so we talked, largely, about nothing at all.

On Friday nights, having nothing much else to do, Eric and I still attended the mixers. We drank beer and watched the others dancing, the fraternity boys whooping it up, and sometimes Eric made a snide comment out of the side of his mouth. He never asked me whether I heard anything from Andrew. Once I noticed a letter on his desk that looked suspicious, the handwriting large and full of loops.

He continued to wear his hat all the time, indoors and out, and to wear the same long brown coat in all weather.

The last mixer we attended was just before Christmas break. There was holly decorating the staircase of the dorm and the railing along the top balcony. The girls were from Emmanuel, Simmons, some as far away as Wheaton. They wore shifts that stopped just above their knees.

Eric said, "Tonight, we should quit farting around."

He went up to one of the girls and asked her to dance. I watched them on the floor. Eric held her close. Afterward, he brought her to me with another girl. They were roommates at Regis. Eric made a joke. "Luca, both of these girls are studying to be nuns. It's our job to convince them they made the right decision." The girls laughed to let me know it was all in fun. We danced with them. "The Crystal Ship." "A Whiter Shade of Pale." For me, there was no sex at all in this. Afterward they said they had to get the last bus back to Regis, so we walked them to the bus stop and waited with them. My girl was named Helen. Eric's was Rose. Eric kissed Rose at a distance from us, under a streetlamp. He ran his hands up and down her body, and she moved into him, like this was what she wanted. Helen and I watched, blew smoke out of our mouths, stamped the ground in the cold. The bus came.

When we were walking away, Eric said, "That wasn't very exciting."

"Kissing?"

"No. That was all right. But they really are going to be nuns."

We walked back to the dorm. Under his bed, Eric had some brandy. "I've been saving this."

"For what?"

"Christmas. Merry Christmas, Luca."

He poured some for each of us.

We sat on the edges of our separate beds, facing one another. He was still in the coat he always wore, and the hat.

"He was something."

"Who?"

"Your friend."

"Yes, he's something."

We drank awhile, silent, as if we were drinking ourselves away from the subject of Andrew.

Then Eric nodded his head, as if all the time we'd been silent, he'd been trying to make up his mind.

"Can I tell you something?" His eyes narrowed slightly and his lips thickened. He was trying to gauge something about me. He adjusted his hat, moved it back on his head, and held the drink between his legs. "I feel like I'm part way that way, too. The way Andrew is. Only partway, though, because I like girls too much. I mean, I hate to say this, 'cause it sounds crude, but I really like to fuck." I heard in his words the slightest phoniness. I'd lived with Eric four months: how often had he fucked?

But I didn't say anything. We both drank the brandy.

"It's the damnedest thing."

He went on staring at me another moment. "Can I tell you what I think is tragic, though? It's all completely and totally in the way we *look*. I can look the way I look—like *regular*—and I can do shit like play rugby and I can get away with any life I want. But Andrew's got to live just this *one* life. He's marked already. And it's going to be really, really shitty."

He looked out the window. He said, "I'm trying to figure out the life I want."

I said, "It's hard."

"Know what else? He said about you, that you're that way, too."

"He thinks that."

"Is it true?"

I believe it was because I didn't say anything that Eric took off his coat. "Would you say we're pretty drunk?" he asked.

I went on sipping the brandy and he tried to refill my glass, but I decided against it, pulled it away at the last second, and some spilled.

"Shit. That's good stuff."

He got down on his knees, very near me, to clean it up. Then he sat up again. He went on looking at me. "If I came over there, would you be mad at me?"

"I don't know."

"I could try it. Then you'd know."

"No. Maybe not," I said.

"Why? You scared?"

I didn't answer.

"Nothing attaches to us," Eric said in a voice just louder than a whisper. "Do you know what I'm saying? When you look like us, things don't attach. I think you have to understand this. It wouldn't mean anything, except, you know, friendship." He took another sip. "We're very free."

Then he came over and sat beside me on the bed.

II

History Teacher

1

My wife, Gina, and I met under what I guess you could call unusual circumstances, though I think the really unusual thing is the fact that we met at all. It was May 1979. I was a graduate student in history at Columbia, just finishing up. My adviser, Dr. Robert Bruner, had been impressed enough by my dissertation to arrange a public reading for me, with refreshments afterward. This sort of thing was not generally done, but he was an enthusiast, eager to launch me in the world. The work he'd been so taken with was called *Happiness in the American Cinema*, which, I think now, didn't really amount to very much. I made a great deal of Dana Andrews's valedictory smirk in *The Best Years of Our Lives*, and built upon it a small theory that, in the postwar world, America had become, if only briefly, too serious a country to consider the notion of happiness as anything more than a bauble. I was entering, again, only this time as a man, the old movie theaters I'd once inhabited with my father and Bob Painter, but the faculty at Columbia didn't need to know that.

Gina was then a first-year law student, in the throes of a painful breakup with a classmate named Neville Barnes. She had been surprised one day to find the flyer announcing my reading in her handbag—not knowing who had put it there—and, considering that discovery serendipitous ("a sign," she called it), had come to listen to me, afterward working up the bravery to introduce herself. How that flyer happened to be in her bag at all that day constituted the first, though maybe not the greatest, of the mysteries surrounding our courtship and marriage.

Robert Bruner was putting his considerable reputation on the line that day to arrange a teaching job for me at a prestigious college. A man from the History Department at Princeton and a woman from Wesleyan were in the audience. The plan was that I was to go on teaching and publishing, I was to be a historian. But after that reading, my only interest was in meeting Gina, who had appeared, an utter stranger, in the back of the room. How things moved forward so quickly is something I will never understand, but after a half hour's worth of conversation, I went with her to her apartment on Riverside Drive and didn't emerge for two weeks. I effected the removal of Neville Barnes from her life, a small, unconscious act for which she feels, still, an unwarranted measure of gratitude.

That act—my sequestering myself in Gina Abrams's apartment— was as uncharacteristic as anything I have ever done. But for a number of years that bold move made for a happy life. Then, in the early summer of 1992, I received a phone call that changed everything. A phone call, and then a trip Gina and I took in response to that phone call, during which we watched a container of ashes dropped into the water of the Atlantic at the tip of Race Point in Provincetown. I place this event before all else because the old historian has not left me. My training taught me that lives contain coded moments that hold in them a kind of template for everything that happens afterward. George Washington became the father of our country largely because he once stood firm during a failure, the retreat of his troops on the Assunpink Bridge. It's a single small moment in Washington's life, but it signified to his troops that he, and therefore they, were going to be able to endure defeat; it could even be said to have altered the tide of the war. And so for me, the phone call, the trip, the dropping of the ashes, and the decision Gina and I made afterward, all of these constitute my Assunpink Bridge, the signifying moment of the second half of my life.

At the time of that phone call, I was what I am now, a history teacher at Williston High School. I teach all four grades, ninth through twelfth, but my prize—we are all given one—is the upper-level Junior American

History class. Williston is located sixty miles west of the town where I grew up, where my mother still lives.

I chose Williston because sixty miles seemed the proper distance—not so close that I would feel bound in any way, nor so far that I couldn't maintain the contact I still wanted. That is, I didn't want an adulthood where my mother could call me at any moment, claiming she needed something (she never learned to drive, though at the point I am writing about she still worked), but it also never seemed possible that I could go through life in one of those severed states in which one's parents exist at a far remove.

Gina and I were married a year after I moved into her apartment; we lived in New York until she got her law degree. When it came time to resettle, Gina went along with my decision. She found a job in a progressive law firm in the midsized city that Williston feeds. She specializes now in what has become a hot legal ticket in Massachusetts, the prosecution of cases involving damages caused by lead paint.

Gina had plans of another sort for herself once. She grew up in a large house outside Buffalo. Her father is a corporate lawyer, her mother a schoolteacher. Everyone did well in her family, as they were expected to. Her two older brothers both live in Washington, D.C.; one is a lawyer in the Commerce Department, the other is part owner of a restaurant in Georgetown. The Abrams children have produced a large enough brood, five children between the two brothers. Gina and I, on the other hand, had no children. Twelve years into our marriage, as we were then, in 1992, we were that arresting couple you see in stores or in restaurants, well-dressed, polite with one another, with a banked sense of intimacy and a tendency to stare furtively at other couples for some clue as to the gap in themselves. We were a couple you would look at and know instantly would remain together forever.

But that is not to say that our coziness, the air we gave off of permanence, was all that comforting to people. At the Abramses' family gatherings, for instance, we were the ones of whom, after a while, it became difficult to ask questions. After they'd inquired as to my classes and Gina's lead paint cases, things generally tapered off quickly. Mine had become, by that time, a face Henry Abrams, the father, stared at too long, as if the more time he knew me, the more vaporous I had begun to seem.

Central to my presence there, of course, was Neville Barnes, but

Neville Barnes's was not a story any of them knew. Gina had naturally kept silent about it, so I was always looked upon—and perhaps still am—as an odd, unsuitable choice for her to have made.

That's a sketch—brief and necessarily leaving out a great many things— of where we were that summer. I was about to end my tenth year of teaching, and was going about the small political maneuvering that would keep me from having to ascend to the chairmanship of my department, an eventuality I had so far managed to avoid. Becoming chairman, as I then saw it, would interfere with those rituals by which I lived, the ability, for instance, to come home right after school and ride my bike, or else run into the hills around Williston, then return to make dinner and wait for Gina to come home. My favorite time of day was that moment, at about six in the winter but somewhat later in the summer months, when I'd stand at the kitchen counter, pour my first glass of wine of the evening, and begin to lay out the ingredients of a meal. Sometimes it managed to come home to me, how this was not the bravest or most daring life I could have chosen for myself. But any life is more complicated than it first appears.

I recall seeing a film once, late in my college career. I'd gone by myself, I remember, and the film wasn't much. It starred Michael Caine and Omar Sharif and took place in some dreamed-of Middle Age with men on horses and marauding armies. Midway through, however, was a scene I have not forgotten. A man and woman are alone in a cottage between two great hills, a cottage, in other words, located in a vulnerable position. There is the sense that some ordeal has been gone through in order to get them there. They have not fallen into happiness, but achieved it, and therefore do not take it lightly. One morning, as they are holding one another in a frosty light, the man lifts his head, hearing something. In his face is a certain expression: he has known a long time this was coming, an army arriving, a call to arms. Perhaps it always underlay his happiness, was kindling to it, an apprehension that the good, calm time had distinct borders.

I offer this example because it captures my own sense of where I was, how I had come to think about my life, at the moment in June 1992 when I returned to the house after a day of teaching and heard the phone ringing.

The woman's voice on the other end was unmistakable, though a quarter century had passed since I'd heard it last. "Is this Luca Carcera?"

There was a formality to the question, a hovering around the words of my name as around a poorly marked monument. If a voice could be said to be putting on its glasses, this was it.

"Yes."

"This is Helen Weston. You probably don't remember me. Andrew's mother?"

"Of course I remember you."

Things speeded up then, as if the next words would do something to me, inflict a wound or a blow for which I'd been preparing a long time.

"I don't know if you're even aware of this. Andrew passed away."

Of course I'd known, known in some part of me. The dull thud I registered was the thud of the anticipated. "I didn't. I'm very sorry."

A silence followed, in which I could sense her waiting for more.

"I knew he was HIV-positive," I offered. "I've been seeing him, summers, I usually go into the bookstore, to say hello."

"Your name was in his book. Your name and address. That's how I found it. You live in Williston now?"

She had developed an edgy, deep voice, like Diana Rigg in her later, vaguely malevolent roles.

"Yes," I answered.

"What's your work there?"

"I teach high school. History." I let out a breath, something that could have been interpreted as a giggle, an old affectation of my father's and one I had unconsciously picked up. The breath, or giggle, was in recognition of the fact that it had been Andrew, not I, who was the accoladed historian of the eighth grade. I wanted to apologize for even this tiny measure of success.

"Are you married?"

"Yes."

A hiccup of silence intruded before she spoke again. "Well, I shouldn't pry. I wanted to invite you. A group of Andrew's friends on the Cape are holding a ceremony. You knew he wanted his ashes dropped into the Atlantic."

"I didn't know."

"Well, there it is. I don't want it, but he wanted it. And so his friends . . . well, the date is June twenty-sixth. And I wondered, since you were in the book." She held something back. I did not go forward, not immediately; waiting, I knew I had not been invited simply because I was in the book.

"You've done well then," she said finally.

"I've done okay."

"You have children?"

"No. No, we don't."

After a moment's pause—I could sense her holding back, with-holding her full approval as she'd once done over the pages of Harold Robbins. Then she said, "They're a mixed blessing, I can tell you."

She allowed then another pause before continuing. "Andrew died in April."

I waited another moment, feeling she was now going to tell me more.

When she was silent I said, "I didn't see him last summer, when I went in. Whoever was behind the counter told me he was sick, but doing better."

"It's a very sneaky condition. I'm sure you've read." She seemed to be reaching, in her tone, for a superiority to the disease that had caught Andrew; then she gave that up. "I've got the ashes. I'd rather keep them here. But Andrew made this very specific request. Can you make it?"

I stared at the calendar Gina and I hang in our kitchen, with the dates of things marked. I am always happiest when I see the large white spaces indicating we have no obligations at all. There was nothing writ-ten on the square marked June 26.

I had no reason to feel obliged to Helen Weston. She had found my name penciled in an address book. Andrew had sent us a Christmas card one year; other than that, there was nothing, save for an unexpected postcard we'd received the year before, chatty and cramped, that I could see only now had been Andrew's way of saying good-bye.

"I'm looking," I murmured.

"Please," she said, a small word from the past, and that was all, fi-nally, that was required.

I couldn't wait, after hanging up, after agreeing to come, to go for my run. I run eight miles and I don't sweat, up hills, into the dense green country around here. Williston is beautiful, but I have never quite been able to lose the sense that I am a trespasser here.

The high school where I teach is staffed like a fiefdom; the principal, a man named Frank Corsaro, grew up and played football here. Several of the staff are relatives of his, and one man, a colleague of mine in the History Department, had the distinction, thirty years ago, of being one of ten young men who lifted Frank Corsaro onto their shoulders at the end of a victorious Thanksgiving Day game. There is a sense of shared histories here that sometimes feels impenetrable.

I chose this place, though. I chose it first because it is beautiful, hilly and lush. There are points on my run where the leafy cover gives way to vistas that are like the landscapes of Thomas Cole: enormous sculpted fields, the faintest shadows of trees at the edge. Also, there is a civilized downtown (a small but well-regarded college makes its home here). But I chose it, finally, because it appealed to me to live out my days in a place where I would always be a sort of stranger.

To chair the History Department would make me, if only briefly, something other than a stranger—would call me out into a public realm—and it was this I put my mind to on the run, a more convenient thing to worry about, certainly, than the death of Andrew Weston. It wasn't easy, though, to maintain the fiction that anything was separate from anything else. Halfway through my run, very much with me was an awareness that the forces of my life converging on this petty thing—my shirking of my duty to become chairman—were larger forces, forces Andrew had helped to build. So I had to think about him.

Andrew had disappeared from my life after leaving Eric Davenport and me alone in the dorm, staring at one another and wondering whether one of us should come to the other's bed. I never called him, and we didn't run into each other at home. Though Eric continued to get letters—I knew because I saw them on Eric's desk—I didn't ask about them. Then Eric and I stopped being roommates after freshman year, and that was the last necessary connection to Andrew. When the epidemic hit in the early eighties, I sometimes wondered if Andrew had been among its victims, but it was no more than a thought. He faded.

After I was married, though, once Gina and I had nestled into our lives as good, quiet citizens of Williston, we started spending two weeks of every summer in Wellfleet. Always creatures of repetition, we settled on a small, leaky house that fronted the bay, and returned to it every year. The cottage had a name, Damp Sands, one of four built on a bluff. (The couple from Avon who owned all four had an old-fashioned, romantic nature and believed in naming houses.) We liked going back, returning to the rooms where we'd made love the summer before, the salt air coming through the windows, the tattersall curtains. The only drawback was that we might run into my father on one of the Truro beaches, an occurrence that would cut into our dreamy isolation from the world. He had come to the Cape, in his mid-sixties, to live.

On the nights when we didn't cook at home, we liked to eat in one of the fish restaurants of Provincetown. Afterward, Gina always insisted on taking the long tourists' walk down Commercial Street.

It was an uncomfortable walk for me, because sometimes men— the sorts of men, anyway, who hang out on Commercial Street—see you with a woman, and they don't care, they assume the woman doesn't exist, or that she's just your cover, so they ogle you and sometimes say things. Other men probably laugh this off, but it's harder for me.

It was on one of these walks, sometime in the mid-eighties, that we stepped into the main bookstore and began browsing. I glanced up to see the man behind the counter flashing me a Cheshire cat grin. I assumed what I assumed, and turned back to whatever book I had picked up.

Then the man said, "Luca."

I looked more closely. This man was taller and beefier than I remembered Andrew being. The sleeves of his T-shirt hugged thick muscles. He was now obviously a habitué of the gyms that had, in high school, been such a torment for him. His hair was cropped short, and he wore the inevitable earring. But yes, behind all that was Andrew.

"Oh my God" is what I said.

I put down my book, stepped toward him, and we shook hands the way men in their thirties do at high school reunions, careful not to touch too much or to reveal, really, anything.

"Andrew," I said.

He looked beyond me, purposefully. The store happened to be full of children. A large family had entered on our heels.

"Which are yours?" Andrew asked.

"Oh," I said, when I finally understood what he'd meant. "None of them." It felt important to draw attention from myself. "So you work here."

"Yes. Here I am. Part owner."

He seemed—there was a light, uncomplicated smile on his face—genuinely glad to see me. The nervousness, such as it was, was all on my part.

"I've been here fifteen years," he said.

"Really?"

"And you? God, what's become of you? What do you do? Where do you live?"

It was cowardly, but I looked up to where Gina was browsing, on the store's upper level. "That's my wife," I said. "Up there."

He lifted his head to acknowledge her. There was—maybe I was wrong—the slightest mocking in the set of his lips.

"We live in Williston. I teach high school. History."

"*Really?* Some of us couldn't wait to get out of high school, and you're still in it?"

I was listening to Andrew more than hearing him; listening, and picking up bits from his clothes and manner. His affect said a great deal about how he'd lived, and what he'd become, since he'd left my room at BC. But there was nothing so surprising about that, or about the macho uniform that gay men were putting on in those days, nothing surprising at all beyond the confidence with which he wore it.

There was, however, something else. It had been there in the detected mocking: a hint of his amusement at me, so that, while I was standing there wearing a frozen grin, doing nothing, I felt like I was in fact dancing furiously for him.

Very soon we seemed to have reached the border at which there was nothing more to say. Not unless we were going to *really* talk. And we weren't.

So it was a relief when Gina came down the stairs. She'd selected a book, the kind she likes, with a fuzzy image of a rowboat or an Adirondack chair on the cover, and had only just noticed I was in conversation.

"Remember I told you about Andrew Weston?" I asked, and heard, in my own voice, a strained familiarity, as if it were important to convince Andrew things were supremely chummy between Gina and me.

"Yes," she said, though I knew she didn't.

"This is Gina," I said. "This is my wife."

I watched them shake hands. The hint of a suppressed comment was in Andrew's face as he wryly regarded Gina's reading choice. We told him we came every summer, and he said, like he might have said to anyone, "Well, *stop in*," and then looked at us in a certain way—taking in our coupledom—maybe pitying us a little but being generous. Clearly, it would not be a huge event in his night, the return of Luca Carcera.

"Remind me who he is," Gina said when we were outside. She was reading the back-cover description of the novel she'd just bought, distracted and ready to begin it.

My heart was thumping, so I was grateful that she seemed so unaware of what was going on in me. "The boy, the one I told you about, who used to come with me on weekends, with my father and Bob?"

"Right. Oh. Then this must have been something for you." Alerted, she looked up at me, as if she had failed me somehow.

"No. Just weird."

"To see him?"

"Yeah."

"You're not surprised, I mean . . ."

She meant that Andrew had turned out to be gay.

"No. Oh, no."

I drove fast that night down Route 6 on our way back to Wellfleet. The windows were open and Gina lay her head against the headrest with her eyes closed and the book she had bought resting against her breast, and I imagined that all that was in her mind was to lie in bed with the bedside lamp on, reading that book and listening to the ocean outside. This was in the days before Gina had decided she wanted a child. She might have been just thirty then, with the assurance of thirty that there is no rush. She was happy with our lives as they were playing out, and she told me more than once that she considered herself lucky.

She believed, too, that she knew me. In her mind—I could very nearly imagine that interior region—she viewed our intimacy, the nakedness of two bodies, the throttled cry of a male orgasm, the passing of two arms on a sexless night over the opposite body in a kind of unconscious and casual beseechment, the embarrassing sounds one hears, too, in the course of cohabitation, and then the talks, the speeches of self-representation during meals, during walks, all of this, along with what she'd observed of me over six or seven years, all of it constituted, in her mind, a kind of knowing. And I was glad then of the limits of that knowing.

But there were pockets of our relationship where I understood that this thing I cherished was based on a necessary withholding, a backing off, a willed and careful absence on my part. The terror of running into Andrew Weston had to do with all the parts of myself I had kept from her, parts that, once exposed, I was convinced would mean the end of our marriage.

That night we made love. I don't need to describe the little things we liked, the tiny measured surprises, the scents I particularly requested she draw up for me. Suffice it to say sex was for me always a solitary act. I do not mean that I was locked away from Gina, far from it. I did not look at her from out of a cold, detached place. But I did not know how to not be myself, how to stop being on guard, how to meld, which I had always believed to be the purpose of sex: that radical and necessary and perhaps devastating loss. Once, maybe, briefly, maybe, but no more. It was too important that I remain alert, that I do whatever was in my power to keep her. If that meant making love like a sentry, eyes wide open, gauging her every response for even a hint of danger, so be it. Such vigilance was sometimes lonely, but still, as I saw it, a necessary thing.

That night, very soon after our lovemaking, when Gina was already asleep and I was about to be, I heard a car approach the house. The likelihood was that one of the other families was coming home. The Wus, who rented Misty Harbor, might be returning with their children from a late evening. I was convinced, though, for a moment, that it was Andrew coming for me. His blandness and indifferent acceptance at the bookstore had been a ruse. The old clutching, accusatory Andrew was behind the wheel of the car, and would honk first but, getting no reply, come and yank at a door I had left deliberately—and for a long time— unlocked.

2

On the night near Christmas in 1967 when Eric Davenport came to my bed, something of course happened.

Let's have fun, Luca. Come on, Luca, we're drunk. It was one thing to kiss a Regis girl under a streetlamp, to run his hands up and down her body, and another to run those same hands up my leg and over my crotch. But the two acts did not constitute, in Eric's mind, the drawing of a line separating light and dark. He held out pleasure the way he'd held out, a moment before, the glass of expensive, secreted brandy.

We were awkward, neither of us practiced. Eric led, though he was new at this as well, having only recently given himself permission to do what, in Milton, in the locker room after rugby, the caked mud still attaching to him, had been merely thoughts. Still, he'd always believed that college would free him and he wasn't wasting time. "It doesn't mean you can't still go with girls, Luca," he said to me once. "It doesn't mean that at all."

Maybe. But it meant something.

It happened only once, and then we parted for Christmas break. Over break, I got a job in a hospital, mopping floors. In the maternity ward, I watched the soft, blanched women hold their babies, the goofy, awkward fathers arriving with flowers, small footballs. Despite what Eric said, I felt this was all closed to me now. Carolyn Lafollette called, we went to parties. I hadn't the bravery to tell her what had happened, how mistaken she had been in her hopes for me.

Eric slept with a girl during the break, a girl he barely knew. It had first happened in the bathroom at a party. Afterward, she had called him. They had done it thirty-six times in a month. (He'd counted.) When we returned to the dorm, and he told me about this, I assumed it meant he'd made his choice, that our one time constituted all the experimentation he cared for, and life would resume its normal pattern. I was relieved. Also saddened, but I chose not to explore that. Classes began, and one night, late, after I'd gone to bed and he'd stayed up, studying, he shut off his desk lamp, took off his clothes, and got into bed with me. Having allowed myself to do this once, I didn't know how to say no a second time. Nor did I want to. Eric's body sidling in next to mine filled me with excitement. I liked the warmth, the sense of being desired. I wanted this to have nothing to do with my waking life; that is, I wanted to go on dreaming vaguely of girls, of the life to come. But I also wanted him to come to me like this, to feel his breathing against me, the closeness of his skin. It was all—contradictions included—remarkably easy for a time.

Then, a month later, after several more sporadic, unannounced late-night visitations—we never spoke of them during the day—the girl called. She was pregnant. Eric had to fly with her to Puerto Rico for an abortion. His funds were depleted and he needed to borrow money from me.

He was depressed after that, and did not visit me late at night again. Nor did I ask him to (to do so would have made me something I couldn't bear to think of myself as being). Eric took on a surly look, grew utterly unconcerned with hygiene, began putting on weight. I would come back to the room to find him sitting by the windowsill, his legs tucked under him, a sullen stare at the view of Hammond Street we shared, his work undone. Late at night, he went out on long walks, wearing the coat, the hat. I felt I could not approach him, his gloom had grown so thick.

I caught him glancing at me from time to time when we were in the room together, though I usually took my work with me to the library, to be away from him. His look had in it what I read as mild disgust. My prescience was that it was more than me he was disgusted by; his philosophy of sexual relaxation had been undone by an abortion.

And without thinking too much about whatever pain this might be putting Eric through, I was glad of it. Now life could resume. What Eric and I had done became an episode, nothing to be deeply considered.

Close to the end of the semester, Eric told me he didn't think he'd be coming back after the summer break. I guessed the reason why. Under his dark mane of hair, under his thickened brows, he said, "I'll just work. For a while. Work and, you know, try to figure things out." He looked at me as if I might have some answer to this. There was none to give. The unspoken grew deep between us in those last few weeks. I always felt we were a half step away from something with the power to change both our lives. Then, when the end came, it came without anything even so formal as a good-bye—his parents came to pick him up while I was out—though I remember, vaguely, each of us making a promise to stay in touch.

Eric did not come back to school. In his absence, I became a model student, with a series of dull roommates. I was mildly disgusted with myself, with rigor, with the good grades. In the summers I returned to Vanderbruek, where they had begun to take me for granted. And on summer weekends, I visited my father and Bob, if anything more hesitant now with them than I'd been before, as if at any minute I'd bust out with the news about myself, news I suspected would break my father's heart.

In the photographs of those days I am barely there: skinny, full-lipped, I have my arm around my father on the summer dock but I am not quite touching him. We are linked that way, two men who knew how to be absent from their own lives.

At home, relations with my mother had taken on an edge. I had begun picking fights with her, I never knew why. Why hadn't she married Biago? Though I never said it aloud, this was the undercurrent of everything. And I knew the answer, one which led directly back to my old desire to keep sex out of both our lives, to allow sex, with all its ability to destroy, to remain the province of my father. She had respected that, at least bowed to it. Now, on summer nights, dateless, I picked on her, aware that, in falling with Eric, I had failed to keep up my own end of the bargain. Her solitude, in the light of this, had come to feel intolerable.

Yet it hadn't affected her beauty. She looked more now like she'd looked in her wedding picture than at any other time I had known her. Something began to come back to her face, the virginal expectation of a woman who does not yet know how it's all going to turn out for her. I asked her once if she had dated other men before my father. She said only one, and she hadn't liked him much, though she'd thought she might marry him anyway. Why? "Because you didn't know sometimes, that there had to be something else." Something else? "Love." She shrugged.

Her story was more comprehensible than my father's. She had held out for love, immersion. I remembered how, during the house-building, showroom-visiting summer of 1962, when the future had seemed to spread before her, she had begun to put on weight. I hadn't noticed it at the time; it was only something, in retrospect, that surfaced. Her body had turned soft, luxurious, and blurred, like she was slipping into the great melting pot of suburban grandeur, where it didn't matter anymore, to be an individual. Had my father picked up on this? Had his leaving been a nudge to return to who she was? Certainly that was what had happened, over time, over the period of betrayal and the brief sexual restoration effected by Biago. Having renounced sex and hope, she had turned skinny again, her face a hesitant bride's. She was again, for good or ill, an individual.

It was not until I had graduated college and, faced with many options, chosen the least imaginative—high school teaching—not until I had moved back in with my mother and we had settled into a life that was like a blinking contest—who could remain stuck the longest?—that I lost my virginity to a woman. A woman at the high school, as it happened, a Biology teacher, Barbara Greene, a few years older, pursued me. My hesitation she viewed as ridiculous, she had no time for it. She was twenty-nine, maybe I would do as a husband.

What Barbara Greene wanted from me—at least, what she wanted sexually—was easy enough to provide. In spite of what had happened with Eric, I had never really doubted that the heterosexual side of me was at least functional. The difference lay in the fact that no particular feeling surrounded the acts with Barbara Greene, no pleasant or desirable aftershock, nothing to draw me deeper in. There was her apartment, the Lava lamp beside the bed, a copy of *Fear of Flying* on the bedside table, and afterward, the feeling that, having done this, I only wanted to go home. Sometimes she asked why I couldn't stay and sleep there. I had to explain, as best I could, that my mother and I had never evolved a language to accommodate such absences. So I went home, and remembered what had happened as being pleasant and utterly insignificant.

Barbara Greene must have picked up on this. Seeing that I was unlikely to work as a husband, she dropped me as a bed partner. But though this hurt at first, I understood that Barbara Greene had given me something I needed, a freedom, albeit temporary, from the psychological grip of Eric Davenport. Things she'd said in bed stayed with me, and brought with them an unexpected confidence. I started to project myself imaginatively outward, into a less curtailed life, and I wonder still what form this might have taken if a coincidence hadn't happened that set my ambitions in a certain direction.

The movies I had seen with my father in the early sixties had begun to appear on television. Sitting in the little room that grew off our kitchen, with the stack of high school themes (English was the subject I taught originally), I watched them, thinking it would be amusing. *Advise and Consent, Birdman of Alcatraz, Lonely Are the Brave.* It was now the early seventies, and those old movies spoke to me in a way that nothing new did. It seemed as though they had risen directly out of the old suburban dream, black-and-white correctives to the inflated expectations of men like my Uncle John. I put down the high school themes and paid attention.

What struck me was that no one in those old movies was happy. No lovers ran into each other's arms at the end; no one, setting out at the beginning to get something, ever quite managed to achieve the desired object. For a time, happiness seemed to have been wiped out as a reasonable goal. In *Advise and Consent*, the stalwart Don Murray responded to the revelation of a homosexual liaison in his youthful Army days by slicing his throat with a razor. Laurence Harvey, at the end of *The Manchurian Candidate*, turned his own assassin's gun on himself. After watching those movies, my father and Bob had gone back to the rooming house, had made the beds, tucked me in, and thought—what? For a time, culture appeared to have been against them. Yet watching those movies as an adult, I began to think they may have provided something in fact more useful: a vision of fortitude, endurance, stoicism, unusual given what most of us think of when we think of that time. *Hold on,* those movies all said, *it's likely to get a good bit worse.* So Burt Lancaster, sucking it up, allowed his birds to be taken away; Kirk Douglas, grinning astride his horse, rode to his collision with the modern world in *Lonely Are the Brave;* Anthony Quinn accepted the inevitability of the cross in *Barabbas.* Always, whatever the circumstances, the ending was the same. The arc of a man's life, in the old, newly lost mythology, went through loss and a separation from what was dear to him, toward a hard-won integrity.

Something took me to the Brattle Theater in Cambridge, the revival houses—the Orson Welles, the Coolidge Corner. I remember the particular excitement of those nights: the notion that I was a high school teacher and something else, something that hadn't been born yet. Finally it occurred to me what form that unborn being might take, and I applied to Columbia. My idea—to study the films of the early sixties to explore a potential sea change in American attitudes—met with their approval.

I first encountered Robert Bruner in a seminar on the rebuilding of Europe after World War II. His biography of George Marshall had won a Bancroft Prize; in certain circles he was famous. Short to the point of near-dwarfishness, his head dome-shaped and sporting a mustache (the only vaguely roguish thing about his small, earnest self), he sat in his chair as if sandbagged, defended against potential assaults, but he grew, over time, open and generous in class. He laughed with us, cupped his hands before him, told Truman stories with glee. Outside the window was New York in its Upper West Side guise, the Hudson River, the Puerto Rican restaurants, comidas chinas y criollas. I had an apartment on 107th Street facing a courtyard where, once a week, a group of recovering alcoholics met. The voices of their inspirational leaders rose up to where I sat, an open book before me: Marcus Cunliffe, Arthur Schlesinger, Allan Nevins, the old great names. This was my life now, a fact I kept waking up to, astonished.

The best moments were leaving class on Friday afternoon in fall, hitting the streets of the Upper West Side, the wind off the Hudson, the light lowered in its preparation for winter, the smells outside Party Cake and the Indian restaurants, the surge surrounding the subway, everyone preparing for the weekend. My own weekend was simple: I went back to my apartment, fixed myself some coffee, read for an hour, made supper, then went to a double bill at the Thalia or the Carnegie Hall Cinema, the

Regency or the Theatre 80 St. Marks, walking all the way. Did people look at me? I don't remember. I had no awareness of myself as a being to be looked at or considered. I think I must have worn a perpetual little smile on my face. The three years of high school teaching had left me with a large enough bank account, which I supplemented with a teaching fellowship. I had found a way to reduce life to a nugget, a discernible project, a goal. Something, I was sure, would come of this.

In his office, Robert Bruner was hesitantly enthusiastic. "Film's new," he said. "Not a lot has been done." He examined me as if trying to figure out if I was up to any task worthy of his participation. He'd resisted service in Washington; feelers had apparently gone out during the Johnson administration, he let me know later. Disgust with Vietnam had led him to say no. "Let me see what you have, when you have something."

Having so little else in my life, I produced good work, though I knew it was small. All I saw was the movies. I drifted through a world so black and white the presence of color began to disturb me. I wanted New York to return to the way it had been when cinematographers like Ted McCord and Joseph LaShelle had seen it, the high still buildings, the pigeons, women in coats. I liked that world of limitations—the man who will sleep with his secretary and then go back on the train to his wife, the presence of drinking businessmen on the train, blondes who sit in the bar car, the dark woods they pass on their way to Connecticut. I could not understand why we had evolved beyond that world; it seemed fixed and perfect.

Robert Bruner once came with me to the movies, inviting himself, on a Friday night, to see *The Victors* at the Thalia. Afterward, it was cold; he insisted we stop at a Cuban Chinese restaurant on upper Broadway. "The scene with Peppard was awfully good," he said.

"Which one?" I asked.

"Where he's waiting for the bus, in the rain, the British family taking him in."

Outside the confines of his office, his classroom, I did not know how to talk to such a man. He seemed diminished, too eager somehow. What did he want from me? His sport jacket hugged his body too tightly. His only son was a medical student in Chicago. He introduced me to tofu. I wanted the evening to be over, but Robert Bruner kept trying to extend it. It was better to think about movies in solitude, to lie on my bed. But on my bed, my thoughts sometimes led elsewhere. Occasionally, the sounds of lovemaking reached me (a sexually active opera singer lived in the apartment below me) or, looking across the courtyard, I watched bodies in the other apartments, the simple movement of men and women on the telephone, watching television, the making of beds. One young man used to watch, deep into the night, a female exercise program on TV, and if I happened to be up, I would study him watching it. If there was a kind of sexual thrill in this, it was the only kind I allowed myself, the voyeurism of a man who doesn't want the act to touch him. But Robert Bruner, it seemed, wanted to deny me even this.

One night, Robert Bruner invited me to a dinner party at his apartment. The guests were Columbia faculty; Diana Trilling was among them. Robert Bruner's wife was pale and tall; she reminded me somehow of Helen Weston, though that could have been the cigarettes she smoked. She gave the impression I was one of many, her husband's acolytes. At the dinner table, I was expected to shine. "Listen to this, listen to what he's doing," Robert Bruner announced, cuing me. The guests listened with mild suspicion (Diana Trilling's eyes might have looked that way characteristically), a tiredness and resentment born of having had dinner with too many bright young men. The discussion moved elsewhere, and I suspected, from his attitude afterward, that I had failed Robert Bruner in some small way.

Around that time, though, something else happened. My reputation in the department was ascendant, the invitation to dinner with Diana Trilling had apparently gotten around. At the reception after a visiting lecturer (the cheap wine, the cubes of Havarti), a girl named Abby Kassell approached me. Abby Kassell was known to be brilliant and unreliable. She'd had to leave the program for a year—mysterious problems, a rumored stay at a mental institution—but the work she was doing on the nineteenth-century anticlericalist Fanny Wright was a departmental legend. Within the graduate program, there were those who were known to be sleeping with one another, and those who were married, and then those, like me, who existed at the periphery, with the whiff of the library about them. I was not someone a star like Abby Kassell had ever paid attention to, until suddenly, at this party, she began to.

She behaved coyly, like she had always been fascinated by me and had only now worked up the courage to speak. I didn't believe this for a second, took it only as an indication that word had reached her of the faculty's growing enthusiasm for my thesis. She had a wide face, prominent red cheeks, and she spoke as if we shared certain subtleties, the burden of being academic luminaries. During the course of that afternoon, she suggested we ditch the party for a walk in the park, which eventually led back to her apartment.

She lived two blocks from me, her place slightly smaller. We lived alike, our nests outfitted in the seminarian rigor of young historians. She was learning to cook Indian, and made something that tasted awful. We drank Jack Daniel's.

At a certain point, I understood that I was doing nothing, and Abby Kassell was doing everything to convince herself she wanted to sleep with me. It is overwhelming when a woman finally decides you are to play that role in her life. In my brief experience, I have never known how to receive it, except to retreat, become a quiet boy, pray that I don't say the wrong thing, reveal the diminishing fact.

"One thing I have to ask you," she said when we had reached her bed. "Please don't touch me. Down there."

It was, I supposed, the revelation of the thing that had sent Abby Kassell into an institution, but I moved quickly past it. Okay. For only the second time, I was sleeping with a woman, but it did not feel that way: it felt, I think, more of a practiced thing. I knew how to please without offering anything of myself. It was not difficult at all to send Abby Kassell into a state of half-open eyes and mouth, the eerie and wonderful and somehow debased silence preceding the words "Oh God." I somehow knew how to calibrate things so that she would never think to open her eyes all the way, to stare hard at me, to wonder who in fact she was sleeping with.

We became, quickly, a couple. A mantle had been laid upon me; I left her apartment, mornings, aware that I had gotten lucky suddenly, everything falling into place. I could say now I had a girlfriend, a serious relationship. There was safety in that, a completion of at least the forms of life; I could not be called out. Abby Kassell liked solitude enough that limitations were built in very early: we saw each other on Saturday nights and usually one other night of the week, dinner at my place or hers, and afterward the elaborately limited sex, which she came to control in a way I never minded. I was still free to go to the movies on Friday nights, to lie on my bed and think, to spend long days in the library, but there was now a charge to these activities. Some weeks she called me on a night we hadn't planned, asked if I could come over. She asked for nothing beyond my body. Large acres of my mind felt unused, unimplicated, yet it did not concern me. We had good conversations over dinner; I had the pleasure of an intimacy with an intelligent woman, and if, at a certain point during the meal, when by her look I knew she had grown bored by the conversation, or by me, and wanted to move on to the next, the purely sexual place, that was fine, too. I was, I guess you could say, an undemanding boyfriend.

I began, after a time, to envision a life growing out of this. I would finish the dissertation, turn it into a book, get a job teaching somewhere, in the same city (preferably this one) as Abby Kassell. We would marry, without achieving an intimacy beyond the easy one we had. I did not know what lay beyond it, or if I did, if some hint floated in the air of other choices I might make, I chose to disregard it.

So I began to see our marriage, the coming of children, the life I would live: Professor Carcera, in a sport jacket, a shirt unbuttoned at the neck, opening a notebook to consult my lecture notes, the office, the departmental secretary, the afternoon coffee, the call home to Abby, who would answer, distracted, at work on something herself. I would pick up the children. I would cook. Of the two of us, she would be the brilliant one, the more ambitious.

"Please don't touch me down there." It meant something, alluded to a past. Another man would have asked questions. What happened to you, as a girl, that you cannot be touched? But the simple language for a question like that was beyond me. I accepted what was put on my plate. The dreams of the future, almost delirious at first, took on another character after a while. I shooed complicated feelings away (memories, primarily, of the simple, and here lacking, emotion that had been elicited by Eric Davenport), finished my dissertation, accepted praise. Would I have daughters or sons? I saw myself pushing them on the swings in Riverside Park, the palpable future in which, I'd begun to think, in a troubled, unvisited region of my mind, I had still not quite managed to come alive.

Robert Bruner's enthusiasm was, in the end, infectious. He had his eye on Princeton for me. That seemed possible. I could take the train, weekends, eat Indian food in Abby's apartment. I could ignore her burgeoning resentment that I had managed to get somewhere first. If I taught at Princeton, I could drag my notes up on Saturdays, grade papers in the Columbia library, find as the locus of my existence the nights in Abby's bed, and the time in which I slipped away to watch old movies. Life, I tried hard to convince myself, need contain no element deeper than cultural analysis and sex. Eventually a boy would be born, or a girl.

So this was the dream I carried into the room where I'd been asked to read from *Happiness in the American Cinema* in May 1979, the subtle, complicated dream in my head as I stood at the podium, surveyed the room, and caught, near the back (there were only thirty or so people there, so it was not hard to catch her) a young woman whose face I didn't recognize. Most of the others were members of the department, professors, fellow students (those who were too jealous didn't bother to show up), Robert Bruner's guests, the man from Princeton, the woman from Wesleyan. We were going to dinner at the Moon Palace afterward; it had been settled. I consulted my open text, and somewhere in me that day were, well, two things: one that inhabited dream, the vision of myself on the train up from Princeton, with my books, my new clothes, my ordered life. But there was also a second thing growing in me, and that was of the perceived inadequacy of this as a dream, its ready-to-handness, as if someone, not I, had envisioned a reasonable future for me.

I did not fully know until that day how much this bothered me, how much was missing from it, how large a measure of disgust attended this neat, contained version of myself. A part of us, I guess, continues to reach out, grasping, even when we haven't given it permission to. Before I began reading, I looked up once again at the strange girl in the back, offered an embarrassed smile, not even sure why I was doing that, but having picked her out somehow, as the person in the room capable of not being taken in by Robert Bruner's florid introduction, by the presence of recruiters, by the unusual fact of the wine and the cheese carted out in celebration of a mere student.

I was someone who had gone to the movies, that was all, someone who had noticed things.

Forgive all this is what I think I wanted to say to her.

3

Six or seven years into our marriage, Gina discovered in herself a desire to sing—not so unusual, perhaps, but given our town's limitations, a desire that left her with few options. After casting about—community theater? a church chorale that wouldn't mind including a Jew?—she settled on a group called the Williston Cantata, an ambitious collection of retired faculty and their wives, along with the usual mix of postal workers, paint salesmen, and civil servants, most of whose children had grown and who were looking for outlets, places to go at night. Given my background in chorus, I kept waiting for Gina to ask me to join her, but she didn't. The Williston Cantata gave four or five concerts a year in ours and outlying towns, and met once a week, in the Baptist church, to rehearse.

That was where Gina was on the night Andrew Weston's mother called, and though I had been asked not to come to these rehearsals or even to meet her outside (she relished the freedom to go out afterward for a beer with her fellow singers), I couldn't help it that night. Grief, or else simple loneliness, made it impossible for me to stay home.

It's actually pretty to sit outside the Baptist church and wait. Farther down the road, closer to the college, are where most of the hip elements of our town lie—the bookstores and the cafés—but here, in the old center, are our ecclesiastical underpinnings: the Baptist church and the Congregational as well as a stone professional building that houses our town offices. There is also, at this end, a second, smaller building with a bar and a bicycle store and a shop called the Bagelerie, which always seems on the verge of failing but never quite does. Our downtown's grace note is the small and well-kept park across from the professional buildings, a park at the center of which is a gazebo and a small plaque honoring our town's war dead. It was here that I took my place, so that I could have a good view, and could spot Gina as soon as she came out.

It didn't take long. She was the first to come out of rehearsal, though she wasn't alone. A friend of hers, a lawyer who specializes in land deals, Chuck Cooper, accompanied her. Boyish and semicorpulent, one of those men who seem to live for their Saturday golf game, Chuck Cooper had a long and complicated romantic past (one of his sons, the issue of his second marriage, was in my American History class at the time). He seemed to be pleading some sort of case to her. Gina listened intently enough, though she seemed stiff, perhaps just from tiredness. Her briefcase looked heavy at her side, and she set it down. Chuck Cooper's romantic approach to women seemed to involve a lot of head wagging and rocking back on his heels, and it was only when I thought of those words, "romantic approach," that it really hit me what I was witnessing: my wife being wooed, in the dark wooded area before the Baptist church, by a local swain.

I didn't really think there was much to be afraid of. In twelve years of marriage, Gina had showed little inclination to stray—this in spite of her sometimes uncontrolled behavior in the years before she met me, behavior that had landed her in trouble more than once. It had been an ego-boosting thing for me to believe that I had tamed her, though she said to me more than once it was life itself that had made her—she wouldn't ever use the word "tame"—less sexually curious. Only once, in our early years in Williston, had she begun a dalliance, with a young lawyer in her firm. She had known enough to end it before it had gone too far, then smothered me with affection and appreciation enough so that I had no choice but to forgive.

So here, now, watching her from a distance, I felt less motivated by fear or jealousy than by a genuine interest in seeing how Gina would behave in a situation like this.

After a few minutes of the head-wagging and heel-rocking tactics, Chuck Cooper took Gina's hand. It was a clear indication that I should break in; still I didn't. Gina lifted her briefcase, as if she were about to break from him, but she didn't remove her hand. Had it been someone other than Chuck Cooper, I might have become worried then.

It was not until Gina started to look genuinely uncomfortable that I broke out of my detachment and called to her. The two of them, startled, glanced across at the park. I stood and moved slowly enough toward them that Chuck Cooper probably believed that his hand slinking out of Gina's and back into his pocket was unseen by me. When I was close, he said the word "Luke," friendly enough. (He has never quite learned to get my name right.) I went on staring at the place where their hands had been recently joined, which was as close as I could come to a chastisement of him.

"What are you doing here?" Gina asked.

"I wanted to take you out somewhere," I said, the innocent husband who had come merely to spend time with his wife.

Chuck Cooper laughed, an uneasy, socially obtuse laugh that made us both look at him. Others were coming out of the rehearsal now, smiling at us, oblivious to the scene.

"This is where I cut out, I guess." I looked at Chuck and thought how he must have lived a life of petty embarrassments like this one, how the little lock of hair falling on his forehead probably made him think of himself as being adorable to women, and how he also must have learned a way of not being present at his own romantic failures. There was that skill in the way he extracted himself.

"I'll see you next week then, Gina." He wandered off into the night.

I wanted to smile then, and assumed we would share the joke of how absurd it was for him to think he might have her.

"So you noticed?" she asked, and I caught a slight embarrassment in her, more than was warranted, as she lifted the hand he had held. I nodded. "Such a sleaze," she said, but not looking at me.

"Want to go somewhere?"

"Like where?"

I nodded to the Bagelerie.

"Didn't you cook tonight?"

"No. Andrew Weston died. Do you remember? From the Provincetown Bookshop?"

She glanced up at my face to gauge how this might have affected me. "Oh," she said, with compassion. "Your old friend."

"Yes, but, you know, it's been a long time. You must be hungry."

She hesitated, I wasn't sure why, something clearly on her mind, or else a wonderment at how I always managed to brush my emotional attachment to things aside. She glanced around, at the Bagelerie. "You want to buy me a bagel?"

"I do."

The store was only half lit. Jimmy, the owner, seen through the window, looked like he was hoping to close early. He has four kids, a wife, formerly a beauty, who'd begun to look a little bleached out. I came in here all the time, and though he didn't know me well, I had managed to pick up, just by listening to his conversations with his cronies, all sorts of details about him, his mother's dementia the latest of his dramas. As we approached, his place began to resemble that Edward Hopper painting *Nighthawks*, except that, in this version of it, the proprietor might be standing at the window, saying: *Don't come in.*

"Are you still open?" I asked.

"Sure. Come on." Jimmy wasn't happy, but he switched on the lights, to brighten things up.

I ordered Gina her bagel, coffee for me. I thought how, from the way she looked—drawn and tired—it must have been nice to have been approached sexually, must have made her feel all was not lost in the fight against time. I could see that it had done something for her, too, though she affected simple tiredness. It was unconscionable but not unexciting to think that if we were to have sex tonight, she might close her eyes and imagine me as the piggish Chuck Cooper.

On the tail end of that thought, I turned away from her and looked out the window into the lush early June night, and experienced a moment of happiness so pure I didn't know how to explain it even to myself. This was my wife, and my marriage seemed, at that moment, safe. Safe for her fantasies, and for mine, safe from the intrusions of others. Chuck Cooper did not realize, perhaps, how impregnable a fortress he had attempted to storm. In the light of this, it seemed we might be safe from other things as well, so I decided to be bold again. "Listen," I said. "There's something."

She paid attention.

"It was Andrew's mother who called to tell me. I never told you much about this, but she was an important woman to me once. And she asked if I would come and—his ashes are going to be tossed into the water, off Race Point."

She took this in, said nothing.

"I gather it's some sort of ceremony."

Still, she was waiting. When I didn't offer anything more, she said, "So. Go."

"No. The thing is, I want you to come."

Jimmy brought the bagel then, and my coffee. He smelled of flour and something else, an odor of grease, like he'd been oiling something before we came.

Gina took a bite. Her brow seemed heavy with thought. I wanted to reach across and smooth it, remove the thick line that had settled across it. But I can't, in the presence of another man, touch Gina. It had always been this way for me, since the very beginning, and I had stopped even trying to probe it.

"What are you thinking?" I asked.

She took a moment before answering. "How we never go any-where." She licked a dab of cream cheese off the side of her lip.

"Come on." I was about to provide her a list, knowing even before-hand that it would be meager.

"No. We do our work, we hang out on weekends, but we don't—*go* anywhere. And when we do, it's to see your mother, or—to some gay party on the beach in Provincetown. I'm sorry, I know this is your friend who died—" She took another bite, kept herself from saying something.

"It would be a trip to the Cape."

"No, it wouldn't be a trip. It would be you dealing with your gay past, wouldn't it? That's what it takes to motivate you out of your little domestic routine, isn't it? It's the one thing that really excites you. And I'm supposed to come along for the ride."

I could feel her foot tapping under the table, a sign of seismic dis-turbance in Gina, and, frankly, I was surprised by it. She looked out the window and chewed. What she'd said was more or less true: it was my "gay past" I was going to explore. She can say those words, and the truth is, they bother me more than they bother her. The separation in years between us—only seven, to be sure—seems to have bridged chasms of tolerance: that I once slept with a man, Gina takes in stride. But her dismissing it that way had never robbed the issue of weight for me. I needed her to come with me because the thought of exploring my "gay past" on my own terrified me.

"It's no big deal," I said.

"No?"

"It's just something I think I owe him."

She didn't look like she believed me.

"I'd like you to come, that's all."

"I'll think about it, all right?"

After that we didn't say much. Jimmy sat at the counter, smoking, in defiance of an ordinance that had recently been passed by the Board of Selectmen. Gina went on eating her bagel, and I really wanted to reach out and touch her, but couldn't. When she was done, I paid and we went outside and, freed from Jimmy's male eyes, I took her hand. She allowed it, no more than that. Her palm felt damp.

"You working late tonight?" I asked.

"Celia Gonzalez," Gina said.

She didn't need to say more. Celia Gonzalez was a Hispanic girl, in seventh grade, who was failing all of her courses. For the past nine years she'd been living with her mother in a tenement near the city where Gina worked, a building whose landlord had already been sued three times for failing to remove lead paint from the walls.

But I had a reason for asking, other than concern for Celia's welfare. I knew what night work did to Gina.

The air smelled wonderful that night, the way it does in early June around here, loaded and still, full of dogwood and the end of the lilacs, so that on the night of high school graduation (then about a week away) it was almost heartbreaking to watch the young healthy seniors step out into the sweet air, in the virtual certainty that life would never again contain for them such a sense of majesty and importance. I stood facing Gina the way I always stand, with my head cocked slightly, a pose characteristic of me, I suppose. I still wasn't sure how serious her little outburst in the restaurant had been.

"I'll see you at home then," Gina said, not looking at me.

"Any chance on earth we can talk about what's bothering you?" I asked.

She hefted her briefcase onto the passenger seat. "As if you didn't know."

She drove away, not looking back at me, not even running, midway up the window, the white flag of a tired smile.

When I reached home, I parked at a distance from the house, pleased that I had gotten there just behind Gina, so that I could have my "Stopping by Woods on a Snowy Evening" moment; that is, so that I could sit and watch from a distance Gina perform her nightly activities. That night, she didn't do anything unusual, but I enjoyed watching nonetheless. Her small actions, that sense of watching someone when she doesn't know she's being looked at, filled me with a kind of illicit pleasure. She opened the passenger-side door and took out her briefcase and started inside, checking the mail in case I'd forgotten to. (I never do.) The house was in darkness. We live on a cul-de-sac, at the end, and the driveway forms an arc from the road to the front of the house and back to the road.

I love this house. It's a modest but I think beautiful dwelling, tan with black shutters and white trim, two-story, a hundred years old. Sometimes, looking at it, I feel the way I imagine the men who inhabited the Hill in the early days must have felt, those men who stoked themselves by standing in their doorways at night, surveying the cleared forest. I have, at certain times, attempted to replicate such a moment, standing in my own doorway at night, but there is always a hollowness that comes over me. It is just not the same; recent history has moved us all on. I inhabit a house that other families have inhabited before me; mine is more a tenancy than a creation. And even if this weren't a house I'd bought jointly with my more well-paid wife, even if I'd lifted it, literally, out of the earth, I doubt I'd allow myself the sense of completion that Meola and Semenza and my Uncle John once indulged. We have passed that simple male moment, I'm afraid; it is unrecoverable. The necessary goal of a man's life is no longer dominion, the settled claim; it is now something else, it is intimacy. A man like me, standing in his doorway, cannot stay fixed on the land and the lawn and the sheltering trees. His mind will go to his wife inside. His mind will go, whether he wants it to or not, to some demand constant and perhaps unanswerable.

With this in mind, I drove up and parked behind Gina's car. In summer, we do not use the garage. I locked both cars, because though we live in a low-crime district, you never know, and because Gina is too casual sometimes, leaving expensive items, articles of clothing, in the backseat. Then I went inside and already I could hear the shower running. So I climbed the stairs and stood close to the bathroom door.

Gina was humming a song in the shower—something I didn't recognize, something from the cantata, no doubt. I glanced around the kitchen, saw how neatly I had everything stacked—the spices, the cookbooks, the oil and the wine—and I tried to remember what Gina had said in the Bagelerie. "My cozy domestic routine," had those been the words? I listened to Gina's song and imagined her soft body inside, imagined her soaping her breasts, and something in me wanted to break out of its own enclosure. Some other man, I knew, would act on the impulse I felt just then, which was to go inside and hold her. I stood waiting, considering, and then I heard the shower go off and then it was too late.

Still, I could hope that the night would follow its customary, desirable pattern. I was used to having things come to me without working too hard for them. Within half an hour, I knew, Gina would have her legs tucked under her while she sat in a soft chair, a cup of tea cooling beside her, and read, deep into the night, the depositions of early-childhood-education experts, medical experts, people whose work was all about the brain. And I, upstairs in bed, had to bone up on a few things for the next day's classes, my classes that were nearing the end. I would drop off before Gina, but at a certain point she would come to bed, and what I then thought of as the secret, silent, truest part of our marriage would be allowed to speak and breathe. Half-asleep, half-awakened, I would feel her nestle in, then draw close to me, wrap her arms around my shoulders, her breasts pressing against me. It had come to me in the nights of my marriage that the heart of a man's life is not in his work or his thought or his actions. It's in that moment I have just described, when his wife is wrapped against him like that, and he's waiting for her hand to lower. Shameful to admit, but there it is. It is a moment rife with the drama of D-Day: *would* it lower? You could never be certain. Never *entirely* certain. So you breathe, and you wait, and should she touch you, all contradictions you may harbor go out the window. Your life, for that moment anyway, is perfect.

For a long time, it had worked that way, and that night, I was almost saved. It almost happened the way I have just described. She did nestle up close to me; she did rub my belly and the tip of my penis whispered against her wrist, inviting her. But as if at that suggestion, she drew her hand away. I felt her stopping, a hush in her breathing, like a decision vocally reached.

After a moment, I said, "What?"

"If I go on, you're going to put on a condom, aren't you?"

I didn't answer, didn't have to. It was what I did. It had been my custom for the last few years, since a certain event. I turned and saw her staring up at the ceiling.

I asked a question that was a kind of joke of ours, a line I had learned from hanging out with her family. "Why is this night different from all other nights?"

She didn't answer. She continued staring upward. I did the same thing.

"I feel you on a big boat," I said, trying again for the light touch. "I feel you drifting away."

"Yes," she said finally.

Then she added: "I think I'm making this decision. I think I've let you save me long enough."

"I never saved you."

"No. You did. And gratitude goes a long way. But I think maybe this is the end of gratitude."

I didn't answer because it filled me with too much black sadness. It felt sudden, though it had been stupid of me not to have seen the signs before.

"I'm starting to think you've gone as far as you can go, Luca. We'll just go on like this forever if I let us, and you'll never complain. Late-night sex where we don't have to look at one another, and you refusing to have a child. You cooking and keeping our little house safe, this is the extent of what you want. Isn't it? And you're just praying I'll settle for this and not ask for anything more."

I didn't answer. Every word was utterly, indefensibly true.

"And if I didn't wear a condom," I asked, "that would make all the difference?"

She simply let out a snort.

I moved closer to her. A part of me was gauging what the chances were of her getting pregnant from one free throw. Another part was thinking how stupid, how indefensibly private a thought that was. But who, with an erection and a little need, really wants to closely examine his own motives? I moved close and tried to kiss her. At the last moment she turned away so that I was kissing only the sides of her lips. In the movement of her eyes toward the window, I caught something, a vulnerable, outward-seeking look that made me pity her.

I kissed her again, and ran my hands down the sides of her body, as if I were warming her. "Gina," I said.

She continued to look out the window.

I wondered if she would let me, and what it meant simply to be allowed. The fact was, our sexual appetites had been pretty evenly matched in this marriage, a surprising fact, given Gina's formidable head start. I was a stranger to the sort of sexual cravenness that was a feature of the hoary Jewish sex jokes Gina's brother Michael liked to tell. ("What's the Jewish definition of foreplay?" "Two hours of begging.") Not me. Though I liked it best, I have to admit, when Gina came to me and woke me out of sleep. I liked that feeling of being the desired one, and if sometimes this called to mind the nocturnal disturbances of Eric Davenport, I tried not to pay much heed to this.

I crawled on top of her, the entirety of my body facing hers, so that she had to turn away from her view of the square of moonlight and confront me. Would she be surprised that I seemed willing to go ahead, condom-less? I decided it was worth the risk.

She was not, I could feel immediately, anywhere close to being ready. Neither was it a night for foreplay. To enter her like this— uninvited, insistent—was to make a raw statement. Something dry in her grated against me. I like the long ascent until there is nowhere further to go. Sometimes I think entry itself is the best part of the act. I always close my eyes and utter a low, satisfied grunt, and I could die there, I really could. The insect who has his head bitten off just after his ejaculation is not an unhappy insect, I'm convinced.

In our early days, I found something surprising used to happen during sex. I found I could outlast Gina. We had, of course, no sense of time (fifteen minutes could seem like hours) but at a certain, fairly reliable point, Gina would close her eyes and begin to drift away. Tiredness and ecstasy had a way of changing places during the act. It excited me to see that happen, to know I had that power. In the moments after Gina dropped off, I felt the sweet relief that nothing more was going to be asked of me, I was free to go on to my own completion in an oddly satisfying isolation.

Eventually that phase of our sexual relations gave way to Gina's greater capacity for consciousness. And in this I always thought of Gina— of this whole time of our marriage—as positing a demand: *meet me*, she might have been saying in those years, as she clutched at me and asked for an involvement beyond the studly, an eye-on-eye communication that had been thrilling and terrifying at the same time.

It was clear I hadn't—hadn't met her, that is—because that night we entered the third phase of our marriage, the phase that reeks of finality. Gina's eyes were open, but she asked for nothing, as though she'd given up on an old expectation. Nor did she make even the beginnings of the sounds of pleasure. It was as if, instead, she were telling me she didn't believe me, that the transformation she was waiting for wasn't available through simple, unsheathed sexual desire. I went on and on, but to no avail. I was nowhere close to coming, and at a certain point, as if she understood how little I had budged from my long-held position, she turned away from me and stared again out the window.

At which point I withdrew. It did not take Gina long to fall asleep, but I stayed awake, thinking. I had assumed the death of Andrew Weston was going to precipitate a crisis, but I had been wrong. The crisis, I ought to have known, was already here.

4

Actually, I don't remember which of us in that stuffy room at Columbia approached the other first. I do remember, after my reading was over, seeing Gina hovering near the back of the room, and I registered that she seemed to know no one there. So why had she come? And why wasn't she leaving? Robert Bruner forced the Princeton man on me. We both were holding little plastic cups of cheap wine. The Princeton man had large ears with hair protruding. He'd written a book about Amundsen and Scott. Over his shoulder I saw the strange girl standing in a corner and sensed—there is no defense or real explanation for this—that it was very important I not let her leave the room without speaking to her.

What I hate is that memory blurs, that it really is impossible to reconstruct things, which is what makes history an impossible science and my attempt to locate the true stirrings going on in me that day in May 1979 a botch. Historians (and almost no one else) are familiar with the word "stochastic"—that is, proceeding by guesswork—and that is what I am doing here. I could make myself the hero and force memory to give up evidence that I was bold, that I told the Princeton man to wait, but if I did that (and I honestly can't remember) I suspect I was waylaid, caught by someone else I needed to talk to, because Gina remembers it differently, remembers waiting patiently for me to be done with the congratulatory conversations. In her mind, she had composed an introduction, never intended to be spoken. "Thank you for this afternoon. There's no real reason for me to be here, I'm actually missing an important class, but I found the flyer advertising this in my handbag and I have no idea how it got there. Someone put it there, and that must mean something. Or else I took it down off a wall somewhere and forgot all about it, and that probably means something, too. But really I'm here because I'm lost in my life, my wrists still hurt because a man tied me to a pair of bedposts this past weekend and then abandoned me for four hours. I'm full of self-loathing and disgust, and you look like the purest, sweetest thing I've seen in about a million years, so do you want to be my boyfriend?"

That is how Gina remembers it, standing in that buzzing room and making note of what history people were like, how they were different from law people, having nothing to say to anyone but wanting very much to talk to me.

In this, in Gina's view, I am, for the fourth time, the passive receiver of a woman's sexual attention (Karen Meola: "Why don't you come out, Luca?"; Barbara Greene, over lunch, in the teacher's room: "We should date"; Abby Kassell, in this identical room, her voice barely above a whisper: "It'd be better to take a walk, don't you think?"), and I don't like that reading, I want instead to see myself for once as the aggressor, so in the text of my own mind I alter things sometimes.

At a certain point, we were close to each other. I remember that much. I was talking to a young man in the program, and I couldn't get away from him; I recall for an instant hating him, for his words and his greasy hair and his pretentious little goatee, and where had such a strong emotion come from in me? I wanted to hit him, to put him out, so I could walk, take the two or three steps to where the strange girl was. She mustn't be allowed to leave.

And then, at the end of a sequence neither of us can construct with any confidence, it was achieved. I was standing before her. She became shy. I was wearing a quizzical expression, Gina says, a pained expression.

The words that came out of my mouth were: "What are you doing here?"

She laughed, they were so inappropriate. She also noted the tone, as if we already knew each other well, and I were scolding her for missing the important class.

"I have no idea," she said, and finally looked directly into my eyes, and decided (she claims) that it would happen.

I do know I put down my cup of wine, and it was like letting go of an allegiance I had assumed would sustain me for the rest of my life. I remember blinking at that moment and thinking I should go and see how the Princeton man was doing.

"Who are you?" I asked.

She told me. And that she was a law student. Something began to trouble me.

Gina claims I said the word "Okay," as if I were taking on, half against my will, a difficult assignment.

Sometimes, in recognition of the fact that a life can always go two distinctly different ways, I construct a kind of anti-afternoon, the one I didn't participate in. It was a May afternoon, 5 or 5:30. The waiters at the Moon Palace, who knew Robert Bruner well, would have been expecting him and three guests. He was concerned at the awkwardness of including the woman from Wesleyan, who was there only to let the Princeton man know he would have to fight for me. We would have eaten that dish Robert Bruner always insisted on ordering, the hot pot, Meat Sizzling Rice. The steam would have risen on our faces. Academia.

Instead, we slipped away. I like those three words, like the look of them on the page. They bring something back to me, May in New York, 1979, *The China Syndrome* was playing at the movies. We slipped away. I think I had only the intention of walking her home, then returning, doing my duty, going to dinner, perhaps making an appointment to meet her later. Was I cheating on Abby Kassell? Abby had left immediately after the reading (to see me get that much attention was difficult for her). To think how little she finally mattered was to see how wafer-thin that relationship, my rock and my foundation, had come to seem.

At the door of Gina's building, I said something. Neither of us remembers what. There was white sunlight on the river, a tanker passing. I had never felt so young, so much a boy, so excited about anything. But I had to get back. Until, suddenly, I thought: *Why?* And back to what? In an instant, it had come to seem a prison, the train ride from Princeton to New York an interminable distance, the man with the hair growing out of his ears and his book about Amundsen and Scott a man I didn't want to know. Even Robert Bruner, for whom I felt affection, came to seem, in that moment, an impediment.

Gina Abrams's apartment was different from Abby Kassell's. Immediately, I sensed money, taste, a kind of social confidence foreign to me. It was in the long block of brownstones on 116th that curves slightly as it approaches Riverside. I sat on a pale orange sofa, staring at the Paul Davis poster for *Threepenny Opera* she had hanging on one wall. Also, some smaller things, photographs, colored glass perfume bottles on a table, the light just beginning to clarify after the late-afternoon diffusion. In the little kitchen, she poured something, and stood in the doorway. I knew I didn't want to leave, this was perfect. "You need to get back, don't you?" she said. "Your big, amazing future." I smiled. She could save me if she wanted. There was some doubt that she felt as intensely as I did.

The rest is more predictable. The kissing. You maybe only kiss in a certain manner when you feel invisible hands dragging you away, the sinking feeling that you belong elsewhere, that what you are doing is transgression, taboo. But the more I kissed her, the more I realized I didn't want the life I had mapped out for myself, and were I to go back now to face an angry Robert Bruner and a miffed Princeton historian, I knew I lacked the will to charm them back into quiescence. We made love without protection, a thing I had never done before. With Abby Kassell, I had always had to wait for her to go in and put in the diaphragm, and Barbara Greene had been a fanatic for condoms.

But Gina Abrams had only pulled me down, become small, buried her head against my chest, made sounds I had not heard before. Going into her, a subterranean world opened to me. I recognized it, while realizing that I had not been there before.

Afterward, I stayed in Gina's body a long time. At any moment, I thought, we would both realize this was all ridiculous, except that moment never came.

As for the rest, I did not call Robert Bruner or the man from Princeton to apologize. I did not go back to my apartment until Gina suggested I might need different clothes, a change of underwear. It had been three days, four. She worried about the classes she was missing, went to one, left in the middle, came back to me. "This is better," she said.

Another time, one night when she got scared, she touched my face. "Don't you want what you were working toward?"

"No," I answered.

"Then what were you doing it for?"

"I didn't know what else there was. I didn't know what else to do." She nestled against me. "But it was brilliant."

I saw it drifting away, *Happiness in the American Cinema*, one of the minor achievements of New York culture, slipping into a crack, down a drainpipe. You had to hold things up if they were going to survive, and I had no interest. When I returned to my apartment, the landlord said they'd had to break in, they'd thought I'd come home and killed myself.

"No," I said, and quietly packed, and paid the last month's rent. (The lease was up in July.) What furniture I had I put on the sidewalk for anyone to take. It was gone in two days. I moved into Gina's apartment. A bookstore on West Eighty-ninth Street hired me part-time. Gina went on probation for missing classes. Her father called, having heard, angry.

There was also the ex-boyfriend, Neville Barnes, the one who had tied her wrists to the bedposts and gone to see, as it turned out, *The Deer Hunter*. Where, here? "No, we went away." He came to the apartment after I had moved in, and she refused to open the door. He came again, banging. Gina had changed her locks after the wrist-tying incident, but he still had the key to the building's front door. The second time he came, I opened the door and imposed myself between him and Gina. I was no tough guy, but I knew this tall, effete-looking man would not be able to land much of a punch. He went away, cursing, and Gina was afraid to go out after that, for fear that he would stalk her.

Her affection for me seemed to increase with every intrusion of Neville Barnes.

But you cannot live forever on gratitude, on the cusp of changed lives. Sometimes I felt an urge to hold the light itself, the light on the Hudson outside Gina's window, because it was this light—light of this exact quality and depth—that was our substance. I had not been aware before this that May's light has a character different from June's, and July's is altogether heavier and denser, that to approach a woman in that atmosphere requires a different pitch, a developed skill, that love and the maintenance of love demands an outfielder's sensitivity to the texture of air.

We held off a long time telling each other our stories. You can be stupid for a while, I've found. Life will allow it. You can believe the narrative will read: *A boy and a girl found each other in a dark wood*, and that the whole peopled past—stepmothers, witches, huntsmen—has left one's innocence essentially untouched. Innocence? Boy? I was twenty-nine years old. There is no excuse, finally, for what happened.

Gina bent to her father's will, went home for the summer, clerked for a judge in Buffalo, the circuit court of appeals. Weekends, she came to me, loaded down with work. "I missed your body," she said. Magic words. All week I prepared, working in the bookstore, running endless miles in the park, ten, fourteen, wanting always to masturbate but not, the cold showers, the solitary meals, books. July, August. "Who were you, before this, before now?" I made up a story composed of actual things that had happened, leaving out others. It wasn't such an unusual life, after all: college, high school teaching, graduate school. "Who were your girlfriends?" There were names, stories I could tell, sentences to cover and excuse whole areas of the past. "In college I was inhibited." "Ever gotten anyone pregnant?" she wanted to know. "No." On the Upper West Side, I nearly ran into Robert Bruner once; he was buying bananas in one of the Korean markets. Even in summer, he wore long pants, a dress shirt. I was in my running clothes, resplendent with sweat, in the body I had grown to love. I did not approach, watched him pay, his slightly squashed head, his body with its aging man's vigor, wondered what the night had been, after I had abandoned him. Had they gone to the Moon Palace anyway? A single letter had arrived, forwarded to Gina's address. "I have never been so disappointed . . ." But on upper Broadway, as I watched him take his bag of bananas from the clerk, I felt the summer wind on my legs, the hairs standing out, a certain magnificence of being I might never have known existed.

Still, there were the stories that waited to be told. "My parents are divorced" was all I had said to Gina. Where my mother lived, my father in New Hampshire. I kept Bob Painter at the periphery, unmentioned.

Neither could Gina quite tell me about the marks on her wrists. We agreed to leave areas untouched. There was time to get to them. Once I leaned to kiss those marks and she pulled me away. "No." "So who *was* this Neville Barnes?" I asked. "Why were you with him?" Questions came at dusk, postcoital, we lay on the bed. It was an unusually hot summer. "Not yet," she'd answer.

In the great old fairy tales, there is a secret held, the hero or hero-

ine goes to huge lengths to cover it. "I cannot spin straw into gold. A little man comes and does it for me" is a pair of sentences to save or destroy
a marriage, but they are not said somehow. Until, finally, a question is
posed at dusk, which ones feels (foolishly) brave enough to answer.

"So where does your father live, exactly?" Gina asked. "Tell me
about his life."

"He owns an inn," I said. "He lives [I had decided to say it, because
why not?] with another man."

I waited a moment for this to register. Then I named the town.

Beside me, Gina stiffened somewhat. A silence followed.

"What is it?" I asked finally.

She asked me to repeat the name of the town.

"Please describe your father," she said.

I did. She was, for a moment, relieved, then seemed frightened
again.

"I'm going for a walk. Don't follow, okay?"

She got up, dressed, went outside. I lay on the bed, waiting. Finally,
after more than an hour had gone by, I went to find her, seeking her in
our usual haunts—the edge of the park, the West End, the bookstores.
When I came back to the apartment, she was at the table, smoking, a
habit she reserved for certain highly charged situations.

"All right," she said, letting out a nervous rush of air. Watching her
sitting there, hunched and still, I had a presentiment of what it would be
like to not love her anymore, to see her in time and space, an arbitrary
figure on whom I had only imposed things.

"Here's the explanation, then," she said, her voice cracking. I put
the cigarette out for her.

On the weekend before my reading, she and Neville Barnes had
rented a car. It was near the end of the semester, they were sick of law,
sick of torts, sick of their professors and of each other. Sensing the end
of the relationship, they decided to go somewhere to save or destroy
it. In the story Gina told me, I could sense her holding something
back, something about her feelings for Neville, whom she described as
evil, unbearable. They drove as far as they could, beyond New York,
into Vermont, New Hampshire, no reservations anywhere, stopped to
eat, to fight. "The Dance of Death," Gina said with slightly exaggerated
irony, and closed her eyes, and tried to light another cigarette.

Finally, they found a hotel. An inn. They had lost, by then, any sense of reserve: fought on the stairs, in the room, didn't care who heard them, who knew; what they said was unfiltered. The proprietors, alerted by the other guests, had had to ask them to quiet down. And because sex was a part of their fighting, the sex was loud and unrestrained as well, cruel, expressive, a thing to draw blood. She closed her eyes when she said such things, but she kept the final details shrouded. I had to guess.

The next day, things seemed calmer. Perhaps they could reasonably allow things to die. She believed it. Even Neville Barnes could be convinced to stop before they reached the precipice. In the afternoon, they started what she referred to as friendly sex. Neville asked if he might tie her up. Yes, all right. It seemed safe enough. It had happened before, was an occasional thing with them. He finished and then got up and dressed. "Where are you going?" Without untying her, he left the room. Nearly four hours later, he came back. *The Deer Hunter* was a very good movie, he said, and described it. She'd peed in bed. She lay in squalor. They shouted, worse than before. Deep into the night. She demanded they leave, he drive her back to New York. He hit her. To survive, she agreed to stay with him. In the morning, they left.

"You understand," she said.

"It was my father's inn."

"Yes."

I stared at her hands on the table. At first, it seemed to matter more to her than to me, and I thought there had to be things she was leaving out, depths to the humiliation she would undergo were she to see my father again. But why should that happen? My father was hardly a part of my life anymore. Still, when I moved to hold her, to reassure her, I felt something I had not felt before, a nimbus surrounding her body that separated it from mine, distrust, a vague sense of disgust I tried to fight, as though Gina had shit on the floor and I had to see it, had to confront her body as an ordinary human receptacle.

This feeling hovered over me. I did not know how to explore it, so it came to have a power it might not otherwise have had. It wasn't until we went to bed that night that one of us thought to say the obvious: the flyer that had mysteriously appeared in Gina's bag after that weekend had been put there by my father. Or else by Bob. I had sent it to my father, knowing he wouldn't come.

It changed things. Just as the words "We slipped away," written on a page, allude for me to a host of other things, so do those words, "It changed things." Gina went back to her job in Buffalo, and I continued my rituals. For a time, I assumed we would absorb this, it would soon cease to matter. But there is only a short, enchanted period when everything you do seems held and protected in God's palm, as it were, and then you understand, again, it is all a chaos.

In August, Gina arrived one weekend with the news that she was pregnant. Except that it wasn't precisely news. She'd known for weeks, had kept it from me, not judging it, from week to week, the proper time to tell me. When an idyll comes crashing down, it crashes entirely. We barely discussed it. "Is that why you wanted to know if I'd ever gotten anyone pregnant?" "Yes, that was when I first suspected." There seemed only one way to go with it, and Gina said she was just checking. "Lest you had this wild desire, I mean, to be a father." I had no such wild desire. It was confusing, more than anything; my reaction was annoyance, like it distracted us from the thing we *should* have been talking about. Which was what? The unspoken betrayal of having chosen, out of all the places in New Hampshire, my father's inn? But then we never would have met, I'd be sleeping with Abby Kassell, going to the movies, checking out apartments in Princeton. So if not that, what was I angry at Gina for? Having had a former boyfriend, a taste for rough sex? Was that the issue?

Gina arranged for an abortion. A friend told her about a clinic on the Upper East Side. On the following Saturday, we sat with other couples, all of whom seemed to be in the midst of a fight, or else entirely unknown to one another. Pregnancy seemed a huge, inexplicable accident, not the result of effort but a rock dropped from a building, onto arbitrary victims. They took Gina into a room and sent her out in fifteen minutes. She'd gone pale and, seeing me, shook her head. "I'll tell you in the cab," she said, and pulled me out of there.

In the cab, Gina fell into a fit of sobbing. Holding her, I saw myself walking solitary across the green Princeton campus, composing my lectures. That pristine life seemed, at least in comparison, holy and simple and good. I'd had no right, really, to get myself involved in the world of real emotion. "It's longer than I thought," she said. "Second trimester. Fourteen weeks at least, they said. They couldn't do it there."

Abby Kassell, I was certain, would have had a completed pregnancy. The History Department at Princeton would have sent flowers. I'd have held my son or daughter, and covered the estrangement in Abby's face, chalking it up to exhaustion. I'd have announced the birth, shyly, and with suitable male embarrassment, in my classes.

Fourteen weeks. Fourteen weeks put us beyond May 7, the day we met. Fourteen weeks put us back in the realm of Neville Barnes.

About this, as about the next step, we were dispassionate. We called the hospital in upper Manhattan the clinic had suggested, and made another appointment for the following week.

She would not stay overnight, but the procedure was radical enough that Gina required, afterward, several hours' bed rest. From a bodega in the neighborhood I had bought a box of goodies: cream puffs, cannolis, which sat, untouched, at the foot of the bed.

Summer was winding down. Soon Gina's law classes would begin again. Her father had arranged things so that she would not be penalized for the transgressions, the missed classes, of spring. Having Gina back for the summer, he had asserted himself. I, the man living in her apartment, had become a villainous figure, to be referred to only in whispers, at the dinner table in Buffalo. They had liked Neville Barnes, both her parents had, very much actually.

Gina, on the bed, sipping from a cup of ice through a straw (they'd had to use anesthetic for a second-trimester abortion), was telling me about the first blow job she'd ever given a boy. She'd been fourteen years old, it had happened behind the junior high school, his name was Alex Bergeron. "I want you to know this about me," Gina said, as if there was, in fact, much more to know. The decade-old blow job she referred to as an indication of "my dark side," which had appeared early. Alex Bergeron had been followed by others. How many, exactly? Well, she answered, she could remember walking with her father one Saturday, early in high school, on the bike path near their house, the two of them coming upon the spray-painted announcement, "Gina Abrams gives good head." This was not her first abortion. No, not her second, either.

And how did I react exactly? It may be hard to explain how, in spite of the evidence of Gina's sexual expertise and the way, little by little, bits of her sexual past had come to me before, I had still clung to something essentially innocent about our pairing. The conditions of love seemed caught up in a fiction: the notion that nothing important in the past had preceded Gina's coming into the room to hear me read. Intuitively she had understood this, understood my particular need, had tailored things so that I should not know too much about where she had been before.

Here then was something deliberate on her part: an attempt to move us a step into the real world, to test what was possible.

Well, so what? a part of me wanted to say in response to her confession. At the same time, the word "whore" appeared, as if from somewhere in the past, a boyish layer uncovered. I brushed it away, yet it was real. It explained Gina.

The irony was that I still clung to my own deception: I had never told her about Eric Davenport. Though that little affair ought to have evaporated by then, I had found, over time, that the only preparation for the intensity of my time with Gina had been those nights with Eric. Yet I had chosen, deliberately, to present myself to Gina as something simpler than I was.

I could have met her then, could have shared my own past as a kind of tit for tat, and we might then have begun to conduct our relationship along difficult, honest lines. It was what she wanted, I believed.

But there were words I still couldn't manage to say. I hadn't the courage. *Eric hadn't mattered*, I'd convinced myself. So a part of me stepped away that night, into a shadowy place. I stayed physically, but a part of me went away, and that split remained, until the night when sex began to fail us as a balm.

5

Gina did, in the end, decide to come with me to Provincetown. "Rather than stay home alone," she said, as if she were giving away nothing. "I'll just work if I stay here. I could use a little sun." But there was no promise of anything beyond company, and I began to get the feeling, in the three weeks between our coitus interruptus and the trip, that I had to prepare myself. We had not had sex in those three weeks, nor did Gina show the slightest inclination or desire. With my eyes even the slightest bit open, it became clear that Gina was getting ready to make a move.

So I made a plan that, even as I was going about the business of setting it in motion, struck me as among the most peculiar instinctual actions of my life. I invited both my parents to dinner in Provincetown Saturday night. They hadn't eaten together in thirty years, as far as I knew; hadn't even been in the same room since our wedding. I couldn't begin to guess what it would be like to place them together again. It was as easy to believe they would be merely polite to one another as to imagine rage and recrimination emanating from the table at Sal's, the restaurant I'd chosen. At the same time, I understood that desperation sometimes incites an action that turns out to be precisely right. Whatever the results of this dinner, I knew the time had come to bring them together again.

It had taken little effort to convince my mother to come. Of course I couldn't tell her my father would be there as well. That was the surprise I felt guiltless enough to inflict. Her access to Provincetown—to travel itself—was still through Emma's big, reliable Lincoln. When I proposed the Provincetown trip, her response was what I expected. "I'll see," she said, "if Emma wants to come."

But calling Emma, which I told her I would do, meant risking an uncomfortable situation. My cousin George might answer the phone. He was living with his mother, as he had been for nearly twenty years.

Uncle John had died seven years before, in 1985. He'd died while still a youngish man (sixty-three), and the fact that George had come, and remained, home was not, in my mind, unconnected to his death. After his return from Vietnam, George had done a number of hopeful things. There'd been a brief marriage (a little girl had come out of that union), and he'd gone to work with Bobby, who'd begun a modest entrepreneurial life of his own by taking over part ownership of the garage where he'd been working since high school. In the meantime, John went on with his committees, his Heart Fund dinners; the appearance of the motorcycles had not impeded his social progress, as he'd once believed it would.

"They're going to ask us to move," John had said, on the day of George's party, with the aunts and uncles all in attendance. Then he'd thrown down his fork, as if the worry had just come over him, like a spasm. "This is not the kind of neighborhood that can tolerate this sort of thing. People don't move up here so they can put up with motorcycles, for Christ's sake." From outside then, I remembered, we could hear their noise.

Of course motorcycles were never the issue. Something else was. Drugs, I suppose, and the whole burgeoning late sixties world into which the returning, rudderless George had collapsed. When it became clear that the neighbors weren't going to ostracize John, it was largely because the other sons and daughters of the neighborhood had begun to experience troubles of their own. A Meola boy was kicked out of college for possession of an illegal substance. One of the DeMarco sons landed, a bit later, in jail. The neighbors circled their wagons and sipped their drinks and buried their errant children. John might have done the same thing.

George came home eventually, left his marriage and the garage and moved into his old room, slipped into a state that could be referred to only in the vaguest terms. No one had an actual name for what had happened to George. Emma referred to him as a zombie; his father, at least in public, referred to him hardly at all. John had every reason to write off his elder son as a bad job of work and know that, gazing across the golf links at Joe Meola or Doc Semenza, he would receive sympathy and shared regret. But that was not the choice John made, though even describing it that way, as a choice, is missing the point.

Sometime in the mid-seventies, John's hair started to grow. A lot of men his age, taking up a fashion late, let that happen, sported mustaches and sideburns; the pictures are embarrassing to look at now. John's letting his hair grow did not seem that sort of deliberate affectation. He suddenly did not care anymore to be the polished, good-smelling man in a suit. His trucking firm continued to prosper—at least as well as it needed to; there was no indication that John was neglecting business. But to see him in his yard on a summer night in the years after George came home (I continued to make a traverse through the Hill, to visit him, during the time when I lived with my mother and taught high school) was to see a man physically unraveling in the smallest but surest way. The tufts of hair growing over his collar, over the tops of his ears, were like the growth at the side of a house that seems at first the result of the owner's loose, laissez-faire attitude, but that later begin to do real damage. That was the effect: if John had been a house, you would have suspected him of rot. In certain lights, you might even begin to believe the house was tilting toward earth.

In the most unexpected of all his actions in those years, John began taking adult education classes, given at night at the high school. He became embarrassed by his own failure to have earned a high school diploma, so he took matters into his own hands. He told me once, in the second or third year of these classes, that he was keeping a notebook of his dreams ("As soon as I wake up in the morning, I go right to the tablet, write them down. Instructor's orders").

John drove George to a clinic two afternoons a week, a bit of information that filtered down to me. The life inside their house in those years became unimaginable. Emma and my mother drew closer to one another; I often found Emma at our table when I got home from teaching, she and my mother commiserating over tea and pecan sandies. "He writes down his dreams," I heard once, from a room away, Emma speaking as though that sentence could be made somehow to line up with the regulated past. "John drives George to the clinic two days a week" was another one of those sentences. "What clinic?" I once asked my mother, but she only shrugged. They were women, she and her sisters, bred to accommodate the tragic detail. John had put up a long fight against falling into the sort of life where such details were the expected thing. Now all that had changed. He and the other men of the neighborhood took up bocce. The grand transfiguration they had expected had not occurred. In the eighties, one by one, they began to die.

That was what had happened to the Hill. The golden age of the middle sixties, the age of the parties, the colored lanterns, the handsome sleek sons, all of this had seemed a prelude to something. It had turned out, instead, to be their high point, the brief sunlit pocket of time before another set of questions emerged: How were the sons to take this a step further? Those questions, when they were answered at all, were answered in the negative. Nothing at all, it turned out, was to come after them.

The daughters might have offered some solace. Brenda, John's little girl born in the high-water year of 1962, was in law school when John died, a fact that ought to have cheered John more than it had. George was the wound; that was all there was to it. I had visited George, once or twice, sat across the kitchen counter from him while Emma, puttering, serving, had tried to force conversation. George had taken to looking at me strangely, waiting for me to ask the questions, which he would answer with one or two words, then wait for the next.

As for John, it was a brain tumor that got him, though it took him a year to die. Visiting him in the hospital, I listened to the slurred, barely comprehensible words, felt the frantic tugs at my sleeve, witnessed John's suddenly shameless nakedness (the johnny kept riding up, Emma or Bobby, in attendance, would try to pull it down, but then it would ride up again). There was a certain phrase he kept repeating, which it took me years to figure out. "Remanwa," he would say, then pause, lick his lips, working up the energy for the rest, "Dowstre." It came to me only after he was dead what he'd been trying to say: "Remember the walks down the street."

Yes. I remembered.

"Provincetown?" Emma said when I called (I'd been lucky; George hadn't picked up the phone). "Oh sure, we love to go there. But we have to be careful, keep her away from you-know-who."

"You-know-who" had by then become the proprietor of a dock-side apartment complex on upper Commercial Street in Provincetown, called Captain Lou's. On a shingle that hung outside the complex, an artist had captured my father in nautical gear: a captain's hat, a peacoat, his enlarged features gazing invitingly at those who sought "Rooms. Efficiencies." That shingle made him appear something of a local wag, though I knew he kept mostly to himself and considered the summer Provincetown crowd a little wild for his tastes. He had by then himself become a kind of widow. Bob had died a year after John, in 1986 (his liver, drinking, a surprise). My father had held on to the inn less than a year after Bob's death, then sold it to the two chefs who had started a successful restaurant on the premises. He'd come to Provincetown for what he referred to as a semi-retirement. Like everything else my father touched, Captain Lou's was apparently an enormous success, with a long waiting list in the summer. From time to time, Gina and I visited him in his apartment, which looked directly out onto the water and had a small deck attached. The outside of Captain Lou's was decorated by a string of colored lanterns, and these hung from the deck, so that at night, sitting with him in his stark rooms, with their white walls (he had never been much for interior decoration), there was the glow of red and green and yellow lights.

For some reason I did not think it would take much convincing to get my father to have dinner with my mother. So I was taken aback when, on the phone, he seemed resistant to the idea.

"Why on earth would you want to do that?" he asked.

"I don't know," I answered. "When's it going to happen if not now?"

"Who says it has to happen?"

I waited so long to respond, he finally had to say, "Luca, you there?"

"I'm here."

"Everything okay?"

"Yes."

"Everything all right with the marriage?"

"Things are fine."

"Good. So why are you planning this dinner?"

The words I forced out—"I'm getting to the age where I need some answers"—were true enough, but balder than anything my father and I were used to. He seemed to be playing with them afterward, a long time, in silence. "What kind of answers? Maybe we could deal with this without involving an old woman who's going to find this, I would imagine, a bit difficult."

"And you," I asked, "you won't find it difficult?"

"I know how to be polite." He chuckled under his breath. "Let's just say a lifetime's worth of learning how to absent myself in certain situations has taught me a thing or two."

I allowed that. I even let him think about it. I knew very well this was not a man who could be coerced into doing things he didn't want to do. I couldn't tell him, either, why it was so important.

"Listen, I think Mom can take it. I honestly do."

He listened, his low murmur giving rise to a question. "What kind of woman has your mother turned into?" It had come out sounding musing, interested, and I thought the thing to do was try to lead him toward the answer, rather than give it.

"Wouldn't you like to find out?"

"Oh God, I hate people who answer questions with questions."

I imagined his face then, the large, caricatured face painted on the shingle of Captain Lou's, peering into the small world my mother inhabited: Hobbs Road with its made beds, its tidy kitchen, its framed photographs of Gina and me, in our seventies haircuts, on our wedding day. It didn't seem fair, mismatching them this way.

"So what I'm hearing is, you'll do this."

"When did you hear that? Did I miss something?"

But then he laughed, and let me know it was okay.

"Depends on where we're going," he said. "And who's paying."

"I'm paying."

"On a schoolteacher's salary?"

"My wife's a lawyer. Did you forget that?"

"No, I don't forget. How *is* Gina?" he asked, as if his voice were putting on a big smile. As if, too (I couldn't ever help but think this), there were aspects of that long-ago weekend when Gina had washed up at the inn that I still didn't know.

"I want a day at the beach," Gina announced, when we were driving to Provincetown. She adjusted her sunglasses, her face behind them appearing a little too stern. "As if there were no deep purpose for this trip," she added.

"You can have all that," I said. I reached to turn on the radio. Gina looked at my hand, while I was doing that, and then, while I was driving, I could tell she was watching me, studying my face. The marvel was, I had no idea anymore what she thought. I wondered if I were still handsome to her. I wondered if she saw my face at all, or something else, something that had come to cover my face and absorb it, a succubus with the name "husband."

Because you never know. One time, Gina and I were making love, she was on top, and I must have been only half hard, I slipped out of her. I watched her going on a few seconds, as if she were oblivious, until I said, "Gina. Gina, wait, I'm not even in you," and she looked at me and started to laugh. "I didn't even notice," she said, and laughed some more, and that moment always seemed, afterward, to speak volumes about the shifting sands of being in and out of love. When you're loved, you hardly have to be there at all, even your absence fills up a space, but when you're not loved, you become too big, just being your normal size turns you into an unbearable weight for the other person. Sometimes, those days, those days of the withdrawal of her affection, I was tormented by that small insight. I felt too big.

We arrived at Race Point when it was still late morning. In June there are still not many people on the beach. It was windy, no one was in the water, the lifeguard entertained himself by talking with two young women. There were families, and couples: older couples, too, gray-haired men who sat, fully clothed, with their shoes off and their toes dug deep in the sand. I was afraid that Helen Weston might come early, she might very well be part of one of these older couples—and seeing me, she might want to come over and talk. I didn't want that, wanted this time alone with Gina, so I moved us toward the end of the beach nearer the lighthouse, the end opposite where we were to meet her. We lay out our blanket and Gina undressed. She had on a new black bathing suit, and when I looked at it she gazed back at me the way she might look at a man on another blanket, a man she knew was staring at her with interest, as if to let him know she accepted the interest, was unfazed by it, and wished in no way to encourage it.

Then she lay down on her belly and closed her eyes. The paperback book she was reading—I remember the pale blue of the cover and the fuzziness of the photograph, but not the title; they all blurred together, Gina's titles (words like "water" and "women," "moon" and "night" and "stone" seemed always to crop up; later on, she became a big fan of Oprah's selections). I remember knowing she wasn't going to read it, she was going to let it lie beside her because she had some other, deeper desire to probe. It was up to me to sit up and notice the other people on blankets, to watch the little kids and mark the absence of Gina's usual ironic comments, which she was fond of making when we were on a beach like this. "Tick tick tick," she would sometimes say, when the two of us caught ourselves watching children, and hearing her say that, hearing her lay a salve of irony on her wound, always made me feel safer.

An hour or so after we got to the beach, Gina turned over onto her back (that I write about this gesture as I would about a larger event says a great deal about the lassitude of that day). Her small behind lifted up for a moment, turned, and then settled. I just stared at her in a distracted way, my balls so full they had almost ceased to exist, but something going on in them with every subtle move of her body. At the seams of Gina's suit, the ends of her pubic hairs showed a bit. They are dark and entirely absent of the reddish tints in her hair. What I did was I traced them where they fell out of her suit. There was no one close enough to make us embarrassed by this. I just slowly traced them with one finger and then—I wasn't sure why—I wet my finger and went on tracing them, just to see if she would stop me. While I was doing this, I looked down the beach at the water and tried to imagine Andrew Weston's ashes in the air. Or better—because I still could not imagine Andrew as dead— as *ashes*—I saw him looking at us. He was here, if he was anywhere, and I saw him regarding Luca Carcera, his boyhood friend, in this extremely odd moment of his marriage, and just shaking his head. What Andrew Weston would believe—I could see this with utter clarity—was that all the unhappiness of my marriage, all the pain I had ever caused Gina, arose out of the simple fact that I'd never been able to admit to myself that I was like him. Maybe this was unfair to the complexity of Andrew Weston's mind, but I saw it nonetheless. And as these thoughts came to a head, I found my finger, as if obeying a will of its own, going deeper inside Gina's suit until it reached the place where she gave way, and then, going even deeper, sought the depth at which her wetness began.

"Stop," she said.

"Why?" I asked.

She squeezed down so that my finger was forced out. I spent a moment staring down at her and then by instinct sniffed my finger and got that intoxicating whiff, and wondered if I was smelling it for the last time. Then I lay beside her and covered my face.

"Don't you miss it?" I asked Gina after a couple of minutes had gone by.

She did not look at me to answer. "That's the funny thing. I don't."

"You don't need it anymore?"

She paused a moment. "Yes. You've cured me of my old dark need."

She shifted, stared into the sun. "Maybe I need it different, Luca." She stopped again, to consider her words. "I'm just seeing us as this old couple who allowed this period of their lives to become . . . their lives." She pulled her suit down, to discourage further forays on my part. Her bush made a soft, spongy mound under the suit that I couldn't take my eyes off of. "I know I can't do that, that's all."

I allowed the pause to absorb the weight of what that last sentence implied.

"And what happens to me?"

She removed her sunglasses to answer. "I have no idea."

The look that followed was one of her looks, thick with invitation and regret, as if she knew, always, how to load her looks with the weight of our history. I'm sure Gina thought I would suffer deeply after our parting, suffer like an animal, completely unaware of why things had ended. The phrase she sometimes used to describe me was "willful stupidity."

"Why are we here this weekend, Luca?" she asked.

"I told you. Andrew's mother."

There followed another meaningful look, as if she knew better than I why we were here, but would wait for me to catch up with her.

"No. There's always a scheme. Always a bigger plan. A way of getting at the past." She paused. "Your parents. I mean, why would anyone who wanted to save his marriage do something like this—force his wife to sit through dinner with his parents?"

"Nobody's forcing you."

"No? What am I supposed to do? Sit in the motel room while you go out?"

"I thought seeing them together might tell me something."

That was where I stopped. There was more to it, of course. It wasn't lost on me that I was married now twelve years, just short of the time it had taken my father to realize he had to get out of his own marriage. Yet the mystery—the unanswered question, could he have stayed?—was one I didn't know any other way of getting the answer to, short of forcing them together.

"Will they know we're thinking about splitting up?" Gina asked.

"Who says we're thinking that?"

She chose not to find that funny.

"I don't know. Maybe. Sometimes I think they both know a lot more about me than I've given them credit for."

"But of course we won't talk about it."

"Of course not."

A line hardened in her forehead, her old anger at my family's close-mouthedness about our history. I smoothed it out.

"One thing I want to ask him," I said, "is why he put that flyer in your bag. That's the thing I've never asked him, and I'd like to."

The line in her forehead, which I'd managed to make disappear, returned.

"Why are you doing that?"

"It's time."

"Please don't."

"I won't ask him when you're there."

"Just don't. Okay? Spare me that."

She sat up. She seemed to be thinking something over. It bothered her much more than I'd have guessed.

"Why not?" I asked. "Isn't this a step in the right direction? Talking about stuff? Getting it out?"

"But why about *that*? Don't you understand this is something you should maybe leave alone?"

"Why?"

I saw her reversing direction, a small deflection that made me intensely curious: why should I leave it alone?

"What's he going to tell you, that he thought we *belonged* together? It's all accidental. Just get that. He did some spur of the moment thing, and it worked. For a while. It could have gone on working if you hadn't been so afraid."

She stared into me a moment, angry now, but anger seemed an improvement on the indifference with which she'd been treating me the last few weeks. "I despair of what's going to happen to you, but I keep convincing myself it's not my responsibility."

She lifted one hand to scratch her forehead, turned away from me to stare into the sand.

Some mysterious thought seemed to overtake her. She finally looked up and said, "I'm going in."

She threw off her sunglasses and half-ran down to the water.

A few moments later, I could see her head bobbing under the water, then lifting up in her steady crawl. I had the feeling I'd received an invitation of some sort, and I watched her carefully, thinking I might join her. Very soon, though, she'd swum out much farther than she should, and seemed to have no intention of stopping, or of coming back to me.

At first, I was not frightened. But as I watched how far out she was going, a small panic started up in me. I ran down to call her in. At the same time, the lifeguard, alerted, blew his whistle. He moved, more quickly than me, down into the water, went in until he was calf-deep. As I moved down to the water, I couldn't help but glance at those calves of his—well-shaped, with a fringe of blond hair to match the hair on his head. Maybe any other man would have noticed them, too, but I had no way of knowing that. That was the problem. Part of me clamped down then, drew inward. I hated when this happened, but it did. It was supposed to be about Gina, and Gina alone. He blew his whistle, and called her in.

I did lift my arm then to signal to Gina, and began to shout her in as well, but a familiar kind of damage had already been done. The gesture felt compromised by the fact that, even as I was making it, I was fighting the onset of another, vaguer set of feelings: was I drawn to this boy, and if that was the case, did it *matter*?

At that moment, as if she were able to sense all this, Gina stopped swimming, treaded water, turned to shore, and stared at where this boy and I were waiting for her. She was too far out for me to be able to read her expression, or for her to read mine, but I couldn't help but feel she must be able to see the depths of my conflict and, seeing clearly, was making up her mind. The only difference now was that I wanted her to see. I had no more desire, or energy, left to hide.

6

On the drive, in June 1986, between the small New Hampshire cemetery where Bob Painter was buried and the gathering of mourners back at the inn, Gina asked me to pull over to the side of the road. "Over here, anywhere," she said.

"Why? Do you need to pee? We're almost there." We had been late arrivals at the cemetery; my father, standing graveside, had gestured to me and then pulled me close and held my hand tightly. Because there was so little to be said there (the crush of mourners, a surprising crowd, my father's need to get back for the reception), I was anxious that we make it back with speed, and not display, by our behavior, any sign of disrespect.

After I had stopped, Gina simply looked around at the woods, which were hot and white with midsummer dust.

"I don't want it to go too fast" was all she said, when she had finally decided to speak. Then she lifted the cloth of her skirt and laid her hand against it.

I looked closely at her. "What's going on with you?"

She glanced at me, and from the way she looked, I could see just how far apart our moods were. I was wearing my one black suit, a maroon tie, and seeing me in this rare guise (we dress casually at the high school) seemed to make her smile.

She pouted her lips, as if to tell me the answer was not so easily expressed.

Gina had not laid eyes on this place since coming here with Neville Barnes, at that point seven years before. She was thirty now. She was still a young woman.

She looked around and sighed with what I read as a kind of contentment, and at a certain point got out of the car and walked a few steps forward before resting against the hood.

I leaned out the window so she could hear me. "Gina, I don't want to be late."

She shook her head, to silence me, to let me know that, for anything like an answer, I would have to wait.

It was, as I say, 1986. When I look back on that time, it's quite natural for me to try to frame it by means of the movies that were playing, but that, I recall, was a lousy summer for movies. The whole mid-eighties, in fact, seem to me a bleached-out, unduly optimistic moment in American history, supported by nothing more than relief at being done with the troublesome sixties and seventies, and the movies may only have been reflecting that. *Ferris Bueller's Day Off, Stand by Me.* What did those movies possibly say to anyone? *Top Gun, The Fly.* No boy, seeing them with his father, could ever use such movies as a way into the dark recesses of the adult world. Gone was any sense of the old American stoicism; we were all expected to be happy now.

Gina and I, six years married then, were probably unwitting exemplars of the national curve. We went through our days as if nothing had been ordained for us but the nurturing of habit. We bought cookbooks and tried things out. We found the cottage in Wellfleet, and, later, we found Andrew Weston. We had our personal jokes, a small encyclopedia of erotic interplay that was ours alone. We were unthreatened because there wasn't anything substantial enough about us, perhaps, to *be* threatened. (Of course that's not true, but we both perceived the threat to be far away.) We were like a new country that had not yet written up a charter, designed a flag, suffered a punishing war. Thus, we could believe—I think we *did* believe—that nothing held us.

Now my wife sat stock-still on the hood of the car, and I sensed something in all of this was about to change, become settled and hard. So I got out of the car and joined her.

She was wearing a small smile. "Do you suppose there's a motel nearby?" she asked.

I folded my arms and leaned back against the car. We had not determined that we were going to stay over, but if we were, I thought it would be polite to stay at the inn.

"What do you want to do in a motel that we can't do at the inn?"

"No," she said, shaking her head almost violently. "I don't want it to happen there. Not there."

"For *what* to happen?"

I hope it's true that every marriage, sometime in its existence, knows a moment like this: a time, not the beginning, but a middle time of renewed wildness, when impulse is given way to, when the presence of another is support enough to do things we would not otherwise give ourselves license to do. Gina shook her head against my words and started running. She ran a long way down the road. She gave way to something. And I simply watched her, amazed as I could sometimes be, a little worried that we would be late for my father's gathering, but knowing intuitively that this—whatever it was—was more important.

She was a long way from me when she turned around. Then she stopped a moment before she began walking again toward me, slowly, like she had all the time in the world. I was aware of the glow on her face, and the soft, relaxed movement of her hips.

When she got to me, she put her face right up to me and kissed me hard. She broke away just long enough to show her delight, then kissed me again. She wrapped her arms around my back and squeezed. She also, for good measure, put her hand down the front of my pants. A couple of cars passed us, but she didn't care. I have learned that when a woman feels this degree of passion, you get out of the way. You let her do what she needs to do.

When she broke away from the second kiss, she rested the top of her head against my chin, and started to laugh.

"Someday," I said, "you're going to tell me what this is all about."

"I'll tell you now," she said. "This has only happened a couple of times to me in my life. It happened while I was watching you at your reading, and it just happened again." She smiled, putting the tiniest of spins on the next thing she would say. "A little bird goes fluttering around my insides."

She looked at me, then bit her lower lip, deciding to be unashamed of those words, freeing herself, if only briefly, from the habit of irony. I thought I was supposed to understand a great deal, based on what she had just told me.

"This little bird?" I asked.

"Okay, so I'm ready," she said, and looked down a little shyly.

Somehow I knew what she meant before she said it.

"I'm ready for that baby we never talk about. My body just told me that. We can talk about this until we're blue in the face, but what my body wants to do is jump you."

"We're at a funeral" was all I could think to say.

"I know, so let's let impulse pass us by, right? There are motels. There are *woods.*"

She gazed up at me with chastening impatience.

"Because *you* want it, right?"

She hesitated, looked at the ground, at the front of my shirt, finally into my eyes. "Yes."

When I didn't say anything, she said, "And you want it, too. I just felt you, so don't tell me your body doesn't want to. And maybe that's the only thing we should be listening to."

"Our bodies."

I looked at her face then, to check for signs of doubt or weakness and, finding none, broke away from her. I went and sat on the edge of the ditch by the side of the road. First I made sure the grass was clean. She came and sat beside me. I had my hands folded and I was looking down at the grass between my legs, not seeing it or thinking anything, really, hoping she would have changed her mind in the brief interim.

"That little run you just took?" I asked. "That was . . . ?"

"That's what I'm not going to tell you for a long time. That's what I won't tell you till we're old."

Gina ultimately knew that I couldn't be forced, so I managed to convince her that if she wanted a baby so badly it could at least wait until that night, until we had paid our respects to Bob, until we were settled safely in the inn, or in that motel she talked about. I meant it, too, at least meant it for the moment, though it scared me. What I actually thought we would do was begin talking about it that night, have a long and interesting discussion of this new thing in our marriage she wanted to introduce. Then we would plan some unspecified date in the future on which we would begin *trying*. We would have years, I guessed, before all this really came to a head. That was what I convinced myself.

Gina meanwhile sat in silence, listening to me, keeping her own counsel, until she finally gave in. And that, right there, her deciding to wait, might very well constitute the turning point in our marriage. If we'd gone ahead and not paid our respects to the dead, if she'd just blasted through toward her own desire, we might have conceived a child, if not that time then another time. I'd have been going to Andrew Weston's ash scattering with a five- or a six-year-old, and though this would have made my torment infinitely more difficult, it would also have made it harder for Gina and me to get to the place where we were so ready to split. Paying our respects to the dead, you could say, has been our undoing, Gina's and mine, or nearly. We sat on the side of the road that day, beside that dusty ditch, and I came up with all the arguments why things could wait, how it would be better to go back to the inn and drink coffee and eat the little sandwiches and shake hands with strangers and join in the ancient rituals of mourning. When I die, I hope some couple coming to mourn me go off and fuck and make a child. That's the advice I'd give them. Go do it. Forget the niceties of grief. I believe that now, but of course, I didn't then.

The inn that day in 1986 (I hadn't seen it in seven years, since before meeting Gina) had gone upscale in a big way. Someone with taste had come along and done the right, subtle things to it. The color, for one, a pale green trimmed in a glossy white. The porch had been extended so that it wrapped all the way around, and didn't merely sit there in the squat, occluded way it had in the old days. These changes were not a total surprise. Two years before, *Yankee* magazine had come and done a spread (my father had sent us multiple copies), featuring pictures of my father and Bob on the long, beautifully tended green lawn that spread all the way down to the lip of the pond. It must have been *Yankee*'s nod to New England gay culture, because Bob and my father, as well as the two chefs whose restaurant now took up half of the ground floor, were un-ambiguously pictured as couples. No spouse showed up in the back-ground, as *Yankee*'s readers might have expected, no gray-haired woman holding a wire whisk and a mixing bowl. It was just two couples, men who seemed happy in each other's company.

Bob appeared big and red-faced, with an expanding gut and a diminishing mane of now mostly gray hair. The sun glinted off his forehead; he appeared to be deflecting it, so that his smile took on a forced, slanting quality. Beside him, my father looked short and trim, his usual impeccable self, a man who could have been at home anywhere, but who had always chosen his homes diffidently, standing somewhat at a distance from them, proud, but able to leave them at a second's notice.

That Bob looked so healthy in those pictures made his death two years later more than a little suspect. My father, informing me over the phone—there had been no prior word of illness—had only sighed when I'd asked, and told me that, all appearances to the contrary, Bob's drinking had never completely stopped, that his liver had finally given out and, as that conversation continued, had hinted at private wounds Bob had allowed to fester for years. "His family," my father had said, and no more.

There were mourners on the porch that day, and on the lawn, mourners within, surrounding my father. Who were they? Unattached men, largely, as if my father and Bob, coming here, had beat the bushes and discovered, among the high school teachers and the retail clerks, the L.L. Bean salesmen and the state college faculty, a gatherable world. Except that it was not so simple. When we went inside, when I found my father surrounded by a crowd of men, he took me aside so that the two of us could have a few moments alone, could survey this room at arm's length.

"AA mostly, what you see," he said. "Bob's crowd."

He was sipping seltzer from a plastic cup, though he had handed me wine. "You'd never know so many drunks could gather in one place. Where's your wife, by the way?"

Gina was at a distance from us, allowing us time alone, still shy of facing my father. She hadn't come with me to greet him. It was a big moment, of course, their first meeting since the wedding. I waited for him to say something more. It was for him, not me, to bring up their former meeting, the whole circumstances of our being together. But he simply gazed at her, his mouth making a small, funny motion, while a heightened interest gathered in his face.

"What do you think?" I asked, indicating Gina with a nod of my head, a nonsense question that grew out of my discomfort.

He looked like he'd been snapped out of a reverie. "Hmm? Where do you *live*?"

"Where do I live? You know that. Williston."

"Yes, but *why*?"

We were not connecting; I waited a moment before saying, "Oh, come on, Dad."

I wasn't sure why my father had chosen this moment to humiliate me for my (to him) disappointing choice of profession, and of life. Maybe, it had come out of his own lack of surety as to where he stood with me. So I changed the subject.

"I'm sorry about Bob."

He gazed at me, and moved an ice cube from one cheek to the other. "No, you're not."

Then he spit the ice cube back into the cup.

"You hated Bob."

"I didn't hate Bob."

He held something back.

"I didn't hate Bob," I repeated, and wished that someone would interrupt us.

"Sure," my father said, and, replacing the sharp look in his eyes with a mild sadness, squeezed my arm and motioned so that my attention was drawn across the room. "See who showed up? Recognize those guys?"

There were three men in a corner, set slightly apart from the others, and I was surprised it took me even thirty seconds to recognize the tallest: the Coke-bottle glasses and Dick York haircut, even if entirely gray now, should have given him away instantly. Wellsie had come, with Eddie Delavoise and Will Monaghan from Vanderbruek. Wellsie was looking at me, too, wearing a smile that showed he recognized me.

"You should go talk to them," my father said. "Relieve them of their misery." He pushed me gently toward them. "Don't worry about me. I'm okay."

"Hey, kid," Wellsie said, once I had worked my way close. "Figured we'd run into you here."

He hit me on the shoulder a couple of times, which was more than

I got from Monaghan and Delavoise, who looked like they barely re-membered me.

"It's great you guys came," I said.

"Ah, we saw the obit in the paper, we figured we'd show our respects." Wellsie adjusted his glasses, surveyed the room once before fixing his gaze back on me.

I thought for an instant of their lives now, scanning the obituaries, cars full of aging men, taking off to funerals like this one.

"Hey, what became of you, what do you do?"

"I'm a teacher. High school."

"You married? Got kiddies?"

"Not yet. Married, yes."

"Late starter, huh? Me, I'm a grandfather. Eddie's a grandfather. We're the old poops now. Hey, where's your wife?"

I turned to find her, and was surprised to see that Gina had joined my father, the two of them now deep in conversation.

Gina was looking not at him, but ahead of herself and facing slightly downward, speaking earnestly, while my father, all close atten-tion, leaned toward her, the better to hear her. You would think—from their positions and the cast of their faces—that she was a woman con-fessing to a worldly, forgiving priest.

"Right there," I said, gesturing. "That's her. You know my father, don't you?"

Wellsie shook his head.

"They lasted together, huh? Him and Painter. All these years."

"Yes."

"Like an old married couple." Wellsie cackled in that familiar man-ner of his, then took in the crowd in the room once more, excited and in-terested where the others only looked suspicious.

"These guys want to go back, but I figure we're here, we're on an interesting anthropological expedition, we should see how the other half lives."

I went away from the simple conversation with Wellsie, something in me released by the sight of my father and Gina together; an anxiety I'd hung on to until now evaporated. Our little scene by the side of the road, now this rapprochement between my father and Gina: things were turning out well at this funeral, better than, in imagining us coming here, I'd ever have thought.

I wanted to join them, but it was clearly *their* moment, not to be intruded upon, so I turned, and when I did, it was Will Monaghan's face I met. I was prepared to love whatever face I'd come upon just then, but that it was Will Monaghan's struck me especially. There was something reflexively hopeful about him that was probably inseparable from the fact that he had never been particularly bright. I knew, for instance, that nowhere in his memory was stored the cigarette he'd smoked with me in 1967, while Wellsie stayed behind and screwed his wife. Or had that even been true? I found I suddenly wanted to call into question all my systems for judging and classifying the past. I wanted to be free of them.

"I remember your wife, Will" was what I said.

His eyes lit up briefly, suspiciously, in a way that assured me of something.

"I remember her coming out when we were all hanging around your pool," I added quickly. "You guys were trying to get me drunk. A long time ago. Nineteen sixty-seven," I added, as if he needed that, as if he needed the year. "She was beautiful."

"You remember that, huh?" Wellsie said, and did an odd thing, gritting his teeth back and forth, and then clicking them. "I hope you don't remember too goddamn much else, 'cause I was full of lies in those days."

I nodded, not wanting to come too close to this, and decided this might be a good time to escape. I told them again it was great that they'd come, and stepped out onto the porch. There were a few people on the porch, no one I knew, so I just held my cup of wine and stood there and looked down at the pond and thought maybe it would be all right. There was laughter to my left. I turned to see two men, and though my father had claimed all these mourners were AA, I knew he'd been covering something, because they were two old, healthy gay men. Why should my father not want to admit to this, that they lived among, and were friends with, such men? It had to be something in me, something he judged still too brittle and unaccepting. These two looked happy to be with one another, so I just watched them and wondered at my own stupidity, how I carried around a sense that if life was to be lived safely, then it had to be lived marginally. Maybe it was time to grow out of this. Maybe. My heart started to beat wildly. I thought of the way Gina had said "a little bird goes fluttering around my insides," and it felt like an accurate description of what was happening to me. I got down, squatted on the porch, and thought: You could be a father, Luca. Instead of a man just waiting for his past to catch up with him. You could do that; it is available, the ability to allow good things to come.

I considered that, on the porch, the way we sometimes pretend to be thinking and considering when we know very well, by the beating of our own hearts, that we have already made up our minds. "Of course you know *Jack*," one of the two smiling gay men said to the other, because a third, a skinnier, chinless man who resembled Don Knotts, had joined them, and I was so happy I wanted to go to them, to tell them who I was, to embrace Jack. At the end of the long roadway leading to the inn, a late arrival was coming—a white sedan—dust was rising behind it and I peeked inside the inn, through the glass, and saw my father and Gina still talking, joined now by one of the chefs. The three of them were in conversation, and Gina was holding a cup of wine, a sign that things in that conversation were going well.

The white car had now pulled up, and a woman got out of it. She was tall and redheaded, thin, in a black dress too stylish for this gathering. She slung her bag over her shoulder and gazed up at me on the porch, and it was only then that I recognized her.

There was the expanse of grass to cover. I stepped down off the porch to shorten this distance. I was not sure she recognized me, or whether she was smiling at the recognition, but she was at least locked in to me, her head held high, with a broad, prominent forehead, and a gaze that seemed uncertain but not shy.

"It's Luca, isn't it?" she said, when she was ten feet away, and put out her hand.

"You've hardly changed."

I took her hand. "Maureen," I said. "It's good to see you. Though not . . ." I instantly added, because she was not, after all, smiling, but of course mourning, and it struck me then by the downward cast of her features that she might be the only one here, my father included, to whom that term could accurately be applied.

"A long time," she said.

Her voice had an unsettling patchiness to it, like that of a foreign actress trying to affect an American accent without attaching it to any specific locality. I knew from periodic reports from my father that Maureen worked overseas, did some sort of business translation work of a peculiar sort. She'd grown tall—taller even than the formidable height she'd attained at seventeen, perhaps an inch taller than me—and her look, in spite of the expensive dress and the carefully structured curls, was masculine and hard in the way of certain Irish girls, in their thirties, who have begun tilting genetically toward their fathers.

"Yes," I answered. "A long time."

We were awkward with one another. She looked beyond me, into the inn, and seemed to be deciding whether she needed to go ahead with an unpleasant task.

"I've come"—she dropped her head as if undergoing an uncharacteristic moment of shyness—"from dropping my mother off at the motel. I didn't see you this morning at the funeral home."

"No. I was late." I had deliberately not said "we," and that holding back—my deliberate withholding of the fact that I had a wife—snagged somewhere in my mind, something I would want to probe later, when I was alone.

"Well, it's good you've come," she said.

"I wouldn't have not been here."

We stared at each other an instant, as if deciding, out of all the myriad routes to follow, which to pursue. One of the routes, of course, was to politely dismiss one another.

It was Maureen who made the choice to move forward. "We should *talk*," she said, as if some old, unfinished business lay between us. "You're a—don't tell me. Lawyer?"

"No, you must have got that wrong. My wife's a lawyer. I'm a—"

"Teacher," we said at the same time.

"Yes. You wrote a book. I'm remembering now." She leaned down, as if to remove a pebble from her shoe. "I can almost remember the title."

"Your father must have told you that."

"Something about the cinema, wasn't it?"

Either she had been in Europe too long, or Maureen had grown pretentious. No one said it that way: the "*cin*ema."

"That's right. But you're the one who's become successful," I said, to get the subject away from me.

"Have I?" She scanned my face with a certain offhand aggressiveness I wondered if she was aware of.

"You work in Europe. You do some sort of translation work."

"That's about right."

"So that prize you won for *Le Petit Prince* paid off."

"God, you remember. We really do have the potential to embarrass one another, don't we?" She smiled with a certain unsurprising hardness, allowing nothing, a Margaret Thatcher sort of smile. "Listen, where did you get that wine?"

"Inside—let me fetch some for you." I took a moment, perhaps feeling the wine a little, or else emboldened by the good feelings I'd been recently indulging. "Promise me you'll stay here. I'd like to continue this."

"I should speak to your father."

"Well then, come in, but—well, you've got to do what you've got to do."

I felt I was talking nonsense, so I led her in. The room—crowded, light-filled—no longer contained my father or Gina. They had disappeared.

"This is strange," I said. "They were here a moment ago."

I poured Maureen wine, myself a second cup. We both looked around the room, and decided silently, and almost simultaneously, that we were uncomfortable here. But even when I managed to get us outside—it was necessary first to introduce her to Wellsie, who was standing near the door—we did not succeed in losing the sense of strangeness that had come over us in the inn. Maybe, I thought, it was our bond. No one else here, after all, could be made to shiver by a beautiful inn fronting a pond, on a bright day in which the water glowed. No one else could remember what it had been to come here in the early days, when there were few guests, and the two men who had been our fathers had been so expectant and unsure, so happy and at the same time wanting. Maureen and I had never given them what they'd wanted in those days; that, too, I thought, might be our bond.

In any case, I understood that we were both, at this moment, trying to find a way around the small, difficult fact of her father's death; there was no way now to go back and smooth things over, to have made those days of transition easier ones.

"Tell me what you do overseas," I asked.

"Oh, it's not very interesting, really. A kind of advanced facilitation of mergers. Nothing very socially useful, I'm afraid."

"You said your mother was here?" I asked, just to keep things going.

"Yes. For the burial only. She wouldn't come here, to this. We all stayed, last night, at this really wretched motel. My sisters brought their children."

"Lizzie and . . ."

"Patricia and Jane." She paused, again beamed a searchlight around the hidden corners of my face. "This wine must be potent." She smiled, in a way that gave me a little hope.

"I didn't see them at the cemetery. Or you."

"Well, you must not have been looking very closely. We've all turned out to look much more like him than like our mother. She remarried, by the way."

"Did she?"

"Didn't yours?"

"No."

We stood a moment in silence.

"And you?" I asked. "You never married?"

She blinked, hesitated, looked surprised—for a moment, I thought I'd actually managed to say something that amused her, until its natural downward draw reclaimed her face. "My sisters did all the marrying. And the childbearing. But I wasn't aware I'm old enough to be considered a spinster."

"I didn't mean . . ."

"It's really all right."

She paused. "Frankly, I'm surprised you did."

I didn't answer, not sure what she meant; on the other hand, entirely sure.

"I'm trying to get this right . . . no children. As yet?"

"That's right. How often did you speak to your father?"

"Weekly."

"From Europe?"

"They do have telephones."

"Good for you."

That little interchange might have come off as a joke, but somehow hadn't. A previously submerged tension had surfaced between us. Still, Maureen pressed on ahead. "Weren't those strange days?"

"Yes."

"The two of us never got along, did we?"

"No. But, I mean, how could we?"

"Trying to avoid hearing them making love. Not that they tried very hard to keep it down." She stared into me. "It never bothered you as much as it did me, I remember."

I shrugged, manufacturing, on the spot, an alternate self. "I wanted them to be happy, that's all."

"Did you?" She looked incredulous, like she had caught me out in a lie, and knew it. "That's the *last* thing I wanted them to be. I wanted them to be utterly miserable, so that my father would come back to us." She waited for me to respond. "Didn't you want the same thing?"

"Yes, I suppose."

"You *suppose?*"

"Yes. I wanted that." Emboldened by the wine, I went further. "I even came up with a half-cocked plan once to win him back."

"What was that?"

"You don't remember my friend, do you? You came with us, I remember, on a picnic. My thirteenth birthday. He was there, my friend. Unmistakably gay."

Maureen nodded. "Yes."

"You remember."

"I do, yes. Blond hair."

"I thought if I could convince my father that, y'know, that things were starting up between me and this boy, this Andrew, that he'd freak out. Completely. And . . . you know."

"Come back to you."

Maureen sipped her wine and stared into my face. "Did you really think that?"

I looked at her. The demand was there to be honest.

"I was thirteen."

"Yes, but it's still colossally naïve."

I paused before speaking. "I was thirteen."

"I got a different impression. From you and that boy. Oh come on, we're not kids anymore. I mean, it was absolutely clear to me that things maybe had started up." Maureen smiled. "No, don't blush. You were thirteen. Don't boys . . . well, in England I know they do."

"Maybe they do over here, too. But not us."

"Well, that's disappointing to hear. I know I didn't show it, but all those years, I mean, we'd come here, weekends, to this place and when you never tried anything, I was, well, disappointed." I looked at her and put up a losing battle against displaying the shock I felt. "I was convinced nothing happened between us because you were . . . I suppose, committed."

I toed the grass. "Gay."

"Yes. Awful word. Yes." She bit the edge of her cup. "And here you were only pretending to be. For your father's sake."

I wasn't precisely sure why, but I could feel—in my stomach, or thereabouts—the way this conversation had begun to press against my earlier feelings of hope and release, undermining them. I wanted to get away from Maureen. "It's always more complicated than we want it to be, I guess."

"It is, yes." Maureen went on looking at me.

Then she said: "By which you mean what, exactly?"

For an instant I wondered: having endured her father's desertion, did she go through life forcing every man to question his sexuality? I had a vision of the poor business types she worked with in Brussels, being twisted into knots by her pressing them as she was doing to me right now.

"Our fathers' sexuality," I finally answered. "First they'd been with women, then with each other. It was confusing, and it made . . . *me*, confused."

"But it's not so complicated, is it? They wanted to be with each other. They just *did*. I suppose all that time with our mothers, that was just a prelude to the life that was always waiting to happen. I mean, it was the early sixties. The dark ages. The pity is that they took so long to find each other. In the meantime, they made the mistake of having *us*."

I waited a moment. "Was that a mistake?"

She seemed to find the question amusing. "Oh, not from our perspective, maybe. But it hasn't been a picnic growing up with this entrenched distrust of men. I let him know it, too." She glanced away for a second, and I remembered the look they had shared, years ago, on the porch, which told me then—and now told me again—how deep and strange and ultimately unknowable their bond must have been. Her lack of forgiveness, after more than twenty years, seemed to have determined who she had become. "I mean, look at us. No children, either of us. Not that that's a crime, by any means. But it does indicate a certain lack of . . . faith in things." She looked at me again, downed the last of her wine. "Yes, I'd say it was a mistake. Men like that shouldn't. Experiment with women, yes, all right. But children? It's just too fucking sad, don't you think?"

I didn't answer. I saw myself, briefly, as I'd been on the porch half an hour before. Fool.

Inside the house now, I could see my father, separated from Gina, making his way from group to group. Maureen noticed, too. "Ah, there he is."

She looked at me as though she might be about to apologize. "Well, we caught up, didn't we?"

"Yes."

"I should go in and speak with him." She consulted her watch. "Early-morning flight tomorrow. To Brussels."

Was someone meeting her there? I doubted it.

"Well, good seeing you again," I said.

"Yes."

She looked at me another long second, put down her cup, went inside. I picked up her cup to throw it away. I watched Maureen, on the other side of the glass, greet my father. They became serious with one another, nodding heads. She towered over him. It was unfortunate that Gina hadn't been with me for my encounter with Maureen—she might have saved it from taking the direction it took—but then I wondered about that as well. What Maureen had brought up seemed inescapable.

I walked down to the pond, far from the party. The water was dark and flat. I stood at the edge of it and thought that time and distance had warped perception in an unusual way: the pond seemed larger than I remembered it. It was mid-afternoon. I was frightened now of facing Gina, terrified of her demand. This was the way it happened to me, sneak attacks shifting my sense of the world and its potentialities. Maureen could have been anyone; a lifeguard on a beach, anyone.

At the top of the hill, I watched Wellsie, Delavoise, and Will Monaghan leaving. Part of me wanted to go and say good-bye to them. The likelihood was that I would never see them again. They walked with the postures of men who have just enjoyed a good meal, men who might be about to put toothpicks into their mouths. I looked at Will Monaghan and felt acute jealousy. How easy, I thought, how remarkably easy life would be if a wife's infidelity was the largest thing I had to face.

Eric Davenport had said, "Come on, this is just something we're doing *now*." He had believed it, too. I could still remember the feel of him under me, the hairlessness, the tracing of muscle and the faint whiff of chlorine. I could be back there in a second, if I allowed myself.

Suddenly Gina appeared on the porch, smiling to herself, I could see. As she caught sight of me, the smile expanded, and she lifted her blouse in an affectation of pregnancy. More than anything then, what I wanted was to cross the distance between us, and I moved one foot forward as if to do so. But then something stopped me, and I stood there, in midstride, for what seemed the longest time.

7

The sky had turned powdery by the time Gina and I made our way down the beach, later in the afternoon, toward the place where Helen Weston had said we'd meet.

On the phone, she'd been vague. "About half a mile down, let's say, out of sight of the crowds." Then, as if to reassure me: "There'll be enough of us, I suspect, that we'll be hard to miss."

After Gina had emerged from her long swim, the lifeguard had chastised her. She'd stood a little back, and listened to him as though he were speaking in another language. Her face looked clear and impassive as the water dripped from her. "Go ahead, yell at me," Gina might have been saying to this boy, and I saw in that instant all the defiance with which she might once have asked Alex Bergeron to meet her behind Carteret Junior High. *To hell with rules,* she'd said once. *There are things I want to know.*

In the motel, changing to come here, we'd caught each other naked for a moment. Without thinking, I'd reached out to touch Gina's back where it had turned red, and she'd looked shocked, as if to be touched naked, even within the precinct of our motel room, was more than she could bear. But then she'd given me a long hard look, and I hadn't known what was in that look. She'd turned away before I could pierce it.

Then we'd both dressed, and finally we were walking down the

long blank beach in preparation for my meeting up with a ghost from the
past, a meeting she was kind enough to attend. I wondered then whether
she didn't think of it as a last gesture, a final letting go, a kind of *Here,
Luca, here is the world in which you've always felt you truly belonged. Go to it.*

"I don't see them. Do you?" she asked.

She hadn't said much since coming out of the water, so even the
sound of her voice—that she was talking to me at all—was comforting.

"No. She said half a mile."

We stopped then, realizing we had walked at least that far. We
could see far enough down the beach to know that no large group con-
gregated farther on.

"Are we early?" she asked.

"I don't think so."

Above us, the Provincetown sightseeing plane made a circuit.
Down the beach, in the distance, the overland vehicles were coming
back from their dune visitations. Gina looked out at the water. The wind
pushed her hair off her face. The thought that at any moment a dozen
gay men might invade our territory made it impossible to touch her, but
I felt the desire anyway, along with a heightened awareness that we were
alone here. Having expected to be taken up by a crowd, relieved of the
burden of ourselves, we were instead thrown back on those very selves.

Gina sat in the sand, and I joined her there.

"You're sure you have the place right?"

"Yes."

"Okay. So we wait."

She put her sunglasses on, and I thought of that look she'd given
me in the motel room, and wondered what would have happened if I'd
gone on touching her. But even here, I could sense it would have been
a deflection, that sex could no longer absorb the entirety of what was
between us. It wouldn't be that easy.

"So tell me about him," she said.

"Who?"

"This boy. Andrew."

I watched her staring straight ahead of herself. I wasn't sure what
she was looking for in asking the question, but I sensed she wasn't in a
mood to accept anything but the truth.

"I guess he kind of attached himself to me. Or me to him. He was the first gay kid I knew. I mean, where it was undeniable. And I thought I could make use of him." I nodded toward her. "My father, y'know? Only it kind of backfired."

She adjusted her sunglasses.

"He drew me in. He made me see things about myself."

Behind the glasses, I could see her eyes lower, though hardly with surprise. I had told her, not long after the abortion, about Eric Davenport. At first, she had only been surprised; then she seemed delighted. "*You?* I can't believe you were that free." Her framing it in terms of freedom seemed the oddest thing to me, but she acted as though she enjoyed knowing this about me; she wanted to know everything Eric and I had done, and even found a way of putting it to use in the early days. We'd see a movie, and afterward she'd ask me, "Did you think that actor was cute?" Something always bound up in me with those questions, and she knew it, liked to take that tightness and tease it out in bed. Straddling me, she would smile a certain way, and I knew exactly what she was thinking.

She had, at the beginning, she said, been turned on by my repressed nature, the parts of me that seemed hidden and scared. She liked to play with them, "loosen you up," she said. In the months after her abortion, we were each trying to look at the other differently; she was trying hard to strip me of my innocence, and, with the information about Eric, I had given her something with which to work.

It was only after Bob Painter's funeral—only after I began my long hesitation around the issue of a child—that she started to get even a hint that it all arose out of something else—not the fun little thing she could tease me with sexually, but a difficult component of my being. Then she had tried to explain to me, perhaps too many times, how sexuality is larger than a single, limited identity, that if I were "gay" she'd had enough experience that she would have known it, that she was utterly convinced by my interest in and ability to become lost in the act of sex that I was at least as "straight" as she needed me to be. As far as she was concerned the problem should have disappeared long ago, died of attrition.

But there are always parts, when you tell a story, that you deliberately leave out.

One thing I had never told Gina was how in the years in New York before I met her, the time before even Abby Kassell, the blissful time when I had relations with no one at all besides Robert Bruner and a set of semiobscure early sixties filmmakers whose movies I watched in the dark, Eric Davenport had returned to my life. His return had come in the form of a call. He was getting married. He wanted to invite me. He'd gotten my New York number from my mother.

I declined, of course. He was marrying a woman in Virginia, a woman he'd met in his life as a salesman who traveled for a pharmaceutical company. They were getting married in horse country, he mentioned. There was no alluding to the fact that he had once slipped into bed with me and worked his hand appreciatively over my belly before lowering it just a bit farther. He had successfully jettisoned all that, and the silences I allowed in that conversation—those silences that were the only way I knew of alluding to the past—he treated like a form of strangeness on my part. "Are you all right, Luca?" I remember him asking.

Of course it was his right to marry the woman from Virginia. I was not so dumb as to think that because he used to jerk me off with a regular form of abandon he couldn't ever marry a woman. He'd always let me know that was his first and primary interest. My concern was more in making room for what had happened to us, and so I could not imagine sitting in some church in Virginia watching him kiss the bride. I was someone who didn't belong there, so I begged off.

And then he began calling again. Not often. Once a year. He had a daughter, and he called to tell me. A year or so later, when his son was born, he made a different kind of call. Something, I knew, had gone wrong with that birth, though he wasn't exact. A melancholy attended the details; I suspected Eric was drunk when he called me. Was the child born with Down's syndrome? Had there been some other birth defect he was too embarrassed to mention? How did you ask such a question, unless the information was offered up directly?

After that, Eric was never drunk when he called, but he began insinuating that work might take him to New York soon, and if that happened, he'd love to get together.

I always said things like "Sure, yes, great," but I dreaded such an occurrence. My life with its tightness and its discipline and its limits suited me. The sight of the neighbors seen across the courtyard in their daily rituals was all I needed of sex. Watching them, listening, was like having sex through somebody else, and it was as though I needed that, required an extension cord for my own drive; it could not reach far enough on its own. It did not know what it wanted.

Because I knew this—because it was the most solid thing I knew about myself—I feared Eric Davenport's return. Feared the thing that might happen should he show up one night, knock on the door. Feared, too, that should the affair resume it would kick me out of the category of a man who had once "experimented" into the category of a man who clearly *was* something.

But he had not appeared—that fabled business trip might have been a chimera. Gina had come instead. Had arrived like a gift I didn't want to look at too closely, until I was forced to. I did not bother to have my number officially changed after I'd moved in with her; I just took hers on, and didn't inform those, like Eric, from whom I wanted to sever myself. But my marriage had still been lived in fear of a thing I had never fully gone through and explored. It was that simple. It was not so alive as to torment me on a daily basis, only alive enough to bring my whole life into question.

Now, here, on this beach, all these years later, I felt called upon finally to be brave, to show Gina some of the things I'd never shown her before. When she'd asked for "intimacy," on the troubled nights of our marriage, it had been this of course she'd been asking for, to know me completely. Yet "intimacy" had always been linked, for me, with a private region that I'd felt, once displayed, would make her want to bolt.

"How much have you ever really wanted to know about me?" I asked, and was surprised that Gina seemed taken aback, unprepared for this.

"About who you married," I went on.

"I thought I knew who I married." Her voice was low and, I felt, suspicious. "I thought it was very clear. Until you got scared. Then you became somebody else."

I dipped one set of toes into the sand.

"I felt like the day I went to your apartment I became an entirely different human being. I couldn't even find the *connection* between who I was with you and who I was before you."

"Luca, we know all this. And anyway, what's so surprising about that?"

"Well, look at you. You were at least somebody, the facts sort of added up. Some sort of line existed between who you used to be and who you became . . ."

"Oh, that's just the old academic in you talking. You want this time line for relationships. You want a *map*. Besides, it's not true. I can't believe you're still stuck back there. I mean, of *course* you become somebody else when you fall in love. Who doesn't know that?"

"Yeah, but how long does that last? How long does this new-person-ness last before the ugly facts of your life catch up and you just feel terror?"

She got up and moved away from me, down the beach.

"What is it? Where are you going?" I followed her, thinking I had begun all wrong, dragging her over the hot coals of the past yet again.

"I'm sick of hearing about *terror*. It's gotten so I think it would be tolerable to be with any man so long as he didn't use the word 'terror.' "

I took her hand, to keep her with me. "Hey."

"Hey what? Maybe I'll go back to the motel. I don't know why I came with you. How do you see this, exactly, your coming to this little ritual on the beach? Explain to me the perverse symbolism in your showing up."

"There isn't any. I want this to work. I don't want you to leave me."

She looked at me a moment, before speaking.

"Oh Christ, I don't believe that for a second. I don't believe you can change anymore. You've got this model of doom in your head and you're just waiting for it to come true."

"Gina."

"It's true. Maybe if you keep me at a distance it won't hurt so much when it happens. So you live this ridiculous safe little life where you're the guy who checks the gas jets at night, who worries about the roof, who wants to put me at a distance and just keep me there except when you want sex, and then you don't want sex to have anything to do with the rest of our lives. Why is that, exactly? Why is sex some separate place for you? Why is it you won't even touch me in public?"

"Shh."

"I don't care if anyone hears. You think there's anyone close enough to hear? Tell me, what's the big issue here? Are you going to run off with some man?"

"No. That's not going to happen."

"Then what's the terror? Huh?"

I stopped then any attempt to silence her. I looked out at the water and felt quiet. What, indeed? The next thing would, I sensed, be do or die.

"I'm not going to run off with a man. But there are parts of me you still don't get. You always thought the gay part of me was some joke, something I did when I was young that was cool. In your view—your sophisticated view—amazingly cool."

She folded her arms. She looked at the sand. "So what you're telling me is it's real. It's always been real. You've just never been able to own up to it."

I didn't say anything at first.

"Let's have it out, Luca."

"Something stayed with me." I stilled myself a moment; it felt stupid and embarrassing, but at the same time, necessary. "That I was capable of that. Capable of some kind of feeling with a man. I know I should have accepted that by now. It's ridiculous that I haven't. But I haven't. I just keep asking, Is this a real life? Or just some fake thing I settled into? It's made me step away, always having to ask that question. And I keep wondering, What's it done to you that I've been only half here all this time?"

She lowered her head. "Half here? Is that how much you've been?"

I paused a moment. "Yes."

Her head lowered further. A couple of tears fell out of her eyes. She fought them.

"What did you see when you were out there on the water looking at the lifeguard and me?"

"I saw a man I wasn't sure I wanted to come back to."

"And him?"

"I didn't see him."

"I thought you might be thinking something."

"What? That you were attracted to him?"

"Who knows? I'm being honest here. I don't know half the time whether I'm attracted to someone, or just feeling scared because I *might* be attracted. But there's the terror, right there. The whole uncertainty of it. If I'd never slept with Eric, I'd probably never give these feelings a second thought. I'd probably think all this was perfectly normal. But when something's been half opened up in you, it doesn't really shut down."

"Why don't you just go be with a man and get it over with?"

"I don't think I want that. I honest to God don't. But I don't know how to be anything but what I am with you, which is clearly not enough."

"No."

"I've always found ways to make it safe. You know that. I thought that, when, in the beginning, you used to have lots of orgasms, that made it safe. You'd stay with me forever, it didn't matter, I was doing enough. Then you looked up from the orgasms and it wasn't enough. Okay, so what else did you want? A house, a life like the one we've got? All right, here it is. Would *that* make you stay? I loved watching you. Getting ready for work, going out to the car, going to your rehearsals, I loved to watch your life. I loved when you came to bed at night and wanted me. I couldn't believe that it kept *going on*. I mean, after all the men you'd had, what was so special about me?"

She shook her head.

"No. All right. I'm not going to fish for a compliment here. But I don't know where to go from here. Tell me, What the fuck is intimacy?"

After a moment, Gina said, her voice low and dark, as if she were speaking against her own will: "This is."

"Is it?"

"Living at this level. Yes. Not hiding away. Yes."

"Okay."

"Okay what?"

I shook my head. She seemed to be looking at me with only one eye open.

"I feel like telling you everything, every ugly little detail. Just like I should have that night you told me your whole sexual history."

She didn't respond, which I took to be a kind of permission.

"Eric came back into my life once."

She turned away from me a moment.

"It was when I was living pretty much in solitude. When I was just hiding like crazy. Going to the movies. The early New York days. Sit down," I said.

"No. I like standing."

"Okay. You know what I used to do? You want to know how ridiculous the man you married is? Or was. *Is.* There was this guy who lived across the courtyard from me. I could see into his apartment. Late at night, he used to watch this show. Women doing exercises. Three in the morning. It was all dark, all the windows in his building and the next building dark, and the only light these women with big hair, in leotards, doing their stretches and their—"

She shook her head, which seemed to have nothing to do with what I was telling her.

"What?"

"Go on."

"So I would watch it with him. And I could never figure out, was I watching the women, or was I watching him watching the women? So into this life, this life where that was my big sexual thrill, Eric calls. He'd gotten my number from my mother. He's married, he has two kids, he's a salesman for a drug company, he says we should get together. And all the time—I'm terrified—I'm thinking, so this is what happens now. Eric Davenport comes and we start up again, and this is what I am. As if I had no will, or choice in the matter. It was like somewhere along the line I misplaced my own sexuality, and anyone could come along and define it for me. You, him, whoever. The guy across the courtyard."

She looked down.

"But he never came. I guess he chickened out. That sort of double life would have been too much for him."

"Unless he just wanted to see you."

I paused a moment. It was the least imaginable rationale. "Yes. Unless that."

"So he didn't come."

"No. You came instead. That girl Abby, and then you. But you see, I could never believe in it, after those first few months. Those first few months were incredible. But if that could happen, if anybody could come along and tell me what I was, how safe was this marriage? I've always believed something was going to catch up with me. I've been living with that doom ever since."

She again looked down at the sand at our feet, something, I could see, hardening in her. "And this is the moment, isn't it? When it's supposed to end. According to your calculations. Right?"

"Except I'm waiting for a miracle. I'm waiting for the reason for it not to end."

"And I'm not enough? I'm not enough of a reason?"

She toed the sand, a barely withheld tension working through her; then she grabbed me by the shirt, very hard. "Do you have any idea, you sonofabitch, what it's like to live with somebody, to *adore* them, to know they are totally capable of answering every need you have, except they won't. It's like living with a ghost. Something's in you. I hate it, because it doesn't even feel real. But you won't let go of it, this unreal thing, you just hold on to it. Just because it's the past, isn't it? Because every little bit of the past has got to be recovered, and cared for. God forbid you should let anything go, even if it means destroying yourself."

She started to hit me on the chest. I grabbed her hand to stop her, and as I did, out of the corner of my eye, I saw a woman approaching from the crowded end of the beach. Something about her was instantly familiar.

I held Gina's hand, and she started hitting me with the other.

"Hold on," I said. "Please. She's here."

Helen Weston seemed to be hobbling, unused to walking on sand, or having worn the wrong shoes for it. She carried a heavy-looking shoulder bag. Her face was rounder, fuller in the jaw than I remembered. When she was about fifteen feet away, she stood still and gazed at me. She tried to smile, though it looked difficult.

"They won't let us do it here!" she shouted against what wind there was.

She tapped the bag she was supporting. "They won't let us scatter them on the beach. We asked, and they won't let us. The *water,* they said. It's not allowed."

I moved toward her. When I was close, I smiled in reply to hers. She seemed to have no awareness of the kind of scene she'd intruded upon, which pleased me. Some old part of me still wanted to make a good impression.

"It was stupid, we shouldn't have even asked. But one of his friends, not knowing any better, I suppose, mentioned what we were doing to the ranger. No, they said. *Illegal.*"

In her face now, I could sense a vague request being made. It was between us a moment, in the air. I saw in her aging features what had always been patrician about her, the part of her that had battled against her own circumstances. She pointed back in the direction from which she'd come. "They're all waiting. Up at the top. We have to go somewhere else. Somewhere farther away. I knew you'd be here, so I came to get you."

Something caught in her throat, and she cleared it, moved the strands of hair that the wind had pushed against her face. "How are you, I should ask."

"I'm fine."

"You look well. Is that your wife?"

I turned to see Gina behind me, still seething but trying to cover it in a way that made her look shy.

"It is. This is Gina. Mrs. Weston."

"Helen." She nodded, smiled in a tired, strained way, as if she were greeting the last mourner at the end of a long wake. "Wretched day, this is," she said.

"I'm sorry" was all I could think to say.

Again, she looked at me as if there were some agreement we might make in silence. I couldn't imagine what it was she was asking for. After a moment, she dropped her shoulders and said, "Well, they're waiting," and it was clear, from the way she said it, how little she thought of the men who were waiting, how much she wished, perhaps, they would go away. "I think we're going someplace secret now. It wasn't what he wanted, of course. He wanted *here*."

Without waiting for us to join her, she started heading back. After four or five steps, she stopped, looked out at the water, then just once back at me. It was a mildly beckoning look that had nothing to do with whether or not we were following her. I knew she was asking me something, but since I didn't know what that was, all I could do was shrug in reply. I saw that she took this as a form of permission.

She reached into her bag and took out a container that resembled a small, blue wine bottle. She unscrewed it and made a short, high accompanying sound, the smallest scream I could imagine. Then she took a step forward and emptied it into the water at her feet. The wind, being wrong for the act, carried the ashes back against her.

"Oh no, no. No. No, please." Her hands flew out to collect the ashes as the wind took them. Enough of them landed on her skirt so that her instinct was to bunch it up, lifting the skirt high enough so that her legs showed, for a moment, far above the knees, an old woman's legs, white and veiny. I wanted to turn away, but didn't. She moved into the water, holding the bunched skirt and then dropping it, when she had gone far enough in. Her skirt was wet.

I moved toward her. She turned around and scanned the sand, with a wild look in her eyes, as if her son's ashes could still be rescued. Leaning forward awkwardly, and as though the water exerted a difficult pull, she began moving to shore and, once there, got down on all fours and began pawing the sand, flinging what she could into the water. Behind me, I heard Gina say, "It's all right."

"No, no it isn't. I've ruined it." Helen Weston's voice had a frantic quality now.

"It's low tide," Gina said.

Helen Weston did not at first hear. It took me a moment to understand.

"Did you hear that?" I said to her, because I was closer.

"It's low tide. The tide will come in and take his ashes from the sand. It's all right." I touched her shoulder.

At that point, she seemed to fall forward, her head against the sand. I kept my hand on her shoulder. It seemed all I could do. We waited.

She wept, and then she opened her eyes. For a long time she lay against the sand. "All right," she said.

But she seemed to have no intention of getting up until she closed her eyes again and seemed to be coaxing herself toward an effort of pure will.

"What a scene for you to witness," she said finally, wiping the sand from her face. "Oh God, what a scene. Help me up, please."

I did.

She surveyed the sand behind her one more time, but now with a different look, as if she would stay there to be sure that tonight, of all nights, the moon and tides did their work.

"All that's left of your old friend, Luca."

"Yes."

I said it as if to affirm her idea of the great friendship Andrew and I had never quite managed to sustain.

She looked beyond me, to Gina. "Did you know him?"

"I met him," Gina answered. "In the bookstore. Yes."

Helen Weston nodded. She gave the appearance of not hearing the last few words you said to her, like her attention couldn't carry that far.

"Maybe I could go and get the others," I said. "Maybe we could say what needs to be said here."

"Oh, they'll never forgive me."

"I think it's a good idea, Luca." Gina touched me on the arm. It was probably unconscious, probably only a way of laying a stress on her words. Nonetheless, it felt reassuring.

"How about I'll do that," I said to Helen Weston.

The men on the promontory were easy enough to spot. They were clustered, some lounged against the railings, and they were not dressed for the beach. When I asked if they were the group with Andrew Weston's mother, they looked at me with an initial suspicion. It faded quickly. I told them I was the token friend from home, a small joke to soften what came next.

"She *what*?" one of them asked.

Another laughed, was hushed.

"She dumped the ashes *here*?"

"It was spontaneous." I did not want to have to make excuses for Helen Weston.

They went on staring at me, a dozen men, four or five of them wearing looks of serious disappointment.

"The main thing, I think, is we should go down there and be with her. My wife's with her now."

The words "my wife" got a subtle reaction, but I'd already noticed a couple of pairs of eyes go to my wedding ring. Some of them started picking up paraphernalia, shoulder bags, books. There had been plans for what might be said, how Andrew's life was to be celebrated. This had been spoiled. They started to follow me.

A tall man sidled up alongside me as we were making our way down the beach. "You were in school with him?"

I nodded.

"What was he like?"

I thought a moment before speaking. "He was miserable. He never told you?"

"Not much."

"Kids gave him a very hard time."

The man's face told me that Andrew had not shared the story of his showerless high school gym class.

The man walking next to me was named Jonathan. He had gray, wispy hair and a long, ruined face, though I didn't think he was any older than I was. Something about him—his voice, his gait—marked him out as midwestern.

"We didn't even know he had a mother until this all happened," he said.

Something prim and reserved was in his mouth, but he was likable.

"Now we know he has a mother. Oh boy, do we know."

I said it, though I wondered at the disloyalty in saying it: "She doesn't want to let him go."

"Oh boy, no," Jonathan said, and shook his head.

It felt strange to be walking with them and to know, as we passed blankets, families, that anyone looking up would immediately associate me with them. They were a distinct crowd, unmistakable. Yet the curious thing was how little this seemed to matter to me now. I felt no urge to dissociate myself, to display to the world any kind of difference from them, and this surprised me.

It took us no time at all, anyway, to cover the distance. Helen Weston was where we'd left her, and Gina was close to her, and it was clear they'd had a conversation while I'd been gone, though whether this had been a warm conversation or a close conversation or simply one that marked time, I couldn't tell.

"Where are they?" one of the men asked.

Helen Weston didn't answer at first, gazed upon the men as if she expected to be chastised.

"The ashes?" the same man asked.

"If you hadn't spoken to the ranger, none of this would have happened," Helen Weston said. She had recovered, and the belligerence she had toward these men was now in the open.

"We *live* here," the man said. "We have to obey the laws."

Her answer to that was to bunch her chin.

Jonathan said, "His ashes landed in the sand? That's what Luca said, isn't it?"

She nodded.

"Well, good enough, you know?" Jonathan said, and reached into his backpack and took out a tattered book of poems. "I brought this," he said, "to read when we had this ceremony. So now we're having the ceremony, just a little different, so I'm going to read anyway."

He read a poem about skunk cabbage, about things dying and being born again in the muck of spring that I thought at first was just a generic poem to read at someone's funeral, and therefore unworthy of Andrew. They had missed him somehow, I thought, as his mother and I had not: the boy who used to scrunch over his boyhood desk, writing, in a way so specific, so spiderlike, that none of these men could probably imagine it. I watched Helen Weston listening to this poem with the identical resistance I felt, as though they were trying to turn Andrew into something less than he had once been.

But then the poem turned, became a celebration of the ugly skunk cabbage's ability to blaze a trail for the pretty, delicate things that come after it, and I understood what Jonathan was trying to do. He was honoring Andrew's guts, and at the same moment that I understood this, I felt Andrew slip away from his mother and me, become what he'd become. He couldn't be taken back just because those were the memories that were easiest for us.

One after another, the men stepped forward and talked about Andrew: his wit, his love of books. One went so far as to ignore Andrew's mother's presence (or else face it directly) and talk about Andrew's sexuality, his insatiability, his ever-readiness for more. There was laughter. Helen Weston's anger gave way, after a few moments, to something that looked like simple pain. Some of the others seemed concerned for her. One of them said this man's name, "Joe," as if to caution him. But Joe kept on.

"He had terrible taste," Joe said. "He'd proposition anyone. Supermarket baggers." The others laughed. "Pimply boys. They'd just look at him. Their jaws would drop." He was clearly the dry wit of the group. "But then, the luck of the draw was, some of them would say yes."

The others managed to overcome their awareness of Andrew's mother, and started to laugh. Helen Weston turned away, stared out to sea. As much as I pitied her then, I thought something had begun to shift. This man, imposing on her memories another, later, more vibrant

Andrew, was doing something important. The truth of the supermarket bagger's dropped jaw was a truth to set aside, even to supersede, the event Helen Weston and I both probably thought of as being central to Andrew's life: the day Mr. McCluskey had called Andrew's mother to come to the school, an incident had occurred, he would have to be taken home.

Each of these men, I thought, would have had a scene like that somewhere in his past, something to let him know that the work of his life would have to be a kind of reconstruction, into which the small, or large, embarrassing moment could be folded. Maybe it was wrong of me to think that, reductive; nonetheless, I did. Their lives would have been marked by a steady *moving past*.

I watched Gina listening from behind sunglasses, and wondered what she thought. In essence, she'd once done the same thing as Andrew had: propositioned supermarket baggers, or their like, forgone high school romance for an exploration of the real thing. But unlike him, she'd gotten away with it, or nearly. She'd met me.

She seemed then closer to them than to me. No death threat hung over Gina, but another kind of threat always had. Had she known him, she probably would have liked Andrew Weston, at least understood him. It was me who was separate, me who had lived a life, it seemed to me then, entirely without courage.

Suddenly, and without warning, they were finished. The last word said, the books closed. The men looked down at the sand. It was then, because I knew I had to, that I stepped forward.

"Umm," I began, weakly, and watched the way they were alerted, surprised that I would speak; Helen Weston, too. "Andrew kissed me once." I watched smiles appear on a couple of faces, Joe's included. "In my room, the night before the two of us were leaving for college. And it was"—I stopped for a moment, gazed at the sand—"a kiss I was embarrassed by for years. It made me afraid of Andrew, and so I think I wasn't a very good friend."

One or two of the men looked bored, slightly, or disappointed, shifting their feet in the sand, paying attention but only just.

"I shouldn't have been afraid. Or embarrassed." I looked at Gina. "I think now I should have just kissed him back. But we don't know that, people like me don't, anyway, we don't know that we can be a little freer than we let ourselves be. We don't know how, most of us, just to once in a while kiss back. And not feel, y'know, there's a mark on us."

I looked up. Gina was still the most interested listener. Helen Weston was not meeting my eyes.

"So. I'm sorry for not being such a good friend."

I leaned down, picked up a handful of sand, dropped it. "That's all I wanted to say." I stepped back.

"That's it, then?" Jonathan asked, and looked around at the others. There were no takers. "Good-bye, Andrew," he said, and ran his foot delicately over the sand. After a pause, he asked, "What's the tide?"

"Low," someone said.

"Then we've committed an illegal act," Jonathan said, trying for an ironic moment to relieve the gloom.

No one was ready to go yet. Everyone wanted to linger, but the group dispersed, some of them going up to the dunes in pairs, eyes downcast, feet kicking sand, others wandering a little farther down the beach.

Helen Weston approached where I was standing with Gina. "Thank you for coming. This was not exactly how I had envisioned it."

I knew she meant the ceremony, but I couldn't help but wonder whether she meant her statement to include a great deal more. There was no pretending Andrew was hers anymore.

"You're a lovely couple," she said, facing me. "Your wife's a lovely girl."

She did not look as though she were ready to leave. "He kissed you, did he?" she asked.

I nodded. She smiled. "He never kissed *me*, you know," she said. "So consider yourself lucky."

"I will. I mean, I'll try to."

She looked at me as if revising the past a little, perhaps seeing more going on behind Andrew's closed door than she'd once imagined.

"Take care of yourself, Luca."

She surveyed the sand one more time, then studied Andrew's friends and seemed to accept that this was not a ceremony in which she could ever fully take part. She went and picked up her bag, and placed in it the empty container, which Gina (or someone) must have put next to it. Then, saying good-bye to no one, she started back up the beach, hobbled by her inappropriate shoes.

When she was gone, Gina stepped away from me, walked down to the place where the bulk of Andrew's ashes had likely fallen, picked up a handful of the sand, and threw it in the water. That gesture struck me then as the most generous thing I'd ever seen. For a moment, I just stood there, watching her, her black hair and her sunglasses and the tan on the back of her legs and the way she had of throwing, like a girl whose brothers had spent some afternoons showing her how. I could have spent a long time standing there watching her, but I knew something more was required, so I went down and joined her.

"That's a good idea," I said.

"You should do it. You can throw farther than me."

"I don't know. You look like you're doing pretty well. Besides, it doesn't matter. The tide."

She adjusted her sunglasses. "He was her only child?"

I nodded.

"How's that woman going to live with this?"

"I don't know."

It occurred to me that I had not asked Helen Weston about Andrew's father, the putative pharmacist from Newtonville, the extra who had appeared in *Six Bridges to Cross*. Still alive? Gone? He had not come, and that said something.

Gina took off her sunglasses and looked at me. Something new was in that look—something quizzical, something that wanted to test the territory, to see if anything had shifted. "So what now?" she asked.

A flood of release went through me, as if that question alone gave me some wild cause for hope. But I realized I might be pushing it.

"What now?" I repeated back at her. "We go and get ready to have dinner with my parents."

I paused, trying to gauge her expression, to see if there were some message she might be trying to send me. She looked very young, skeptical, as yet unconvinced of something in me. Yes, it would require more.

8

At six, we met my father at his apartment and walked the ten minutes or so down Commercial Street to Sal's. We had determined to be early, to be waiting for my mother and Emma when they arrived. Seeing him would be a shock for them; I was braced for it, though my father kept downplaying the event with jokes about "Luca's silly plan." Still, he had dressed well: a shirt so white it seemed iridescent, gray, comfortable pants, a dark blue blazer. His hair, still abundant, was only speckled with gray, and he moved between us with his age-tempered sensualist's swagger, appearing (his old trick) at the same time alert and dreamily thoughtful.

With Gina, he was mildly flirtatious; for me, he always retained a slight mocking smile, as though he were still waiting for me to do the thing that would clearly define me. Walking to the restaurant, I had the feeling he was barely covering his resentment at being dragged back to the domestic world he had so definitively left, yet which I insisted on re-creating tonight. In the cobbled entrance to the restaurant, we gave our names, the proprietor nodded to my father; they were casual acquaintances whose businesses ran along the same street.

Gina wore a yellow dress spotted with small flowers, a dress that clung to her body. She'd taken off her sunglasses and gazed around at the waiters, the early diners, the light on the water. There was a small, not unpleased bewilderment on her face, as though she had no idea what I wanted tonight, but had a front-row seat on a scene from which something at least interesting might be discovered. Again, we had said little on the way back from Andrew's ceremony, little while we'd gotten ready for this, but a charge now existed, and Gina, I knew, was waiting for something from me.

"So, is Luca treating you in high style down here?" my father asked her.

She barely smiled at my father's little joke, his habitual teasing of my perceived frugality. "We have our special place," she answered.

For an instant, my father seemed to be staring into our intimate life, turning it over, imagining it. As always, there seemed a question on the tip of his tongue, one he held back from asking. "That dive up on the moors," he said.

"Oh, it's not a dive," Gina said. "Funky, but not a dive."

"You two could stay with me, you know. If money is an issue."

"Money's not an issue," Gina answered him, then glanced at me, and I felt again what I'd felt on the beach, during Andrew's ceremony, after the appearance of Helen Weston: that surprising sense that she had shifted some, and was now in a place where she was prepared, if needed, to defend me.

My father then began to keep his eye on the entrance, and I detected signs of nervousness in him. He checked his watch, and I thought if there were a mirror nearby, he'd glance in it. His hand went to his nose; he rubbed at it, and when I caught him at this small grooming gesture, the look he sent back was resentful, but only for a moment.

"There's still time," he said to me. "I could escape, and you could give them the dinner they're expecting."

I didn't feel I had to answer.

"How long has it been," Gina asked, "since you've seen her?"

My father gazed at the ground.

"You two are married . . . ?"

"Twelve years."

"There you are. And as I recall, the warring parties were seated at opposite ends of the room."

"We did that, yes. Luca wasn't sure."

He scanned Gina's face in a manner that gave no indication of what he was searching for. They had developed, in the brief times they actually saw each other, a natural kinship, as if each recognized in the other a companionable looseness, an approach to life far from my own.

"We met each other's eyes for a second. I remember that much. Then we started throwing rice. Or something."

He turned then to the entrance with a more somber, anxious attitude.

Gina, noticing it, turned to me: was it worth it, forcing these two people together again? I didn't know. Perhaps it would have been better, after all, for the two of us to have had dinner alone together, to talk over the day's events. If Gina was ready for a new level of intimacy, so was I. That is, I was ready to meet her in bed, to paw over all the vast, unconsidered territory in a way we hadn't in a long time. Who knew where it might lead? But a plan had been set in motion.

It was too late anyway, because Emma and my mother had just then turned the corner, and were standing in the entrance to the courtyard, two small Italian women, both wearing white, heavily made up and with gold jewelry, wearing smiles of simple, evening-out anticipation, which they offered first to Gina, then to me, then, with the frozen-faced shock of the guest who realizes the surprise party is in fact for him, they arrived at the figure of the man beside me.

"Oh God, why'd I let you talk me into this," my father half-whispered.

The women were not moving. Their pocketbooks both lifted in some kind of mock defense. Finally Emma was able to turn away from the sight of my father to address me. "What'd he, just show up? You just run into him here?"

I shook my head. My mother, meanwhile, seemed to be searching, surreptitiously, for an exit. Her lips had become, in an instant, lushly, abnormally red.

I approached the two of them. "I invited him," I said.

Emma clicked her tongue and stared at me as if she were scolding a small boy for a thing he should have been ashamed of. There was in her look, too, some incredulity, as if this action of mine called into question everything she had ever believed about me.

I took my mother's hand. "Listen," I said. "I'm sorry. I should have told you."

She still would not meet my eyes. She licked those red lips, sternly dignified for a moment, and turned away.

"I'll get the car, Dorothy," Emma said.

"No," I said.

Emma had already started to go. I followed her out into the street as she fished in her bag for her keys.

"You must be crazy, putting your mother through this." She turned back to the entrance. "Dorothy, come on," she called. There was one more look for me, some confusion riding now under her dismay.

My mother wasn't following, and we both stepped back inside to see why.

In the short time that Emma and I had taken outside the restaurant, they had met. My father had stepped forward, or my mother had. He was smiling, leaning slightly forward, one of his hands had gone out, as though to take my mother's unproffered hand. She was looking upward, though, it seemed, not directly at him, as though she were surveying the scene beyond him, the restaurant with its quickening movement and the light against the water. Was she caught there, or had I detected some willingness, a decision at least, to remain?

"Dorothy, what are you waiting for?" Emma called.

My father looked across the courtyard at Emma then, a slight glistening in his eyes, a hint of his old superiority. "I don't think she has such a problem with this, Emma," I said.

"Yeah, maybe I do. Maybe I'm the one's got the problem." Still, she didn't budge.

Finally my mother turned to us. It was impossible to read her expression; too many things seemed to be warring there. She looked, still, somewhat trapped, and like she was seeking a neutral space, a place where the tumbling issues of this scene didn't press so hard. But it was also impossible, for me anyway, to miss another aspect of her look, a small eagerness, or willingness, to *have* this scene.

Beyond her, six or seven steps away, Gina leaned against the restaurant wall. A tall, leafy bush grew there, and she had snipped off a frond, was crushing the small leaves between her fingers and looking at me. Her eyes lowered; she shook her head slightly, the crushed leaves fell at her feet.

At that instant, the curly-headed maître d' rounded the corner and considered us.

"Your party all here?" he asked me.

"Yes." I nodded, and though Emma felt stiff and uncertain beside me ("Crazy," she said, and shook her head), I put my hand against the small of her back and motioned her forward.

We were seated in a corner of the deck, and since we were five, there was some confusion as to what the seating arrangement should be. My mother and Emma finally took one side of the table, Emma still engaging in mild, fussy protests; Gina and my father faced them, with Gina and my mother sitting across from one another on the far end. I took the extra chair.

As soon as we were seated, my father leaned toward Emma and said, "Listen, I just want you to know this wasn't my idea." He lifted his hand off the table to stress his point. "I was dragooned into this just like you were." Then he nodded toward my mother, to show her he meant no offense by this.

Emma arranged her silverware, her pocketbook, glanced off at the other diners, and didn't speak, though her tightened lips gave every appearance that she would have liked to.

I motioned to the waiter, and said we wanted some wine. I took a quick glance at the list and chose one, and saw from my father's small reaction that he was disappointed by my choice. Even here, in the midst of this tense scene, the old epicure in him still wanted satisfaction.

"So. I'm sorry to have embarrassed you all," I said.

"What'd you want this for?" Emma asked, a little too loud and eager, with her hands splayed out.

They all looked at me for just a second, but there was no answer I could give them. What pain there might have been at this table was subsumed into my own pleasure that this had been achieved, that they were seated across from one another, that no one had run away from this scene; that, for an hour or so, I might be able to pierce an old, private mystery: was there anything still between them? It was a son's small selfish wish, to know that, for my own purposes, and then to move on.

"You okay, Mom?" I asked.

"Fine. Mm-hm."

Emma lowered her hands. "Won't it get cold out here?"

"No," I answered. "No, it's protected. And besides, it's warm. Isn't anybody going to say hello to Gina?"

Emma sent Gina a chastened greeting, reached one arm across the table to touch her hand. My mother smiled at her.

"Okay," I said.

The menus arrived, blessed relief. We all burrowed in. "What's good here?" Emma asked, and put on her glasses.

My mother couldn't concentrate on her menu, a fact Emma immediately picked up on. "Dorothy, you probably like the scampi."

"Yes," my mother said, and Emma, as if that single syllable represented some mirror of my mother's troubled inner state, turned to me, with an unmistakable look: *See what you've done?*

"The mussels here are fantastic," I said.

"I don't like mussels," Emma said. "Too briny."

The waiter arrived with the wine, poured us each a glass. We drank, each of us, immediately, and it was up to my father to comment, "Not even a toast."

"What do you want to toast?" Emma asked, looking askance at him.

My father shrugged, and sipped his wine. His head tilted meaningfully toward me, his eyes rolling slightly upward, in recognition of the fact that things, so far, weren't going particularly well. Beyond him, I expected the same sort of look from Gina, but her gaze seemed to be fixed exclusively on my mother, as if she were monitoring her reactions to each new sally.

"So how've you been, Lou?" Emma asked suddenly, with no visible softening of attitude.

"As you see," my father answered, looking up.

"What do I see?" She scowled, perused the menu one more time, closed it, turned to me. "They have something simple here? Flounder, something like that?"

"I'm sure you can order something simple."

" 'Cause I can't handle anything too rich tonight. Dorothy, get the scampi."

My mother glanced at her, for the first time, like she might resent this sort of control. That opening in her face lasted only a second. But when the waiter came she ordered striped bass.

"So you heard about my tragedies," Emma said after the menus had been cleared away. She leaned forward, rested her elbows on the table, as if she were settling in.

My father lifted his chin toward her, defensive for the first time. "I'm sorry about John."

"You never came to the funeral."

"No. I was unable to attend." He took another sip of wine and said, "Bob was sick."

At the mention of Bob's name, Emma shifted her head toward my mother. "Ya, he passed on. We heard."

My mother cocked her head, as if merely interested.

"Who told you about Bob?" my father asked. "Luca?"

Emma nodded toward me for only a second.

"I'm talking about George," she said, and lowered her head, allowing it to sink meaningfully into her neck, "when I'm talking about my tragedies."

"What happened to George?"

My father seemed here genuinely startled. I had given him the basic facts about George, but Emma's tone indicated something beyond what he knew.

"He's home, isn't he, Emma?" I asked. "Is something new?"

"Home, yes. He's home. No, nothing new." She reached for a piece of bread from the basket the waiter had left, then, at the last moment, aborted that gesture; behind that little display, I could sense an anger at my father for not having remained intimately clued in to the family dramas. "What can I tell you, he's like . . . lost. Doesn't go out." Her lips bunched into each other; she gave the appearance of accepting something and expunging it at the same time. Then she looked across the table at my father, as if the chief encounter here tonight were between the two of them. My mother might as well not have been present.

"So that's my sad story. At least, thank God, I've got grand-children, from Bobby. Four of them. And Brenda's a lawyer. Not married yet, but okay." She knocked the table. "So how about you?"

"Well, I don't have grandchildren, if that's what you're asking."

Gina lowered her eyes a moment.

"You live here now," my mother said. Her stare fell on my father, as if studying him hard for signs of the man she used to know. I paid keen attention, though it had begun to seem as if other things were going on at this table, things that rendered the fact that they had once been married a secondary concern.

"Yes, Dorothy, I manage some apartments up the block here."

He finished those words, held her eyes a second as if another question might follow, then added some wine to everyone's glass. "I'm alone," he said carefully. "*Sono solo.*"

Emma took that in. The skin around her eyes bunched. "She's with Vinnie now," she said quickly.

My father tilted his head.

"From Vanderbruek," Emma added.

"Vinnie Fratolino?"

My mother nodded.

"His wife died?"

Emma shook her head. "Bedridden. An invalid."

My mother turned away from us, stared out a moment at the water through the plastic covering, then returned to face my father. She lifted her chin, sipped her wine. The movement was as if to banish any sense of shame or apology, and I watched, too, the manner with which Gina studied her, as if at any moment she might begin to smile.

"How is he?" my father asked.

"He's good," Emma answered.

"I asked Dorothy."

"He's good." My mother spoke this time, and I saw some color start up in her face.

"How long has this been going on?" I asked.

"A long time." Emma had answered, again, for my mother. "His wife's bedridden, what's the poor man to do?" She shrugged. Her second glass of wine was nearly finished.

"We're going to need some more of this," my father said, and gestured for the waiter.

By the time my father caught the waiter's attention, he was bringing the food, which detained us a moment, the sighing and the digging in. Before our second bottle of wine arrived, my father poured the last of the old bottle into my mother's glass. Emma watched carefully, concerned that my mother not imbibe too much, lest she fall again into the arms of this charming, faithless man. Yet her concern seemed misplaced. Nothing at all was going on between them.

"The Armenians just sold your house," Emma said.

My father tilted his head, acknowledged only a slight interest.

"Got four hundred thousand."

"No kidding?"

"Turned out to be a good investment, huh?"

"Yes," my father said, though it was clear, to me at least, that he was only humoring her. "Yes, I guess it turned out John was pretty smart."

Emma finally picked up on my father's tone. Her face seemed to close around it and turn, briefly, hostile. Then something else, a kind of visible second thought, came along to replace the hostility. "He wanted too much, John," Emma said, words that arose directly out of whatever silent perception she'd just had.

"What's that?" My father glanced over in a pose of innocence, not having studied, as I had, the recent fluctuations in Emma's expression.

Emma looked at him to let him know the conversation, for her at least, was not glib. "He wanted Paradise," she said.

"Yes," my father answered, taking in her meaning finally, even allowing a little silence, so that history could take its place—not much, in his value system—at the table. "He thought all we had to do was move into those beautiful houses, and everything would be great." He dove back into his cod.

Emma watched him. She looked for a moment like she wanted to fight. Then she seemed to give that up, too. "Ya, that's what he believed, all right."

Still, I could tell she didn't want to give my father his victory so easily. His attitude of laissez-faire, of ambivalence, oughtn't to be allowed to triumph; the loosened hold was not finally the absolute value before which we were all to bow here, tonight.

What made this position hard for her to maintain was that here my father, who had done so little to make the world hang together in any specific way, had at least a functioning, moderately successful son beside him. That I had not, in reaction to his abandonment, ended up like George was an example of the world's injustice, and she seemed, for a moment, to silently rail against that fact.

"How's your spaghetti?" she snapped at me.

"Good."

"That's all you wanted?"

My father seemed to feel as much as I did the roots of Emma's disturbed state. "Bobby, though," he offered. "Bobby's done all right."

"Who do you talk to?" Emma asked.

"Luca keeps me informed."

It was a lie; I couldn't remember talking to my father about Bobby for years. He had another source.

"Bobby's made a lot of money." She laughed. "He's big and fat, you should see him." Then she shrugged. "You know what John wanted."

My father wiped his mouth summarily with a napkin, nodded his head as if in recognition of the sum of all John had wanted.

Emma glanced at him, accepted what he offered. It was nowhere near enough, but perhaps she knew she would get no more.

"You seen where she lives now? Dorothy?"

"I haven't been invited, no." My father's smile was tiny.

"Hobbs Road," Emma said. "Small, very small."

He nodded. "Do you mind it, Dorothy?"

"No. It's enough for me."

Again Emma sighed, as if the whole problem of her sister were lodged there in that too humble, insufficient word "enough."

We were quiet then. For a while, our food was eaten in silence. My father glanced over at my mother, watched her eat, carefully noting that she seemed to be all right, a vestigial concern seeming to be working through him for an instant. Gina gazed beyond him at me, a slight questioning in her face: Where was this going to go now? Did I have some particular place toward which I wanted to push it?

I did, but I wanted the evidence to surface on its own. Did Gina expect me to ask a specific question? And what would that be? What question would not embarrass them into silence or subterfuge? In old age, did people become merely polite with one another? They ate, both of them, delicately, as if careful to prevent any display of their animality from showing forth. I had a sudden memory of the night I had interrupted their lovemaking, our first night in the new house, my father lifting his body off of hers with his blunt arrow of an erection and her soft, white, liquid-seeming body below him. The image held before me a moment, as these two older, somehow less vivid people cut through the last of their dinners. I wanted to know, quite simply: would it have been possible for him to stay? And if that were so, did it constitute permission for me to stay, too?

"Well, that's all for me," Emma said, and pushed her plate forward. "Stuffed."

"Me, too," my mother parroted, though a moment before she had looked to be eating happily enough.

"Would you two care for coffee?" my father asked.

I felt a blow in the stomach that the evening was ending too soon. Let them say yes. But both women shook their heads.

"Keep us up," Emma said. "We're two old women now, Lou."

"Yes. But you look pretty good for old women."

The second bottle of wine must have had its effect. Emma looked, for a second, before she visibly crushed the impulse, like she wanted to smile. "We get around, Dorothy and me. We travel sometimes."

"Do you?"

"Sure. Amish country. Where else, Dorothy?"

"We go to the beach."

"Oh, sure. But I'm talking big trips."

She nodded in silence a moment, as if to lay before my father the vastness of their widowy itinerary.

"And you? You're alone. And you don't mind it?" Emma asked.

"I don't. No."

There was a second long silence.

"How about dessert?" I asked. "We're paying."

"No, you're not." Emma scowled, and reached for her bag. Before we could stop her, she'd taken out a wad of cash and placed it on the table.

"Emma," I said. "We're paying."

"Too much," she answered. "Too expensive. You two have got your future to think of."

"This meal's not going to kill us."

"Put it away for your children."

I had no response to that; nor did Gina.

"Please, take it, Emma." I lifted the wad and pushed it toward her. "Our children will be okay."

Emma lifted her eyebrows. "You got something to tell us?"

"No."

"So what's holdin' up the works?"

After a brief pause—what possible answer could we give?—my father spoke. "Maybe they don't want any, Emma."

"I don't believe that. You two don't want to have kids?"

"Emma," my father interrupted again, "this could be a private subject for them."

"Right." Emma snapped her pocketbook open, peered inside. "So I won't open my big mouth." She looked a moment at Gina, editing some impulse before turning away.

"We never gave it a thought, did we, Dorothy?" She continued to search in her pocketbook, as if for some buried object. "The minute you were married, you know, that was the next big thing. And anybody who didn't get pregnant right away, that was some big problem. But today, there's this long period where, I don't know, what happens?" She smiled, as if this were something in the way of a joke.

"People try to get to know one another," I answered.

"Oh yeah?" She stared at me a long moment, assessing. "Don't worry about that. One way or the other, you get to know each other. Kids don't get in the way of that." She looked around at my mother, my father. "If these two had waited to get to know each other, you'd probably never have been born."

My father closed his eyes, slowly.

"What'd I say?" Emma snapped her pocketbook shut. "It's true."

My father opened his eyes, looked at me, then at my mother, shook his head.

"I think it was smarter, the way we did it," Emma went on. "Give children a chance to be born. The rest, gets taken care of."

"The getting to know one another." The words came from Gina, a surprise. She halted a second, took a sip of wine. "I think I agree."

"So you know him now," Emma said, and made a motion with her hand, as if we should carry on.

"I think it's time for the check," my father said.

"What, this embarrasses you, Lou?" Emma, not looking at him, shook her head, then went on. "I just worry. About the young people. They try to get it so perfect."

"Well, that's a kind of evolution, isn't it?" my father said, a little testily. "I think they're smart."

Emma gazed at him, paused, then chose not to respond.

"We tried to get it perfect, too, didn't we?" he went on. "Just in a different way." He placed his fingers on the rim of his wineglass, turned it. "Paradise."

Emma's face for a moment seemed frightened, and surprised by the way he'd been able so swiftly to turn the conversation away from grandchildren, where she had so clearly triumphed, to the field where he had the advantage.

"Dorothy's got the right idea," my father went on. "You find somebody, the hell with the rules."

Emma looked out at the water. Whatever fight existed in her seemed to be steadily depleted. My father looked at my mother as if what he'd just said had been magnanimous, and ought to earn him credit.

"All I can say," Emma said, "is you two better hurry, if you're interested. They say, today, the problem is half the time with the men. Not enough sperm."

My father glanced down at his plate, allowed the comment to be carried off by the wind.

"We accepted too much, Emma," he said then gently, but still with the inevitable edge. "Don't you think?"

Emma looked at him as if some assault might follow.

"Maybe," she said, when she had finally decided to speak. "The one thing I wish is, I wish we'd never accepted that war. That's what I wish."

My father only nodded sadly, perhaps feeling he'd pushed Emma further than he'd intended, though this had been the place toward which the conversation had always headed. We all moved the last of our food around our plates.

"Well yes," my father said finally.

"Luca never had to go," Emma said, without resentment, simple fact. "You never did a thing to keep him from going, did you?"

"No," my father answered carefully. "He was in school. And he had a high number in that lottery, as I recall. Wasn't that it, Luca?"

"Yes."

"Luck, I suppose," my father said, though he didn't mean it.

Emma nodded. "Ya, that was the thing. Neither of them ever wanted to go to school. He tried. John tried. Remember, you used to come over and try and help George, Luca?"

"Yes."

She made a dismissive gesture with one hand. "Always wild, that one. And now, not so wild."

She placed one hand over the other, and tapped gently on the lower hand, as if calming herself. "Where's that check?"

I lifted my hand for it, and when it came, paid without Emma having a chance to offer her money again. Yet that impulse seemed to have left her as well. She barely noticed my paying, stared out beyond the plastic covering at the water. Suddenly, it seemed, no one was in a hurry to leave.

"You all right, Dorothy?" Emma asked.

"Fine."

Emma nodded. Her charge had been kept safe for the evening, but something else had been opened up. She looked as though she wished my mother would go home, so that she could continue to spar with my father.

It was my mother who moved her chair out, signaling by that action that the rest of us should follow. There was a shuffling movement. We all stood, and moved, stately and slow, out into the restaurant's courtyard. The family apparently waiting for our table was dark—a husband and wife and two black-eyed young sons, each of whom held his mother's hand, or maybe she held theirs, with a fierce claim that set off a wave of longing in me. I tried to catch the woman's eye, but she was fixed on the empty table, on the good of her family, and had no interest in this other, lesser family filing past her. Then we were standing outside the courtyard again, pretty much where we had started. I took in that the night was over, that this was all I was likely to get, and a gut-clenching sadness came over me. I put my hand on my mother's shoulder as if to ask her to stay. But what did I want? For them to scream at one another, to assert the validity of their old union? Who would that serve but me? My father surveyed the street, men in couples drifting by, the beginning of the long gay Provincetown night. He would not make any display for us of what his own interest in this night might be.

For an instant then, I resented that part of him in the old, adolescent manner. In that same instant, I was not above believing that if he'd only resisted it, and stayed with us, a whole block of history might have gone differently. Undistracted, I would never have become friends with Andrew Weston. I might have been able to save George, guide him through the wilderness of *The Great Gatsby*, earn him his student deferment. John, unheartbroken, might still be alive. Ridiculous. Something had been at work already in those days, the failure inherent in John's old book of dreams. Ridiculous to think that things hadn't already been set in motion the day my father left. Still, there was a question there for me on that street: was it better, sensing an oncoming failure, to stay or to bolt? I felt certain for an instant that what my father had lost in severing himself from the common fate was greater than what Emma and John had suffered by sticking to it.

"Well," my father said, as if he had given this long enough and now wanted to resume the better part of his evening. "Was this what you wanted, Luca?"

The question had a kind of haughtiness to it, as if he'd suffered a little in giving me this much, been intruded upon. Also, as if there were something amusing in me, a grown man, having insisted on all this.

I accepted defeat—at least, defeat for now. "Yes, that was fine."

The night called to him, clearly.

"I'll take you guys home, how's that?" I turned to Emma and my mother.

"Don't be silly, we've got the car," Emma said.

"No, I'd like to see you home."

"What, you're gonna drive with us, then how will you get back?"

"I'll walk."

"Too far. And what about Gina?"

I turned to her.

"No, I don't think so," Gina said. "I'll wait back at the motel."

"You don't mind?"

"No." She wasn't looking at me when she answered, so I couldn't be sure whether this had displeased her.

"It's silly to take us back," Emma said. "You don't think we can find it on our own? It's the Holiday Inn."

"Dad, will you be home, if I drop by on the way back?"

"It's no wonder you don't have kids yet," Emma said. "Where else you gonna stop tonight?" She looked from side to side on the street. "Be careful one of these men doesn't grab you."

She looked around to see if the joke registered, realizing only after she'd said it that my father was "one of these men." The chagrin in her face was gone, though, in seconds.

"Lou, you take care of yourself, you hear?"

"I will, Emma."

There was a silence then.

"Dad, you didn't answer me."

"About being home?" He looked vaguely annoyed. "I can be, yes. How long will you be?"

"An hour?"

He turned away, no answer, but I knew he'd be waiting.

"Gina can see me home," he said, and took out a cigarette.

"Still with those?" Emma asked. "Everybody else gave them up."

"I'm still with them, Emma."

It was time then for my parents to say good-bye to one another, the first time, I realized, that this had ever formally happened. My father, about to light the cigarette, suddenly thought better of it. A smile appeared on his face that seemed to have been summoned there. He gestured with his chin toward this unimportant woman, this shade of the past. His eyes suggested this was something he would like to have over with. The white apartment, and who knew what else, waited.

My mother's smile, in reaction to this, grew wide and face-transforming, as if she would meet his tentative warble of a good-bye with something full-throated. But she took no step toward him, made no sound, and in that negative movement indicated—to me, anyway—that if she was a ghost to him, he was a greater ghost to her. He might evaporate into the crowd now, it didn't matter. Once she had been married, that was all. Let's go home.

My father was left standing then, in a pose of arrested movement, and from the look on his face, I could tell that, of the two of them, his had been the greater vulnerability to this scene. A surprise. The cigarette dangled a bit foolishly from his lips, and, noticing this, he cast it out into the street. The evening before him looked, suddenly, less certain. My mother had already begun walking toward Emma's car.

Gina followed her, to say good-bye. Emma remained behind, seeming on the verge of making some kind of apology to my father. "I'll wait for Gina," he said. Emma sauntered off, after saying "G'night, Lou." I looked at him and said, "I hope this wasn't too hard for you."

The displeasure on his face showed for a moment. "Don't know what you wanted it for, is all." He wasn't looking at me. "I'll wait for Gina," he repeated.

I felt a little guilty leaving him then, but the others were ready to go. Gina, having said her good-byes, met me on my way to them.

"Wait up, okay?" I asked her.

"This hasn't been enough? Why don't you just let them go home?"

"I want to go see how it was for her."

"Didn't you see?" she asked. She looked at me, as if marveling all over again at my willful ignorance. "He's dead to her," she said.

"Yes." I touched her arm. "Listen. Wait up, okay? I won't be long. Watch television or something."

She looked at my hand on her arm, made an unhappy face. "Aren't you supposed to be taking care of your marriage, or something?" she asked.

"Yes. Yes, I am." I sent her a look, containing something I hoped she saw.

Whether or not she did, she moved past me, went to my father, and I caught up with my mother and Emma on the side street where Emma's Lincoln was parked.

"Can you squeeze this thing through these narrow streets, Emma, or do you get stuck?"

They were neither of them in the mood for a joke. Emma had been walking with her eyes downcast, thought pushing up against the skin of her face like the movement of oatmeal at a slow boil. My mother hardly acknowledged my presence, seemed in another world.

"You want to drive, Luca?" Emma asked. "I think maybe, with all that wine, I might run somebody over."

"How about you, Mom? Feel like a driving lesson?"

Still she didn't respond, took the backseat. When we were in the car, beginning the drive, Emma said, "Well, I thought I'd die when I saw him, but I gotta admit, he looks good. What do you think, Dorothy?"

In the backseat, my mother settled herself. We drove down Bradford Street in silence.

"She won't say," Emma said to herself.

After a while, she continued: "You think he was insulting John?"

"No. I don't."

She shifted in her seat. "I had to tell him about Vinnie, Dorothy. Otherwise I was afraid he might make a play for you."

Through the rearview mirror, I watched my mother, in profile, staring out the window.

Emma had not meant it; her face looked creased and drawn now, and her mood such that only a joke—even a feeble one like the one she'd just made—would stanch a whole other set of feelings.

"Course, now *you* know, and that was something she didn't want."

"It's all right."

"A mother and son shouldn't hide from one another. You hear that, Dorothy, he says it's all right." And, after the nonresponse: " 'Cause she was worried, you know?"

We arrived at the Holiday Inn without having said anything more of substance. I parked the car while they went up to their room. By the time I arrived, Emma was putting on a nightgown; my mother was in the bathroom.

"You wanna talk to her, Luca?" Emma asked with some severity, as if something had gone on in my absence.

"I'll let you have some privacy," I said. I motioned to the balcony outside the room. "I'll wait out there."

The wind was still soft, and it was not yet dark. From this point on the beach you could see far enough so that the arching hook shape of Provincetown was visible. A set of low clouds gathered over the bay. Occasionally, a car passed below me, tires making a sandy crunch. A group of little girls returned from the beach. The wind had a late June freshness to it, that beginning of summer feeling. I heard a tapping behind me, and saw my mother standing there, ready for bed, in her bathrobe.

"It might be too cold out here for you, Mom."

She opened the glass doors and stepped out, shuddering and then letting go of that, as she realized how warm it was.

"No. No, it's all right."

"I guess I owe you an apology," I said.

"Why?"

"Come on."

She looked out at the water of the bay. "People still swimming," she murmured.

I waited a moment. "What was that like for you?"

She hesitated, looked at me as though the question unsettled her more than the preceding scene had. "You needed to see it," she said.

"Yes," I answered, surprised at anything so direct coming from her.

"That was why I stayed."

"Well, I'm grateful."

Again I waited, while she turned away from me, looked below her, her gaze fixed on the parking lot, and somewhere else.

"I think I always wanted to know where you were with it. With him."

"You could have asked."

"I know. But I've never been good at that, have I?"

Still, there was no response, just a slight, otherworldly smile that told me she was going to need further prodding.

"I'm sorry. I guess it was selfish of me."

She looked at the water, nodded, leaned forward against the railing. I did the same thing. I was remembering the tepid conversations we used to have in the years when we lived together, even the years after college, when I'd come home and taken up my teaching life. I felt a moment's nostalgia for those days, broken by my mother's next words.

"Gina wants a baby, doesn't she?"

A shock, but I answered quickly. "Very much."

It was clear she wanted the next words to come from me.

"How do you know that?"

"I just do. Why won't you give her one?"

I looked into her eyes to see what she knew about me. "You're going to be just like him," she had said once. But all of that seemed forgotten now.

Inside, Emma was puttering close to the glass doors, desperate, I could see, for some snatch of our conversation to reach her.

"I guess I've always been afraid," I said, "that I might do what Dad did. I guess I've always been on guard against that."

I was giving her one more chance to remember that she'd once seemed to know things about me. She gave no indication that she did. "Why would you do that?" she asked.

"I don't know. Men do."

"Not all men."

"No."

"You don't have to be so careful."

The words felt strangely wounding, coming from her.

I paused before speaking. "Well, I feel like I've been careful for both of us, Mom. Too careful, maybe." I paused again, trying to gauge what was registering with her, how much of the past was coming back to her. "But now you and—Vinnie?"

She shook her head, as if Vinnie Fratolino had no bearing on what we were talking about.

"You're happy together?"

"Emma shouldn't have mentioned that." She glanced away from me; her focus returned to the parking lot. "It's innocent, really. He comes, and we keep each other company."

I nodded, stupidly. Perhaps she was lying; I couldn't know. "If it's more than that, maybe you deserve it."

I waited another moment before going on. "People kept trying to keep you from your life. First him, then me."

She looked inside then, and I thought this might be a signal that she wanted this conversation to be over. But she surprised me by going on. "He looks good, doesn't he?"

"Yes."

"It's too bad his friend died."

"Yes."

"Did you get what you wanted tonight?"

"No. I didn't. People don't give up their secrets so easily. But I think maybe if I knew then what I know now. I mean that he means so little to you anymore—"

She nodded, as if I was getting it right.

"If I knew that then, maybe I wouldn't have stood in your way."

"Why do you think you stood in my way?"

I halted before saying the word I don't think either of us had spoken in twenty-five years. "Biago." Then I moved my head, as if her memory would need to be prodded.

She stared directly into my eyes for several seconds. Something in that simple look made me feel I had to keep talking; either that or collapse.

"I was afraid for you to be with another man. I didn't want to see you get hurt again. But it was more than that, too."

Her eyes asked the next question.

"I guess I didn't want either of us to have anything to do with—can I say it? With sex. I thought if I could just bat sex away from both of us, we'd be okay."

She paused before asking, "And did that work?"

"No."

Her next words seemed to finish for me: "Of course not."

"So. I'm sorry."

She did not say what I expected, did not diminish the thing I had done, did not reactively forgive me. Instead, it seemed I had opened it all up for her.

"You coming in?" Emma was on the other side of the glass door, exasperated now, motioning us in. "It's cold out there, isn't it? Dorothy, you'll get pneumonia."

It was strange the way my mother stared then at her sister.

"Are you okay, Mom?"

She glanced down. I touched her arm. Inside, Emma had turned away, gone to sit on the bed. When she turned back, and our eyes met, it was as if she knew, intuitively, what subject we had reached, and was frightened of it.

"I didn't know it would be so hard for you. I'm sorry for bringing it up."

"It wasn't just you."

"What?"

"The reason I didn't marry him. It wasn't just you."

"Who else was it?"

She shook her head. "It's nothing. It's over."

"What happened, Mom?"

"It was something John did," my mother finally said. "With Biago's business. With the banks. He tried to keep Biago from getting a loan he needed. That was when I decided I couldn't go through with it."

She paused a moment. I looked down.

"John didn't mean it. He was just scared. He thought Biago would hurt him with the neighbors. They were too important to him."

She opened the sliding glass door, stepped inside. I followed, and Emma, relieved, glanced up at both of us, though her next words were hesitant and a bit guilty-sounding. "You two patch everything up?"

We neither of us answered right away. Finally, to relieve the silence, I said, "I think so."

"Good." Emma flicked the television on. It was barely prime time; perhaps eight-thirty.

"You ready for some TV, Dorothy?"

My mother looked up at me. "He'll be waiting for you, won't he?"

"I guess he will."

"So you better go."

At the door, we were far enough from Emma that I thought I could speak without being heard. "I feel like I've opened something up for you, now I'm leaving you with her."

My mother simply shook her head. Beyond her, Emma sat, the glow from the television against her. She had shut off the bedside light. She, too, glanced up at me, perhaps feeling safer now, as though, with my leaving, the evening's danger had at last passed.

Before leaving, I asked if they wanted to meet for breakfast the next day. It was Emma who waved me off. "Stay with your wife, you've put her through enough tonight."

I leaned forward to kiss my mother. At the last moment, she offered me her cheek. Then she closed the door behind her.

As I was walking away, crossing the parking lot, I heard a voice calling my name. Emma had come out, onto the motel's passageway. She was three floors above me. "Be careful," she said. I stood there a moment, understanding that she had come out for the purpose of acknowledging what we had both seen when I'd been out on the balcony and our eyes had met, our mutual complicity in my mother's fate. There was nothing to say, but for a moment I saw the Hill through another lens, and my recent adulation of the "common fate" took on another meaning. A breeze lifted Emma's bathrobe, and she held it down. She waved me off, finally, and went inside.

A half hour later, I was climbing the steps that led directly to my father's deck. He was waiting there, having gone from cigarettes to a fat, fetid cigar. An open bottle of wine was beside him. From his chair, he took me in without moving. The light was from a single bulb on the porch and from the string of colored lights surrounding his deck. He removed the cigar, licked some shards from his lower lip, and then reinserted it; that was his greeting. I sat in the empty chair beside him.

"I've been expecting you," he said.

"Yes."

"At the end of this long, ridiculous evening."

A boat must have gone by somewhere out on the bay; the waves pushed against his pilings.

"Was it ridiculous?" I asked.

"Yes."

"Well, then I apologize. Which is what I've been doing all night. But all right, here's one more."

He paused, puffed, seemed to be considering. "Accepted. But I don't know why you had to put her through that."

"I think it was easier for her than it was for you."

"Do you think so?"

"I do."

"Why?"

"I don't know. Just got that impression."

He smiled, as if to diminish what I was saying, to show how it bounced off of him. I looked at the way his skin had hardened and reddened over time. There was still a power in him that came out in small, frightening movements of his face.

"You retain this notion that your mother still has a hold on me, I think." He paused a second, giving me not quite enough time to respond. "Forty-two years old, you'd like us to retreat to that nice house, and say it's all been a bad dream." The smile returned, the absurdity of the sentiment. "And apparently I can't convince you otherwise."

I nodded my head, studied the planks of his deck. We both sat there, silent awhile.

"What?" he asked.

"Nothing."

"No, there's a question."

"There are a million, but maybe I should go back to Gina."

"Yes, maybe you should."

"How long ago did she leave?"

"A while. I expect she'll be home now."

He flicked the ashes off his cigar onto the deck. "I don't know why I ever agreed to this," he said.

"You were curious."

"Oh, was I? Thank you. Because I'd wondered."

"You were. You wanted to know how she turned out." I paused a moment. "I think it's more my fault than yours that she turned out the way she did. Lonely, I mean. Being romanced by Vinnie Fratolino."

"He's not a bad guy. But how is it your fault?"

"I didn't want her to marry that Biago. God, that terrified me."

He smiled.

"It terrified me, too. It's just it was such a *raw* choice. It was strange, but I wanted her to retain some of that elegance I thought she'd aspired to, not make a choice so directly from the crotch." He checked with me to make sure I accepted that. "I don't know why, but that offended me." He shook his head. "But it was none of my business." He lifted the hand holding the cigar to scratch his forehead. "You should have known it was none of yours."

"Yes. Clearly."

He tilted his head toward me, some generosity working in him. "Want some wine?" He poured me a glass without waiting for my answer.

"This is better than that swill you ordered in the restaurant. 'Tears of Christ.' Christ is shedding tears because the wine is so bad."

I drank a little of what he offered me.

"So. Tell me." He leaned toward me, mock-conspiratorially. "*Are* you and Gina going to have children, or is it none of my business?"

"This seems to be on everyone's mind tonight."

"Well, it was a theme. In the restaurant. Don't tell me you didn't notice your wife's reaction."

"I'm not that thick, no. I noticed."

"This is an issue? What is it, was Emma right—a low sperm count?"

"I haven't been tested. We haven't been trying, Dad."

He halted, puffed, chuckled. "*Sorry,*" he said, and made a mock grimace. "I should know better than to pry."

I took another sip of the good wine. "Well, I should be going," I said.

"What did you make me wait here for, if this was all you wanted?"

"I don't know."

We both hesitated a moment before the next thing that might be said.

"What will you do?" I asked. "After I go?"

"Finish this wine, I suppose."

"Then bed?"

"No. No, I expect I'll go out."

"To?"

"Oh, there are places." He took another sip. "Places where I'm known." He glanced at me, to let me know, lest there was any doubt, what sorts of places he meant. "Do I have your approval, or would you like to keep me from that as well?"

I smiled. "No, you can go."

"Thank you." He paused. "You know, I don't blame you for giving me a hard time when I left. I can't imagine what that was like for you, in that rooming house. And Bob was a scary man when he drank. He scared *me.*"

He bit on something, a shred of cigar stuck in his mouth.

"But so much time has passed." He sounded annoyed now. "You've grown up, you've gotten married. One would think you'd understand all this by now, and avoid scenes like tonight."

"One would think."

He sent me a look to let me know he didn't appreciate my tone.

"It hardly matters now who we live with, or don't live with. People make their little arrangements, Luca. Don't kick yourself too much that she didn't marry Biago. If she'd wanted to, she would have, believe me. Your mother's always known how to take care of herself that way." He lifted his eyebrows so that I should understand. "I hope I'm not shocking you."

"No."

He looked me over a moment before going on. "She chose, anyway, to be part of that group, her family. To not go against, or stand outside of it. That was more important to her, to live a life of acceptance. So she let them set the rules. With me, it was the opposite."

He lay his cigar down on the edge of the small table beside him. "You were very young, and I suppose you believed that big houses, neighborhoods, these constituted something very solid. I suppose you believed that."

"I did, yes."

"I watched you ally yourself with John, I didn't miss that. And why not? A solid man, who cared about things, as opposed to a—well, what was I?"

I sipped some wine, waiting to see where this might be going.

"But ask yourself this. Where does life come from? Hmm? Who got you to your wife, after all? Did John do that? John couldn't even take care of his own children, for God's sake, never mind *you.*"

I caught the jealousy there, the sense—new to me—that he had been aware of the competition with John for my young soul. I caught, too, the sense of a plea, as if for an acknowledgment he'd never asked for before. But I chose to pursue the other thing he had brought up.

"Speaking of getting me to my wife. I always wanted to ask you about that. That flyer you left in Gina's pocketbook. Why'd you do that?"

He lifted the cigar, smiled craftily. "Oh, *I* didn't do that."

He puffed.

"Bob was the one." He let that sink in. "Looking out for you. He worried about you. Was afraid you didn't know how to live. Or . . . well, that you didn't know how to get in touch with that part of yourself. Perceptive, eh?"

I was silent for a moment. Bob Painter had been my benefactor, if that was the word. Jesus.

"Did Bob know . . . I mean, did he get it? Gina was with a guy who tied her up and left her. Jesus." Something normally censored in me felt loosened by this news. "She was kind of a whore in those days."

The word had slipped out. Immediately I saw, from the way he looked at me in response, that he was shocked I'd used that word, shocked and disapproving.

" 'Whore'?" he asked. "Did I hear the word 'whore'? I haven't heard that word in years."

He went on looking at me. I sat and merely endured it.

"Because she was with a man, that made her a 'whore'?"

"Dad, you don't know the half of it."

"No, I suppose I don't. But, Luca . . ."

I got up, took my wine to the railing, sipped some. He looked my body up and down and smiled, as though he didn't know the slightest thing about me. "Good Lord," he said.

"All right," I said, to ask him to stop.

"Tell me about your marriage."

"No."

"Well, clearly there's something to tell."

"No. Not much. Terror. That pretty much sums it up. Gina hates me for using that word, but there it is. For years, I thought I was like you. That I was going to leave her for a man. Stupid. Why should that happen? I slept with a boy. In college. I liked it. It was a kind of love, I guess. Things like that hover over you. They don't let go of you."

My father's eyes had widened; then they went back to normal and he puffed his cigar with great, renewed interest.

"It's the rare man who gets through life *without* something like that happening, Luca. If not the action, then at least the desire. That's the sense I get anyway."

"I don't think that's true."

"No? All right, let's say it's not. Where does that leave you, then? Waiting for someone like Bob Painter to show up?"

He smiled at that.

"No, I don't think so," I said.

"I don't think so, either. Believe me, you'd have been suffering a lot more than you appear to have suffered if that was the truth about you."

He paused.

"I know whereof I speak. Which leaves you with the fear. That lovely manly fear that sleeping with a man *makes* you something. Something irrevocable. Women don't seem to have that."

"I know."

"But if a man even once, and, God forbid, *likes* it . . . well, that's it, isn't it? A lifetime of uncertainty."

"Yes," I said, after another pause.

He continued to stare at me, moving the cigar around in his mouth. From one of the apartments he managed, laughter came, a male party.

"You haven't understood the first thing about sex, have you?"

"I guess I haven't."

The party below us threatened, for a moment, to become raucous.

"Shall I tell those guys to keep it down? Does that sort of offend you?"

"No."

"So this is why I don't have grandchildren. This 'terror' of yours. Tell me, why hasn't Gina left you?"

"I don't know, actually. Why don't we stop this, okay?"

He paused, puffed, picked up the wine. "Why, Luca? This is a place where I might actually be able to help you out." He scowled, looked to the side. "I thought your generation was actually doing some good work in this regard. If in no other. Blurring the lines a little bit. Making it all not quite so rigid. But apparently, you're the last holdout. Fifties morality. Fifties sexuality."

"Are you going to go on insulting me?"

"I'm just thinking of that poor girl. Having to live with this uncertainty of yours."

"She would have had a fine life if you hadn't interfered. Or *Bob*." I stopped there a moment. "Bob. Why'd he do that?"

My father made an astonished face, as if the answer should have been obvious. "Because he loved you. Simple as that. And knew you were closing in on yourself. We could both see that. All those summers. This beautiful boy. Who never brought a girl. Or said a word. Who kept to himself. And swam. And swam. All over the dam. It broke his heart. Bob was an eloquent soul. 'The kid should be getting laid.' Well." He took a hearty puff on his cigar. "We got you laid."

"Thank you."

"Oh, it was good for you. And don't assume Gina's life would have been so wonderful without you. You know what she did at Bob's funeral? *Thanked* me. For *you*. It would appear she loved you. Maybe still does."

Again he looked hard at me. "Luca, it is a far cry from living your life in a state of complete misery, believing that it's the *wrong* life, and feeling that because you once got it on with a man, you're something *less* than a man. Ask any crowd of red-blooded heterosexuals how many are secure in their masculinity, see how many hands go up."

He paused.

"So here I am lecturing you. On the subject of sexuality, of all things. How this evening has gone."

He took another sip of wine, sat back in his chair, as if resettling. "But I'll tell you something I do know. Close off one side of your sexuality, you close off the whole thing." He settled back. "There's one valve, Luca." He smiled craftily. "One valve, controlling both spigots." He seemed to like that, having said it. We listened to the water for a few moments.

"Do you remember the night I interrupted you?"

He didn't, clearly.

"First night in the house, I came into your room, you were making love to her."

"It's coming back to me. Dimly."

"You know what you said to me? You walked me back to my bedroom and said, 'That's the sound of happiness you hear.' "

He nodded. "Yes, it's coming back."

"You were lying."

"Was I?"

"Well . . ."

"I don't believe I was lying. No. No, I recall that was a very happy night."

He went into it for a second. I could see it in his eyes. Then he deflected it. I'd seen that action in him many times, that unwillingness to land in the soft place. He simply stared at me then. I wanted to see what would come next. Finally he looked exasperated. "What shall I tell you, Luca? That I loved her? I did. All right? That I was capable of living that life? Yes, I was."

The party noises below us subsided briefly, then there was a burst of laughter. My father looked annoyed by it.

"You lasted a long time with us. I was twelve. You were together fourteen years. That's longer than I've been married."

"So where's your Bob Painter, hmm? When's he going to come into your life, is that what you're thinking?" He gazed at me as if he might be willing—for an instant only—to consider me in some way other than his accustomed way.

"Where'd you meet him?" I asked. "How?"

He paused. "Do you remember the Vanderbruek bus?"

"I do." I smiled slightly. "Numb Nuts and Dry Balls."

"One day you leave your house and there he is. Simple as that. Ugly man." He checked with me, for agreement. "A drunk. Three little girls. A man who drank and hung out in rest stops on his way home from work, picking up men. Then going home and drinking himself into oblivion. That was his life, Luca. Absurd. But there you have it."

Carefully, he folded his hands.

"There you have what?"

"It's never the way we want it, Luca. It's an absurd, absolutely nonsensical thing."

"What is?"

"Well, *love*. The way it lands on the inappropriate. You should have seen him that day. On the Vanderbruek bus. We'd just moved into that house. Ab*surd*. Except he looked at me a certain way and I understood something, instantly." He checked my face to see how much I perceived. "No one else was *asking* me for anything. Not your mother, last of all her. But in this strange man's face, I saw something so simple, so *attractive*. An utterly honest exchange. It threw the whole way I'd been living into relief. I could have turned away." He settled deeper into memory. "But I didn't."

He shifted in his seat, made a grimace.

"That stupid face of his. I wanted to punch him sometimes. But I understood what he kept telling me, I *got* it, finally. If you're not alive emotionally, what good is it? I didn't want someone like him to be the one to make me feel. But . . ." He paused. "Either way it's the same, I suppose, Luca. You give yourself to a neighborhood, to a way of life, or you give yourself to a person. Either way it amounts to the same thing. Your Uncle John knew how to be alive in *things*. For a while. Or, anyway, he managed to fool himself that he was. But in the end, I think not."

He smiled sadly, affirming the perception I'd had at the restaurant that he had managed to keep in touch, after all, to track John's life as if it had been important to him as well. He moved his hands slowly to his thighs. "Are you alive in this marriage, Luca?"

I waited a moment, considering. "I think I could be. I think I'm haunted. But I think I could be."

"Well, that's all, isn't it? That's all there is to say."

He turned away. The men at the party below us seemed to be going out for the evening. It seemed to have tired him, this exchange.

There were sounds from the sea. Another party, on a boat. We heard them shouting to one another. Women, men. Then it was gone.

"Shouldn't you be going now?" he asked.

I looked at him, not wanting to go at all.

"Gina is no doubt waiting."

Something was in his face that I hadn't seen in a long time, the kind of look a man's face wears when he's just admitted something and is waiting for your judgment. Except it was difficult to piece together what my father had just admitted. Or to sense what he was asking for. Forgiveness? I didn't think so. An acknowledgment of what his life had been? That was closer, though not quite it. Only toward the end of this long pause did I begin to suspect that it was simpler than that: tonight he didn't want to be left alone.

I moved toward him. At the last moment he turned away from me, perhaps embarrassed by the too-direct sense of having made a plea.

I allowed him that. "Your night won't wait for you much longer," I said.

"Oh, I may have taken in enough tonight, Luca. It may be that bed is the only thing waiting for me tonight. Bed and TV."

"Okay, then." I touched him on the shoulder. "Do you want me to stay?"

"Of course not. No."

He put his hand on my hand, patted it, then pointed my way out. "Be careful on those steps."

"Yes."

"My best to Gina."

"I will."

From the steps, I waved to him. He nodded his head.

We have two children now, Gina and I. We got lucky, given our ages and the history of Gina's abortions. Two girls, they're six and four as I write. It didn't take much, just a loosening of the gates of Fortress Carcera and then the house filled up. The rooms. I still go around at night, obsessively checking things, even more so now. Gina thinks, as always, I'm a bit crazy, a bit fixated on things over which I have no real control. Their names are Anna and Francesca. We live more or less the lives of everyone else around us, indistinguishable from the other couples with their girls and their boys, their minivans, the couples at the edge of the soccer field. They cling to me, their small hands on my neck. Sometimes it seems ridiculous to me that I once considered an existence devoid of them, but I did. I face every day the ghosts of my former life, the fear I used to carry around with me. At times the old fear seems negligible and at other times it seems like the realest thing I've ever known. It's a mistake, I think, to believe you're ever cured of terror. All you've done is master it. That's all.

I continue at the high school. I did my two years as chairman of the History Department, then returned to my lesser role as teacher, the hours being filled at that point by a baby daughter. For a few years, Gina lightened her load at the law office, but this fall, when Francesca enters kindergarten, she'll go back to full-time.

What happened that night, to change things? What happened after I left my father and went back to Gina in the motel? We didn't have our beautiful resolution. For one thing, Gina wasn't even there. She'd taken the car and driven to Wellfleet and sat on the pier there and smoked cigarettes and considered leaving me. She remained there a couple of hours, bought herself an ice cream, wept. Helen Weston, while I was gone fetching Andrew's friends, had told Gina a story about me, about me coming to their house in the days of Andrew's banishment from normal junior high school life. About what it had been like for her to see me come, silent and dutiful. She'd gotten it all wrong, of course; she'd thought I'd been doing it out of some great altruism—me, who, in Helen Weston's view, could have participated with the other boys, could have enjoyed all the benefits of a red-blooded American life. She could never have guessed I'd become Andrew's friend as a way of courting my own marginality, which for years had been the true, great romance of my life.

Helen Weston told Gina she'd fallen in love with me in those days, and later that night, when Gina told me that story, she said, "That's what you do, Luca. You make people fall in love with you because they take your fear for empathy." She was right, of course. She'd once believed something similar, that my attentiveness as a lover had risen out of undiluted passion, where it had been, instead, a deliberate attempt to keep her from asking questions. So should she leave me? She'd sat on that pier and smoked cigarettes and thought a long time about that.

Finally, though, she'd gotten cold. That is why marriages last, I think. Not because of great decisions or even, most of the time, because of the persistence of great passions but because at some crucial moment someone gets cold, and needs to come in. I am not ashamed to admit that is why Gina returned to me; I'm grateful. She'd gotten in the car and driven back, unresolved, and there I'd been, waiting, a little panicked that she wasn't coming back at all. You carry a scenario in your head. We would make love, I'd thought. We would make love and this time I'd be open and undefended and everything would be fine. Except she wasn't there. For an hour I'd waited, watching anxiously every car that passed in front of the motel.

When she'd come inside she didn't at first even look at me.

"Where were you?" I asked, my own voice sounding to me small and scared.

She told me about Wellfleet and about how she'd gotten cold. She made herself ready for bed. She wore pajamas.

When she was lying in bed I went and sat there. "My father told me it was Bob who put that flyer in your bag."

She didn't say anything at first.

"Are you surprised?"

"I always knew that," Gina said.

"So why didn't you tell me?"

"Because we had to keep things a certain way, remember? Secret and careful." She pulled the blanket over her.

"Why are you doing that? Covering yourself?"

"Should I not?"

"No. You should not." I pulled the cover down.

"It's cold, Luca."

"You should have told me."

"Maybe. Yes." She stared at me without blinking. "He came in after Neville had tied me up. He heard me crying. He came in and untied me. I never told you that." She was unashamed.

"He saw you naked?"

"Yes." She said it in a way that made me embarrassed of the question. "I always knew it would have been him. At his funeral, I asked your father." She waited, as if for my reaction. "There are things you should have told me, too. About being half here."

"Yes."

"Do you have any idea how that hurts?"

"Now we're even."

"Are we?"

"Sure. Yes. You don't have to be the whore anymore and I don't have to be the secret homosexual. We don't have to be that weird couple we always were."

She stared into me a second.

"Or maybe we can still be those people but something else besides. After tonight, it doesn't seem to matter to me who the fuck we are."

Still, she waited.

"What's the something else besides?"

I leaned forward and kissed her.

She gave me one of those kisses that says, *maybe.*

I unbuttoned the top of her pajamas.

"How was it with your father?"

"Shh."

"No, I want to know what it is he said."

"Is this what intimacy's going to be like? All this talking?"

I pulled down the bottoms of her pajamas.

"It's cold."

I covered her but I didn't go in. I kept kissing her until I knew she wouldn't resist anymore and then I made sure she was wet. When I was inside her, she said, "Go deep. Go as deep as you can."

I did. I knew she was looking at me all the time we made love. I knew she wasn't going to allow herself to lose herself; she wasn't going to give me an easy time of it. It was like making love on trial, but I didn't mind that. I didn't mind at all that I had to put my own neediness on display. If I had to make love like this for the rest of my life, I reasoned that would be okay, too. I'd be this needy, desperate guy, yes, but that was at least better than who I'd been up until now.

When I splashed into her she put her hand on the back of my neck. I will remember this forever. The gesture of acceptance. The way another person moves just a little bit. I believe I began to weep. She patted my back and said, "Shh." Then her hand lowered and we started again and this time she was a little more with me. I had this feeling I was going to fuck my way into her good graces, but that is never the whole thing. Never. I knew what was waiting after this, another kind of spilling. I knew I would have to keep meeting her forever.

I would like to tell the story about what happened to us after that night, about our little girls and about the life we live now, about my father, with whom I have grown closer, and my mother, with whom I have not, but in the end I suppose the important thing is that I have stepped into it. I have taken a step, and the requirement now is that I not slip back, not allow myself to return to the place where I was outside things.

The light, though, the closing light falls over that scene of the two of us in that motel room. I remember Gina didn't come even the second time, and I began to get scared. I told myself it was only my old watchfulness, which I needed to let go of, but even so, when we started the third time, I became fierce, it was like a thing that had to happen. I needed something more from her, so I worked like a demon, and when I realized it was going to happen, she was at last going to give herself over to me, I found a little smile came unbidden to my face. Then an image appeared before me. I hadn't asked for it. It just arrived. It was an image of all the couples I knew, the living and the dead, in a kind of weird parade. My father and mother, Emma and John. My father and Bob Painter, my mother in some close embrace with Vinnie Fratolino. I remember feeling, for a moment, a terrible resistance. Then Gina said the word, *yes.* I closed my eyes, and joined them.

Acknowledgments

The journey of this novel began in 1995, when I read a letter to the editor of the *Dallas Sunday News*, in reply to a forum on gay issues conducted by that paper. I am indebted to that letter's anonymous author, who grew up with a gay father, as much for his tone as for his sentiments, both of which ignited something in me.

Thanks are owed to Howard Sasson, Joe Giardina, and Ken DiMaggio for research; to Joann Kobin, Mordicai Gerstein, John Stifler, Betsy Hartman, Marisa Labozzetta, and the late Norman Kotker for invaluable help in listening to the work while it was still in progress; to Deb Futter for her initial faith and for her encouragement; to Sloan Harris and Lee Boudreaux for their always watchful shepherding, for their patience, and for their insights.

A debt stands, as well, to the great black-and-white cinematographers of the early 1960s—Russell Harlan, Ernest Laszlo, Boris Kaufman, and Burnett Guffey—for inspiration at a point when it was needed.

And, as always, to Eileen, Nicola, and Sophia, for their continuing endurance and grace.

Recent History

Anthony Giardina

A Reader's Guide

A Conversation
with Anthony Giardina

Random House: What do you mean when you say that *Recent History* tracks the movement of men's lives from physical dominion to a greater concern with intimacy? What's the next developmental stage for men, then?

Anthony Giardina: One of the trickiest things I've found in my life as a man has been to try and track my own progress against my father's at a similar time in his life. When my father was fifty, which is what I am, he was building my mother her dream house; he was forcibly lifting the two of them, and their children, up a class. Their relationship may not have been great, but maybe it didn't matter so much. They were a corporation, a couple in synch with their times. At fifty, I'm not building my wife her dream house. We tend to talk much more about our relationship, about the mental health of our kids; we may want more on the physical plane, but that's never the number one priority. In this, I'm *almost* in synch with my times. That is, in an age when we, again, seem to be measuring ourselves by what we own, something is eating away at that as an unquestioned goal. No thinking person, in a relationship, can miss the demand that's out there for more intimacy, more emotional honesty and nakedness. We're asked now to *meet* one another, sexually and emotionally, in a way our parents weren't asked to, at least not by the culture in which they lived. So I wanted, in this novel, to look at a couple who are really suited to each other in most ways, yet who harbor, on the male side, a potentially crippling secret. In the old world, that secret would have been allowed to fester somewhere under the surface. Its potential for harm would have been there, certainly, but in an age when marriage had a deeper social component, it wouldn't have the potential to kill, which it does here. So this couple has to look at intimacy itself, what it means, what secrets mean. For me, the novel is about intimacy's potential for destructiveness as well as its potential for good. It's a very hot piece of coal we're juggling at the moment, but you'd never know that from the prevailing discussion. You'd think intimacy was the cure to all our ills, rather then the double-sided thing it is.

RH: Does *Recent History* posit that all men, straight and gay, have a homosexual side to their personalities? How do you think a male readership will react to this?

AG: I don't think all men have a homosexual side to them, no. But I think the labels "straight" and "gay" are about as useful in describing men's internal lives as the labels "conservative" and "liberal" are in describing the politics of the average American. Most of us are somewhere in the middle. But this is not a comfortable thing for men to discuss; in fact, it's hardly discussed at all. At dinner parties I've been to, women seem to feel pretty free to let on that they've experimented in their youths with other women, but when the discussion turns to the men, the guys clam up. (In fact, when I describe the plot of *Recent History* to my male friends, a curious silence ensues.) So how do I think a male readership will react to this? Not to be too pretentious about it, this is the ur-history of men I'm writing about, the suppressed history, the things I imagine a lot of men have felt but have had to suppress because it's never been an acceptable part of the campaign biography. I imagine men will read this book on subways with a brown paper bag wrapped around the cover, but they won't be able to put it down.

RH: How does a straight father of two decide to tackle such a controversial subject? In what way are you venturing into uncharted territory?

AG: The novel came out of a letter I read in the *Dallas Sunday News*, some years ago. The son of a gay father wrote in to defend his father against what I assume were some inflammatory anti-gay letters that had already been published in the newspaper. What struck me about that letter was its tone, how difficult it must have been to write—the fact that a straight man was standing up within an extremely conservative community to defend his father's choice. But look, it's exactly a married father of two who should be writing a book like this. A gay man is not going to write it because he's probably going to (quite naturally) want the main character to come out. It's only when you're writing from within the mainstream that you can summon the appropriate tension for a story like this. Let me give an example of what I mean: Last New Year's Day, I found myself standing in the corner of a kitchen at a party with four or five guys—all straight, married, fathers—and one of us started talking about an experience he'd had as a teenager when his family had moved to Buenos Aires. He was followed by a man one night, and though he was frightened by it, he found himself, also, excited, and it was this latter emotion that had trailed him for the subsequent thirty-five years. One by one, the others of us joined in. We'd all had one haunting, unexplored foray into the other side of sexuality. And as I stood there listening, I understood that what made this discussion fascinating was the level of fear underpinning it. In each of the voices was a heightened sense of: How much am I exposing myself here? How far am I stepping out of the proscribed circle of acceptable male heterosexuality? It's not that a gay writer couldn't capture that level of tension, but I wonder how many gay male writers would be interested in the dilemma of the straight male world trying to figure itself out. Here I am using those labels "straight" and "gay," and I don't mean to, but we haven't evolved useful alternatives. Maybe this book represents a modest attempt to move that discussion forward. In ten years, I hope we've added some new words to the vocabulary of male sexuality or, better yet, quit characterizing it altogether.

RH: What *are* men thinking about when they look at another man?

AG: Any number of things, though the thoughts aren't necessarily sexual. But we're really not so different from dogs; so many of our instincts are doglike, and have to do with the desire for supremacy, with wanting to topple others. At the same time, we get tired of being alpha, and sometimes maybe it's desirable to have others topple us, which is, of course, a historically female way of thinking. Some of this nudges directly into the sexual. I'm always astonished by the thoughts my therapist friends tell me their patients say in therapy, especially when the patients are free-associating. It's wild. Sexual fantasies involving the [male] therapist from men who are leading authentic heterosexual lives. But it's all part of the huge rush that forms each moment of our waking lives. I once wrote in an essay that "99 percent of life takes place in a territory to which no one has yet given a name; it's a space created by two individuals, while they are looking at each other and not speaking." That's the territory I've always believed fiction should be dedicated to exploring. There's lots of things fiction writers are doing that historians and sociologists can do as well. But the secret life of our times, that's the exclusive province of fiction.

Questions for Discussion

1) How damaging does *Recent History* suggest secrets are to a marriage? Could Lou have kept his secret and maintained a good marriage? Could Luca have kept his? How much does the answer to these questions have to do with what we expect of marriage today?

2) Luca says at one point that the main flaw in his marriage is that he has never "fully met" his wife. What does that mean? Is Luca overestimating the need for a level of emotional intimacy in marriage, or is that need really not as strong as he believes? Is the novel making any suggestion that the current demand for intimacy among couples may not be an entirely good thing?

3) How good or bad a father do you think Lou Carcera was? Are there some things he did well in bringing up Luca? Had he been more honest about himself, how much do you think that really would have changed things for Luca?

4) What is the author suggesting is the difference between men's lives today and men's lives in 1962, the time when Luca's father leaves? Does Luca overestimate the differences, or have the changes been as real as he believes?

5) Is this a novel about homosexuality? If not, what do you think the author is using homosexuality to say about all forms of sexuality, or about relationships in general?

6) Would Luca have the same, or similar, problems in his relationships if he didn't have "the haunt" of homosexuality?

7) Is the author suggesting that all men have a homosexual side? One critic said that Giardina "understands something that, in the context of our post-Freudian culture, seems almost revolutionary: our sexual history is not always worth the importance we assign it." Do you think that's true? Does Luca's sexual history really offer him a guide to the potential, or lack of it, in his relationship with Gina?

Further Reading
Anthony Giardina

Though a vast and well-documented canon of gay literature now exists, the specific subject of *Recent History*—the manner in which the two tides, gay and straight, meet and mix in the individual body—hasn't yet produced a significant body of literature.

Of what does exist, the most sensitive treatment I've come across is Michael Cunningham's *A Home at the End of the World*, about the enduring, sometimes erotic friendship of two young men. William Maxwell's *The Folded Leaf* explores the same territory, though having first been published in 1945, it is sometimes maddeningly elusive about the subject of homosexuality. (Until, that is, one amazing sentence near the end.)

The gay novels that have taught me the most—and that say the most trenchant things about the straight world—are Mark Merlis's *American Studies* and David Leavitt's hilarious novella *The Term Paper Artist*, collected in the volume *Arkansas*.

Among the literature of earlier periods, I like Marguerite Yourcenar's *Alexis*, Thomas Mann's *Death in Venice*, and D. H. Lawrence's *Women in Love*, though, even after several readings, it still baffles me exactly what Lawrence was suggesting is possible between straight men. The fault, I'm almost sure, is mine, not Lawrence's.

Finally, there are a number of plays and films that have treated this material. At the top of the list of plays would be David Rabe's *Streamers*, strong in its presentation of the sexual currents drifting around an army barracks during the time of the Vietnam War, and David Mamet's *Edmond*. The French film *Wild Reeds*, directed by Andre Téchiné, may be the most open-minded film I've ever seen about young male sexuality, as well as being, in and of itself, a wonderful movie.

About the Type

The text of this book was set in Janson, a typeface designed in about 1690 by Nicholas Kis, a Hungarian living in Amsterdam, and for may years mistakenly attributed to the Dutch printer Anton Janson. In 1919 the matrices became the property of the Stempel Foundry in Frankfurt. It is an old-style book face of excellent clarity and sharpness. Janson serifs are concave and splayed; the contrast between thick and thin strokes is marked.